For Victoria,

Hugh Whitaker forced himself to run faster. He knew this was insane but he was sure he was following a thylacine! Yep, he was sure it was a thylacine… perhaps better known as a Tasmanian tiger, last seen in the 1930's. But something was wrong... he realised he was running in circles, round and round, as if searching for something, but what was he looking for.

Confused, he stopped and ran his hand through his sweaty hair, before pushing his specs back up his nose. He had no idea what was going on or where he was.

"Yo, Hugh… Hugh Whitaker!"

The boy spun round.

"Spencer, you're..." His voice faltered as his nemesis, Spencer Tate removed his sunglasses and slid them into his breast pocket, revealing his dark, piggy eyes.

"Dead," Tate snarled, taking a step towards the petrified boy. "Is that the word you're looking for? Yes, you fat pommy brat, I am dead, thanks to you and that stinking *abo* girlfriend of yours. You stole the thylacine from me. It was my thylacine, you stole it from me and then you killed me stone dead! Dead! DEAD!"

Spitting each word like a dart, the ranger moved closer to Hugh as the boy started to back way, trying to ignore the sound of his heart pounding in his chest as an overwhelming sense of panic threatened to engulf him, backing away until the ground disappeared from beneath his feet.

"Argh!" Hugh screamed as he fell through the air. His arms flaying as he tried to snatch at roots, twigs – anything within reach to break his fall as he spiralled into darkness, waking with a jolt as he crashed towards the ground.

He lay there for a while, motionless, grimacing as he realised he was gripping the sides of his bed, jarring his damaged arm which was still tender from a fall several weeks before. He shivered, clawing at his sweat soaked pyjama top as he screwed his eyes shut tight, his breathing slowing with the realisation he'd woken from a nightmare. Spencer Tate *was* dead, the result of a tragic accident and the thylacine... his thylacine was safe.

He turned his head to glance at the small clock standing on the upturned tea-chest he was using as a bedside table. The red LED display glowed in the gloom, 02:30, Hugh groaned, it was hours before he needed to be up. He turned over on the damp bedding and closed his eyes with caution, dreading the possibility he might relive the nightmare again.

Chapter Two

With the memory of last night's trauma banished from his thoughts, Hugh followed as his closest friend, Connie, an Aboriginal Tasmanian girl, led the way into the High Street. Not that the narrow road he was riding along resembled any main thoroughfare he was familiar with. Cars could just pass one another in safety, with little more than a cat's whisker between them, its width was so restricted.

With just over a week of the summer vacation left, Connie had agreed to show him the quickest route to the pick-up point for the school bus. The distance to The Sullivan Academy, the nearest high school, was about seven kilometres, too far to ride by bike twice a day.

Hugh smiled to himself as he compared the local 'town' of Sullivan's Creek to Wimbledon, the London suburb he'd left just a few months before. The High Street consisted of a drug store, an 'op shop' or as Hugh knew it, a charity shop, the local newspaper office and a unisex hair salon which was, in truth, a barber shop whose owner rented a chair to a mobile hairdresser a couple of days a month to accommodate the local ladies need for a trim, colour rinse or occasional perm. On the other side of the road was a hardware store where you could purchase anything from a packet of batteries to a chainsaw or saucepan. This was next to a saloon bar called 'Thirsty Work', which picked up additional trade by renting out a couple of rooms to backpackers during the summer months and, at the end of the parade of shops, the school pick-up point where a temporary shelter had been erected to enable the students catching the school bus to leave their bikes in relative safety.

Hugh made a mental note to 'Google' this bloke Sullivan as soon as he got the chance. Connie had told him that Gordon Sullivan was a Scottish explorer who had first charted the area, but there had to be more to him than that as everything in Warrugul National Park seemed to be named after him.

"Hey, what do you think about your dad asking grandfather's permission to date my mum?" Connie called over her shoulder as she rode around a blue mottled Australian Cattle dog standing in the kerb barking at nothing in particular as his owner took a long drag on a cigarette.

"You haven't mentioned it since he asked her out, I just wondered if you were okay about it."

Hugh shrugged his shoulders, the action unseen by his friend who was several metres ahead of him.

"Of course I don't mind. I like Angie very much. If they make one another happy that's fine by me. I can't remember the last time he..." His words went unfinished as a large notice caught his eye.

Slamming on the brakes, Hugh dragged his feet along the ground, throwing up a cloud of dust as he tried to stop in the shortest distance possible.

Startled by the sound of a honking horn behind him, Hugh swivelled in his saddle.

"Hey, you bloody idiot! You trying to commit suicide or something? Bloody fool - stopping in the middle of the road like that," the driver of a grey van shouted as he swerved the vehicle to avoid the boy.

"S, s, sorry," Hugh called, raising his hand in apology, shuffling his bike closer to the kerb as he spoke.

"Connie," he yelled, as she continued pedalling along the road, unaware of the events unfolding behind her. "Connie!" He watched as her curly hair bounced against her back as she pedalled away from him. "Connie!"

"Yo," she called in response, glancing at her reflection in the warped window of the hardware shop as she passed.

"Connie," Hugh screamed, his voice becoming shriller as his agitation grew.

Connie looked over her shoulder, her bike wobbling in a dangerous manner as her front wheel clipped a discarded soda can standing in the middle of the road like a soldier holding the line, prepared to be crushed by a passing car.

"What!" She snapped, trying to get her bike under control without putting her feet on the ground.

Hugh was frantic.

"Quick, look at this," he waved his arm, beckoning her back as he propped his bike up on one if its pedals.

Connie sighed, "What's he seen now?" She grumbled under her breath as she glanced at her friend, her bad temper disappearing as fast as it had arisen, he was so red in the face he looked like a tomato. Even with the drop in weight he'd accomplished since he arrived in Tasmania a couple of months before, his cheeks were still flushed from the physical exertion of riding his bike on what was turning into the hottest day of the year so far.

Checking for traffic, she completed a semi-circle with the precision of an equestrian dressage rider and started to retrace her steps.

"Wass-up?" She asked, planting her feet on either side of her bike without bothering to dismount. She stared at Hugh, the redness visibly draining from his cheeks. It was a cliché, but he now looked as though he'd seen a ghost.

"What's the matter?" She repeated, alarmed at his pale expression. "You look awful."

"Look! Look at that."

Connie stared at the news-stand outside the Gazette's office. The local rag's latest headline was emblazoned across the centre of the board.

'Rare Mineral Discovered in National Park'.

"What do you think it means? It's not telling us much."

Hugh shook his head.

"Dunno, but it doesn't look good. Come on, let's find out," he suggested, rummaging in his pocket for some loose change. "How much does the paper cost?"

"Um, a dollar twenty-five, I think."

"Okay, I've got two dollars, that's more than enough," he said, counting the coins in his hand.

Hugh hurried towards the door of the small newspaper office.

"It's fine, I'll stay here shall I? Keep an eye on the bikes," said Connie, directing her comments at his back, her voice thick with sarcasm.

Standing at the reception desk, Hugh listened to the muffled sound of music playing from behind the closed door in front of him. He scanned a list of advertisement rates while he waited for someone to appear. Not that he was complaining, the air conditioned room was a pleasant contrast to the heat outside.

Several minutes later he emerged clutching a copy of the Gazette. Blinking in the sunshine, the bright light uncomfortable after the dull, artificial environment of the building he'd just left, he hurried over to where Connie waited with the bikes.

"Quick, what's it say?" She demanded.

Unfolding the newspaper, Hugh angled the broadsheet so they could read it together. The bold, black headlines seemed to jump from the page.

'*Rare Mineral Discovered in Warrugul National Park,*' with a by-line, '*Exploration Licences Granted*'.

Hugh started to read the article aloud.

"The Tasmanian Government grants exploration licences. Full story page six."

He cursed under his breath as he struggled to turn the large pages of the broadsheet.

"Here, let's use the bonnet of that car," Connie suggested, pointing to a muddy station wagon parked nearby.

"Good idea."

Placing the newspaper on the flat surface, Connie held one side of the paper as he flicked through to page six. Skim reading, he scanned the array of vertical printed columns.

"Did you know the average width of a newspaper column is the optimum line length for the human eye to read and absorb the information. It's a proven fact".

Hugh glanced up at his friend, his expression one of incredulity.

"What on earth are you on about?"

Connie nodded her head at the paper, "It's true. It's something I picked up in English lessons."

Hugh raised his eyebrows.

"Gee, you learn something new every day," he retorted.

"There's no need to be sarcastic."

Ignoring her remark, he returned his attention to the newspaper, tapping a column on the far left of the page.

"Found it," he said, starting to read the article aloud. "Geological surveys indicate large quantities of a rare earth mineral - Scandium," he glanced at Connie, who shook her head. She was none-the-wiser; she'd never heard of the mineral either.

"Okay," he nodded, as he glanced back at the article. "Err, where was I? Ah yes, rare earth mineral - Scandium has been discovered at four sites across Northern Tasmania. Licences to drill exploratory bore holes have been granted. Scandium, which has a higher melting point than aluminium, is sought for use in the space industry, in particular, in the manufacture of spacecraft and satellites. Blah-de-blah-de-blah. The Gazette's chief reporter, Sasha Albright, has discovered that a licence has been granted to drill a bore hole in Warrugul National Park."

"Oi! Get away from my car, you cheeky blighters," shouted a red faced woman waddling towards them as fast as her swollen legs could carry her obese frame.

Hugh threw her an apologetic look as he scooped the paper off the station wagon.

"Sorry, it was my fault. I just wanted to look something up," he explained.

"Huh, well how 'bout you go look something up in a library. Or better still go and lean somewhere else!" She retorted, aiming her electronic key fob at the station wagon with as much venom as if she were zapping someone with a Taser stun gun.

Connie looked around.

"There's a wheelie bin over there," she said, nodding to a blue garbage bin on the other side of the road. "We can use that."

"Great."

Hugh followed her across the road, the newspaper screwed up and stuffed under his arm as he pushed his bike.

"Come on, let's finish reading it," Connie suggested, taking the paper from under her friend's arm and smoothing the pages as flat as possible.

"Right, once again, where were we?" Hugh ran his finger along the printed line.

"Four licences have been granted to drill exploratory bore holes," he repeated. "Well, I guess they could come to nothing," he added, trying to sound optimistic.

"Yeah, but even exploratory bore holes will need a mining crew, equipment, lorries and such like. That'll mean a lot of strangers and a big disturbance in the park." Connie shook her head. "We need to get back and tell the others. I'm sure Grandfather can't be aware of this as he'd have mentioned it." She tutted, remembering her grandfather had mentioned his whereabouts for the day at breakfast. "Damn, I've just remembered, he's at the ranger's station. He's got a meeting with Doug Langdon. I guess we could ride over there if you're up for that?"

Doug Langdon was the senior ranger employed by the Parks and Wildlife Services in the area. He often used Connie's grandfather, Joe Sampi, to help with tracking and casual labour when needed.

Hugh nodded, easing the straps of his backpack off his shoulders, as Connie folded the broadsheet as best she could before shoving it into his bag.

Connie's grandfather, Joe Sampi was an Aboriginal Tasmanian elder. He, along with his neighbours and other aboriginal communities across Tasmania had kept the biggest secret in the world. They had protected the thylacine, the largest carnivorous marsupial of modern times, from extinction.

Wrongly labelled a sheep killer, the thylacine had been hunted to the edge of annihilation by white settlers during the late 1800's and early 1900's, leaving the world to think the last known specimen had died in 1936. Hugh and Connie now shared this secret. Having seen the thylacine for themselves, they pledged to keep the knowledge of the species a secret in order to protect it from exploitation.

If anyone knew what to do about the mining company, Joe Sampi would.

They pedalled as fast as they could towards the ranger's station. Although he still found strenuous exercise difficult, Hugh was amazed how much his stamina had increased since his arrival in Tasmania. He smiled as he remembered his former sports mistress, Miss Frobisher threatening him with a week's detention if she caught him walking the cross country course again. His face creased into a broad grin as he increased his speed. Miss Frobisher's threats were a lifetime ago!

"Hey, it looks as if Doug Langdon's already left. At least his Land Rover's not here," Connie observed as they approached the squat, white building which now doubled as the ranger's station as well as Andrew Whitaker's laboratory – come – veterinary examination room.

As a veterinary oncologist, Andrew Whitaker had accepted a year-long secondment to assist in the 'Save the Tasmanian Devil' Project. This iconic black and white marsupial was in danger of extinction from a contagious cancer. Daubed Devil Facial Tumour Disease, the condition was fatal. Once infected, grotesque tumours developed around the mouth and head of the devils, often causing them to starve to death. Whitaker had joined the international team working to develop a vaccine, as well as acting as a veterinary surgeon for the small local community.

The sound of Connie's voice dragged Hugh from of his day dream with a jolt.

"I hope that doesn't mean Grandfather's gone walk about or something," she mused. "This is important."

"G'day kids," George Toba greeted them as they walked into the building by poking his tongue out at them. Hugh laughed, returning the gesture.

George, and his older brother, Mikey lived with their father, Napoleon in the cabin next door to the Sampi's.

"Charming!" George retorted, his response good natured as he continued the banter. "So glad you respect your elders," he laughed.

"G'day," Mikey smiled as he glanced up from the computer screen.

Connie walked around the other side of the desk and peered over his shoulder.

"Watcha doing?" She asked.

Mikey lent across the screen, hiding its contents from view.

"State secret, I'm afraid. If we tell you, we'll have to kill you," he teased.

"Yeah right," she laughed. "You and whose army?"

Mikey's expression became more serious.

"If you must know, we're applying for the position of trainee field officers. Langdon gave your grandfather the head's up, just as he promised, when he was here earlier, so do us a favour and keep your fingers crossed."

The position of trainee field officers with the Tasmanian Parks and Wildlife Service was a two-year program comprising of full-time paid work and on-the-job training, a fantastic chance for the boys who, since leaving school had encountered limited opportunities to gain regular employment.

Connie nodded.

"Of course, that goes without saying. Changing the subject, do either of you know where grandfather is?"

Mikey nodded towards the room Andrew Whitaker used as his laboratory-cum-examination room.

"If I were you I'd leave him alone for a while," Mikey suggested. "He had a big pow-wow with Langdon earlier. He's been in a foul mood ever since."

Connie frowned.

"Damn, that's not good, but this can't wait, Mikey, sorry."

"Did I hear someone talking about me?" Joe Sampi laughed, drying his hands on a towel as he came out of Whitaker's lab. The tall Aboriginal Tasmanian almost blocked the doorway. Not that there was an ounce of fat on his muscular frame, toned from decades of manual work. His dark features creased into a broad smile, revealing a row of white teeth. His granddaughter, Connie and her mother were his pride and joy.

"Grandfather, have you seen this?" Connie demanded, snatching the newspaper out of Hugh's grasp and waving in front of the old man.

Sampi took a step backwards as the local rag was thrust a little too close to his face for comfort.

"Easy girl," he chided.

"Sorry, Grandfather," she whispered, blushing under Sampi's gaze. "It's just, well, we've got a major problem," she gushed, glancing at Hugh, becoming more animated by the second.

"Go on, tell us what you've done now," Mikey teased. He saved the on-line application forms he and his brother had been working on in order to listen to what had got them so riled up.

Hugh directed them to the article on page six.

"I hate big newspapers like this," Sampi muttered under his breath as he struggled to control the huge sheets of paper. He wrinkled his nose as the black print ink stained his fingers. "These pages seem to have a life of their own," he laughed.

"Here," said George, pushing some mugs out of the way to make space on the desk.

"Okay, page six you said." Sampi frowned as he looked at the headline emblazoned across the top of the front page before turning to the main article inside the newspaper.

"I can't read this," he retorted in disgust. "The print's too damn small!"

Mikey leant across the desk and read the article out loud.

"Bloody hell," George exclaimed as his brother sat down.

Joe Sampi was the first to break the silence which had fallen over the room.

"I've got to be honest, Doug Langdon mentioned this to me earlier, that's what we were arguing about."

Hugh and Connie exchanged worried glances, the reason for his apparent bad mood had been revealed.

Sampi explained that the Gazette was handed the information from an un-named source before an official announcement could be made, which meant Landon had to arrange the meeting this morning to brief him.

Hugh looked at George and then Mikey, it was obvious from their expressions they were less than happy at being kept in the dark.

Sampi threw the boys an apologetic look.

"I'm sorry, I know I should have said something after Doug left but I wanted to tell everyone this evening, when we all got together, and anyway, the news put me in a foul mood."

"Err, we noticed, Joe," Mikey said, "sorry, but we knew you weren't yourself, even without you saying anything."

"What's it mean, Grandfather?" Connie demanded. "The thylacine, she's in danger isn't she?"

Ignoring the question, Sampi crossed the small room and stared at the detailed map of Warrugul National Park dominating the wall to the left of the doorway.

"Right, from what little detail Langdon was able to give me, I think they will be drilling here," he tapped the map with the tip of his finger.

"That's bloody close to Sullivan's Rise," Hugh observed, stepping closer to the map for a better look.

"Language, Hugh," Sampi reprimanded.

"Sorry, Joe. It's just, well, that's the place we've seen the thylacine and her pups most often. It's the location of their favourite den."

"But... but if that's where they intend to drill we are right back to square one," Connie exclaimed.

Yeah, we've risked out lives protecting the thylacine for nothing, Hugh thought.

Connie looked across the room at her friend who shrugged and shook his head, she'd said it all, there was nothing more he could add.

"Whoa," Sampi said out loud, patting the air in an attempt to diffuse the charged atmosphere.

"Connie, Hugh, do you trust me?"

Hugh couldn't resist a quick look around the room, George and Mikey were staring at him. It was almost as if they were willing him to dare challenge Joe. He could see they were ready to jump on him if he gave the wrong answer.

"Of course we do, Grandfather," Connie piped up. Her voice tinged with indignation at the question her grandfather had asked.

Hugh relaxed, there was no need for him to respond. It wasn't that he didn't trust the old man, but the mining company would bring work – regular work, something the aboriginal community were in desperate need of. He couldn't blame them if they viewed the news differently to him and Connie.

Sampi inhaled before speaking.

"We," he looked at George and Mikey as he spoke, including them in his statement. "We have kept the secret of the thylacine for a long time." He shook his head as he spoke, looking jaded, exhausted even. "We, err, I mean you," he smiled at Connie and then at Hugh, "have survived Tate's shenanigans."

An image of the dead ranger crept unbidden into Hugh's mind. He gave an involuntary shudder. The sight of the ranger, with his pockmarked skin and dark, piggy eyes would haunt him forever.

"That's putting a spin on events," Hugh whinged under his breath.

"We will survive this, the thylacine will be kept safe. I... Sorry, I mean to say *we* will see to that. I don't know how or where, but we will find a sanctuary for the species and then the thylacine and her pups will be kept safe and sound."

Engrossed in Sampi's speech, no one heard a vehicle pull up outside the ranger's station.

Grabbing his laptop bag and the phials of blood he'd brought back from his trip to the Menzies Institute for Medical Research in Hobart, Andrew Whitaker hurried inside, his tuneless whistling stopping in an instant as he detected the charged atmosphere within the building.

As part of his work on the vaccination development programme his visit to the state capital was needed in order to attend a briefing on the Institute's progress thus far, as well as being an opportunity to update other attendees on his work.

The vet looked at the other occupants. Hugh and Joe Sampi were standing next to the map of the Park, while Connie, Mikey and George stood on the other side of the desk, all eyes focused on him.

"Err, I've only been gone a few hours but by the look on your faces World War Three's been declared in my absence," Whitaker joked, his poor attempt at humour falling flat.

War would be the lesser of two evils, Hugh thought to himself in a petulant manner.

"Okay," Whitaker continued with slow deliberation. "I've missed something here. Does someone want to fill me in... Hugh, err, Connie perhaps?"

Hugh grimaced, inhaling through clenched teeth.

"I'm sorry, Dad, but you're not gonna believe what's happened."

Whitaker's face fell. Since their arrival in Tasmania a few weeks before, his son had suffered from smoke inhalation, fractured his arm, 'rediscovered' a species presumed to be extinct and thwarted an attempt to capture and sell the thylacine, what more could go wrong?

"Go on, tell me what trouble you two have gotten yourselves into now?" He asked, looking from Hugh to Connie and back again.

Mikey laughed out loud. The raucous sound filled the room, diffusing the charged atmosphere.

"We know them too well, eh, Andrew. That's what we said," Mikey chuckled.

"Dad! Why do you always think the worst?"

His father pulled a face, "The evidence to date son, I rest my case."

The room erupted in good-natured laughter.

Whitaker placed his bag and blood samples on top of the newspaper, obscuring the article which had been the subject of such heated debate.

"Is someone going to enlighten me, or at least give me a starter for ten so I can guess what you've been up to?"

"The-thylacine's-in-danger-again," Hugh garbled, his words an incoherent mess.

"Pardon?"

Whitaker looked across the room at his friend and colleague, Joe Sampi who raised his eyebrows.

Hugh tutted in frustration as Connie interjected.

"He said the thylacine's in danger."

"Why, has she been spotted by a member of the public?" Whitaker demanded.

"No, nothing as straightforward as that," Sampi replied. "Connie, can you get Andrew a drink, he must be gasping." He waited for his granddaughter to return before explaining what had happened.

"Doug Langdon called in to brief me about an article in today's Gazette." He pointed to the newspaper under the vet's bag as he repeated the story for Andrew's benefit.

"You've got to be having a laugh?"

Sampi shook his head.

"I wish. I was showing the other's where I think one of the bore holes will be sunk, I'm afraid it's quite close to Sullivan's Rise."

Whitaker swore under his breath.

"How's this been approved?" He demanded. He continued without waiting for an answer. "Right, we know the existence of the thylacine is still a secret but we are lucky we are taking part in the research project. Perhaps we can use that to our advantage? The slightest disturbance to the environment and the eco-system might be enough to send the Tasmanian devil population over the edge." He ran his fingers through his hair, "Bloody hell, what have the Government done!"

Chapter Three

Connie was reading the letter Andrew Whitaker had brought from her mother. Angie had been gone for just a few days but, to mother and daughter, it seemed like an eternity.

Angela Sampi, Connie's mother, worked at Hobart General Hospital. As the sole member of the family to command a regular wage, she could earn a lot more working in the capital than she could in the local hospital. Perhaps if her father, Joe, was able to get more regular work with the Parks and Wildlife Service she could find a job closer to home, but at the moment she and Connie were forced to live apart.

Hugh observed his friend from the other side of the room as she re-read the letter for what seemed like the umpteenth time. He couldn't work out her mood. She seemed elated when his father had produced the letter from the side pocket of his laptop bag, but now... he couldn't tell. Her face was obscured by her hair which had escaped from the clip she had placed in it that morning. He smiled to himself, he loved the way her hair hung like that when she was bent over her work or reading a book.

He sighed as he watched her. To a point he knew what it was like to be separated from his mother, but unlike his mum, who had committed suicide when he was four, at least Angie would be home in a few weeks.

"Problem?" He asked.

"Huh?" Connie looked up, pushing her hair back behind her ear. "What'd you say?"

"I asked if there was a problem?" He repeated. "Not bad news I hope?" He nodded towards the crumbled piece of paper she held in her hands.

She smiled, but he could detect a sadness in her eyes that wasn't there before.

"Mum says the hospital is short staffed. She's having to cope with double shifts, which in some respects is great as we need the money." She looked away and stared out of the window. "We always need the money. As it stands I doubt she'll be able to come home as planned at the end of the month."

"But that's weeks away," Hugh replied in an attempt to sound optimistic. "Anything can happen between then and now, don't you worry."

Hugh turned his attention to his father who was attempting to help, or in Andrew Whitaker's case, hinder Mikey and George as they put the finishing touches to their on-line applications. Joe Sampi had gone to meet their father, his close friend, Napoleon Toba, who'd been asked to follow up on reports of unattended cooking fires at some of the popular tourist haunts. The last thing anyone needed was another forest fire like the one they had fought before Christmas. Not only had it devastated a swath of vegetation, it had claimed the life of a male thylacine.

Hugh crept closer to Connie and sat beside her, his back pressed against the cold brick wall.

"Bet your bottom dollar they won't let us help them protect the thylacine when the mining company moves in, what with school starting and all."

Connie tutted.

"Stop being such a dill. They'll need all the help they can get and we've proven we can look after ourselves." She was thoughtful for a moment. "You know, even the most arduous initiation ceremony the aboriginal community could expose us to wouldn't be a patch on what we've been through while trying to protect the thylacine."

"Initiation ceremony?" Hugh looked puzzled, "initiated into what?"

Connie smiled.

"Aboriginal tradition," she explained, "to mark the passage from childhood to adulthood."

"Do these things still go on?"

Connie nodded, "Sometimes. For boys at least."

"What happens?"

"It varies from one language group to the next. Initiates are decorated with body art and jewellery, and sometimes a physical reminder of the event is given." She ignored Hugh's horrified look as she continued, "an area of the body could be marked with an aboriginal symbol, the nose or ears pierced or sometimes a tooth removed.

Sometimes it involves circumcision and even incision on the back or chest."

"Yuk, that's disgusting," Hugh remarked, unaware how insensitive he sounded.

Connie glared at him, "Anyway, as I said, I think we've more than proved ourselves."

"Yeah, me too," he added, making a mental note to research initiation ceremonies when he looked up Gordon Sullivan.

He studied his father who was laughing with the two young men, their banter interrupted by the shrill trill of the telephone.

"Warrugul Ranger Station."

They listened to a one-sided conversation as the vet answered the phone.

"No, sorry, Doug, both Joe and Napoleon are out, checking on reports of unattended fires I believe."

They watched as Whitaker nodded his head as he spoke. "Okay, thanks, I'll pass the message on and I'm sure either Joe or Napoleon will fill you in. Bye, Doug, bye."

Whitaker replaced the handset on the cradle, oblivious that all eyes were focused on him.

"Dad!"

"Err, oh, sorry son, I was thinking."

"Guess that was Doug Langdon eh?" Mikey asked, stating a fact they'd all cottoned on to.

Hugh felt as if he would burst if his father didn't hurry up and tell them what Langdon had called for. He scrambled to his feet before offering Connie a hand up, which she slapped away with a laugh.

"Dad, for goodness sake, what did Doug want?"

Whitaker scanned the room.

"Sorry, Mikey was right, that was Doug Langdon. He called to say they've named the company granted the exploratory drilling licences.

It's the Tasmanian Mining Corporation. And it seems they are pulling out the stops by initiating a damage limitation exercise. They admit the article in the Gazette should never have been published, it seems the information was leaked - at least that's what the mining company claim. To make amends they are holding an emergency public meeting at the Academy tonight."

"But that's miles away," Hugh interrupted. "There's bound to be loads of people who can't get there, that's not fair!"

"It's the only place around here big enough to hold a meeting like that," Connie explained.

"Oh right."

Whitaker continued, "It seems the Tasmanian Government are far from pleased the news was broken by the Gazette in this way. The process or should I say procedure is to brief the local councils and impacted government departments before any announcement is made public. The Tasmanian Mining Corporation is holding our meeting at seven tonight. We, it seems, are the last of the impacted areas to be addressed.

George and Mickey exchanged glances as Hugh muttered under his breath, "Bloody typical," he said.

Whitaker glared at his son.

"I've assured Langdon that we'll be there as he can't make it; he has to go to the Animal Health Laboratories in Launceston."

"You can count on us too," said Mikey. "Dad will want to go, that's for sure."

Connie leant over to Hugh and whispered, "Bet you never thought you'd be setting foot inside the school before the start of term, eh?"

Hugh shook his head, "Not in a million years. Come on, let's get outta here. I can't breathe, I need some air."

Leaning on the wooden rail, Hugh gulped the warm air. He felt as if a band had been placed around his chest and was constricting his lungs.

"It's not fair."

Connie stood next to him, watching her friend in silence.

"It's so unfair," he repeated. "We've fought damn hard to save the thylacine."

Connie nodded.

"But you know neither Grandfather nor Napoleon will let any harm come to her. They, um, I mean, we won't rest until she's safe."

"I've gotta see her. You'll think it stupid, but she needs to know we won't let her come to harm. Coming?"

Connie didn't bother with a response, she cleared the steps in one leap, grabbing her bike from where she had left it when they arrived earlier, propped up against the fence.

With a laugh she was astride her machine and pedalling before he'd picked his off the floor from where it had fallen.

"Sullivan's Rise?" He shouted at her back.

"You bet."

They waited in silence for almost an hour, hoping the thylacine would make an appearance. They knew if they were going to attend the public meeting they couldn't leave it much longer to head home. Hugh was about to ask Connie the time when the female thylacine meandered out of the trees and flopped onto her side, her pups following a moment later.

"Everything is done with such grace isn't it? Connie observed, "I mean the way she moves."

Hugh stared at the animal for a moment, "Yeah, you're right, effortless."

"Wow, the pups have grown in a few days," Connie observed.

"Yeah, I can remember reading in the book you leant me about Australian wildlife that the offspring stay with the mother for about nine months so they'll need her protection for a while longer. I'm not sure if that's good or bad at the moment, with the mining operation, it means all four of them will be in danger."

Connie's face clouded.

"Gee, that's an awful thought. I wish you hadn't said it."

They watched the thylacine as she lay in the shade of the trees. Her stripes, which ran along her body to the tip of her tail, broke up her silhouette, providing the perfect camouflage in the shadow's thrown down by the trees. It was little wonder that no credible sightings of the thylacine had been verified by the outside world for almost a century, she was almost invisible to a casual glance.

Hugh and Connie were transfixed as the pups gambolled around their mother, surprised that the smallest one appeared to be the most dominant, jumping onto its siblings and nipping them as they played.

"In all the times we have seen them I have never heard them utter a sound."

Connie cocked her head and listened as she thought.

"You're right. I'll try and remember to ask grandfather, he'll know if they bark or whatever."

The thylacine stood up.

"Look, something's got her interest."

Connie looked over her shoulder.

"I can't see anything."

"But something's spooked her," Hugh reiterated, "look, she's heading back into the shadows, her pups are following."

"Perhaps she caught a scent of something she didn't like, your after shave maybe?" She teased.

He started to say he didn't shave, shoving Connie in a good-natured way when he realised she was messing about.

"Come on, she's gone. We might as well head back."

Chapter Four

By the time they arrived at The Sullivan Academy, the hall was half full. Pausing in the entrance, Hugh couldn't help wondering where all these people had come from.

A large stage dominated the far end of the hall, framed by long red curtains hanging from floor to ceiling, a theme repeated around every window giving the room a claustrophobic air. Neat, evenly spaced rows of chairs dissected the floor on either side of a narrow central aisle. A baby grand piano stood to the left of the stage, hiding the stairs that led onto the wooden platform. A small lectern had been placed in the centre, its modern metal construction at odds to the general decor of the room. Four chairs had been placed to the right, facing the auditorium. No doubt, he assumed, ready for the guest speakers.

Hugh followed Mikey and Connie into the hall. A glossy brochure had been placed on the seat of every chair, a compact, close printed page had been inserted into each booklet, the A4 edges visible beyond the rim of the brochure.

Joe Sampi led the way to the first empty row, standing to the side to allow Mikey, George and Napoleon to side-step along the line to take their seats.

"Hugh, if you sit next to your dad, then Connie and I'll sit on the end. Don't want you causing too much of a disturbance if you don't like what you hear." His voice was light, but Hugh detected an undertone which indicated this wasn't the time or the place for either he or Connie to let their heart rule their heads and say what they wanted.

"Grandfather, as if we would!" Connie exclaimed, a look of affronted innocence flashing across her face.

"Yo, Connie!"

The young aboriginal girl swivelled on her heel to see who had called her name. She waved to a red haired girl sitting two rows in front.

"Who's that?" Hugh whispered.

"Jennifer Talbot, year prefect. You'll like her, she's a laugh."

They edged past Joe Sampi to take their seats, picking up the brochures before sitting down.

"This didn't cost tu'pence h'penny," Hugh murmured, flicking through the booklet.

"What's tu'pence ha'penny?"

Hugh smiled as he explained to Connie about pre-decimalisation coinage.

"It's two old pennies and a ha'penny or half penny."

"Ah, I see," she said, a look of confusion on her face.

Hugh flicked through the brochure.

"It's a play on words, it means it's expensive."

The booklet consisted of high definition photographs of state-of-the-art mining equipment ranging from Caterpillar digging machines to Jaw Crushers and SuperMiners, to name but a few.

The environmental section started with a bold mission statement, *'The Tasmanian Mining Corporation is an ethical company'*. Our pledge is to leave the environment in the same state, or preferably an enhanced position to what it was prior to our arrival.

The article explained it was of paramount importance to the CEO, Laura Goodman and the Board of Directors of the Tasmanian Mining Corporation that they work with the blessing and co-operation of the local community.

The corporate spiel went on to say that their 'Indigenous Heritage Program' has received State wide recognition for its on-going commitment to honouring Aboriginal heritage and indigenous traditions, at the same time ensuring the Company remains at the forefront of profitability while utilising cutting edge technology'.

The penultimate page of the brochure carried a map of Tasmania dotted with tiny red circles indicating where the company had projects either underway or in development.

"Looks as if they have a finger in a lot of pies," Whitaker grumbled, reading over his son's shoulder.

"Yeah, they aren't going to be a pushover are they, Dad? I wouldn't like to meet her on a dark night," he added, looking at the adjoining page which carried the names and photographs of the speakers. "She frightens me."

"Who?" Whitaker looked at the photograph. "Ah, Laura Goodman, oh I don't know, she looks a bit hot to me."

"Dad! I thought you were dating Angie?"

"I am, son, I am. But I can look can't I?"

Hugh tutted, shaking his head in mock disapproval.

Connie stood up and looked around.

"Hall's almost full," she said.

"I'm not surprised, darl," said her grandfather, jotting a note on the front of the brochure. "This could impact a lot of people," he added, removing his damaged watch from his pocket and checking the time. "Almost seven, they'll be starting any minute."

"See you haven't had your watch repaired," Hugh joked, pointing at the broken face and missing strap.

"What, this unique and valuable timepiece? I'd be lost without it, Hugh, there's no way I could let it out of my sight for repair," Sampi joked, but there was more truth to the statement than he would ever admit. His damaged timepiece had been a wedding gift from his late wife, there was no way he was ever going to be parted from it, even on a temporary basis.

"Yeah right! Unique eh, it's un-wearable. Ah well, perhaps you can start a new fashion trend – or not!"

The old man grinned at the boy, "That's character, Hugh, and unlike your watch, which if I remember is broken. Smashed when you fell out of that, err, um... tree!" He laughed, referring to the first time Hugh saw the thylacine and fell into a sink hole, breaking his arm when he hit the ground. "This one works. Bugger, it's stopped," Sampi confessed, holding the damaged timepiece to his ear as he glanced at the clock suspended above the entrance door. "It's a quarter past, they're late. It's turning into a typical public meeting, shambolic!"

Mikey nodded over his shoulder.

"You spoke too soon."

Hugh turned. He recognised the obese woman leading the way down the central aisle as the one who had told them off for leaning on her car. She'd had her hair done and was wearing thick blue eye shadow which clashed with the purple floral dress she wore, but there was no doubt about it, it was her.

Hugh felt a slight pressure on his arm.

"Is that?"

He raised his eyebrows to acknowledge Connie's unfinished question, yep, she'd recognised her too.

Napoleon leant in front of Andrew Whitaker in order to get Joe Sampi's attention.

"Isn't she that awful council woman who wanted to pull our homes down and drag us off to some estate in Devonport?" He asked, nodding in the direction Hugh was looking.

"Yep," Sampi snarled.

The obese councillor was followed by a tall broad shouldered man with short, strawberry blonde hair, Hugh guessed he was similar in age to his father, though the snazzy, bespoke tailored suit looked as though it cost as much as his father made in a month. Judging by his muscular arms, which were evident even in the well-cut jacket, he was used to working out on a regular basis.

The general hub-bub began to peter out as the audience became aware of the procession making its way down the central aisle towards the stage.

The strawberry blonde man was followed by a slim woman, at least a head shorter than the man in front of her. It was clear her outfit had been chosen with precision. Her immaculate peach linen suit clung to her body in all the right places, showing off her perfect hour glass figure.

"Wow!" George exclaimed.

Connie tutted, "Down boy, put your tongue away, George. She'll not give us a second's glance, that's a genuine Louis Vuitton bag slung over her shoulder which'll have cost a small fortune. That's not taking into account her outfit which wasn't off the peg or from the local op shop and looking at the size of diamonds in her ears..."

"Believe me, my dear," said Napoleon, "neither of my boys are looking at the diamonds in her ears," he joked, his eyes travelling in the direction his sons were looking. "Yep, she's a classy looking Sheila."

"What's an op shop?" Hugh asked.

"What? Oh, it's a thrift shop, you call them charity shops don't you?" Connie replied.

All eyes were on the woman as she walked towards the stage, her stiletto heels clicking against the parquet flooring as she walked, her hips swaying as if she were a seasoned model walking along the cat walk. She strode forward without a glance to the right or the left, following the rest of the party up the small flight of stairs onto the stage. Stepping in front of the obese woman, she sat beside the strawberry blonde man and crossed her legs, studying her audience with interest.

The overweight woman remained standing, waiting for the last trickle of conversations to finish, pulling, self-consciously, at the floral fabric of her dress as she waited.

"She looks nervous," Connie whispered from behind her hand.

Hugh nodded.

"Good evening, ladies and gentlemen." She paused for a moment as she dabbed the perspiration off her top lip with the edge of a small embroidered handkerchief. "Um, thank you for taking the trouble to attend this impromptu meeting this evening. For those of you who do not know who I am, let me start by introducing myself." Her eyes darted around the auditorium as she spoke. "I am Councillor Felicity Kameron, Mayor of Warrugul."

Hugh turned to Connie and sniggered, "Whoops, that was the Mayor's car we used as a table. Ha ha, official car to a wheelie bin - it's downhill all the way!"

The woman in front of him swivelled in her seat and shushed him quiet.

Felicity Kameron continued to speak.

"It was not the intention of Warrugul Council, or the Tasmanian Mining Corporation to spring a meeting like this to announce we are one of the four communities identified as potential mining sites." She rocked on her heels, swaying in an alarming way for someone her size as she spoke. "But, um, events overtook us." Her eyes darted around the hall as she continued. "I am pleased to announce that we have two very important representatives here this evening from the Tasmanian Mining Corporation who agreed to attend the meeting at such short notice."

"And whose fault is it that the meeting is held without notification," Sampi grumbled to himself.

Kameron droned on.

"There will be opening statements from the Chief Executive Officer followed by the Head of the Legal Department with an opportunity to ask questions from the floor at the end of the meeting. Let me start by introducing the CEO of the Tasmanian Mining Corporation, Miss Laura Goodman."

She started to tap the palm of her hand with the tips of her fingers, nodding towards the audience in an attempt to encourage them to clap as she perched herself on the edge of her chair, a worried look crossed her face as if she were concerned it may collapse under her weight.

Laura Goodman waited for a moment before standing, her eyes scanning the expectant audience in front of her. Connie was correct, she had chosen her outfit with care, electing to look elegant and feminine rather than power-dressing in one of her range of bespoke two-piece trouser suits she wore to the board meetings and presentations she attended. The money she had spent on a personal stylist several years ago had been money very well spent.

"Good evening, ladies and gentlemen," she paused, smiling for a second before continuing. "My name is Laura Goodman and I am the CEO of the Tasmanian Mining Corporation. I'd like to thank you for giving me the opportunity to speak to you this evening. And to start by making two apologies." She paused again, glancing at the floor for a moment before lifting her head and holding the gaze of the audience. "I apologise with all sincerity for the way in which the news of our exploratory bore holes was announced. That was not our doing and I can assure you that it is not the way we, in the Tasmanian Mining Corporation, work." She paused again, lowering her eyes for a moment before continuing.

"My, she's good," Sampi muttered, his words were little more than a whisper but they were loud enough for Hugh and Connie to hear.

"What do you mean, Joe?" Hugh asked.

"Shush, not now," he said, "I'll explain later."

"My second apology is for the absence of our Aboriginal Heritage Officer, Richard Pirlatapa who has been called away on a personal emergency.

"Yeah right," Mikey muttered.

Napoleon nudged his son, "Shush," he said in a hoarse whisper.

"Heritage officer, my eye," grumbled a man a couple of rows behind. "Why are we pussy footing around with crap like that," he demanded. "What we want here is jobs. Not some protection around a few scratches in the rocks or some faded finger painting."

"Oi," Mikey exclaimed, turning in his chair to get a look at the man who was speaking.

"Leave it, Mikey. He's not worth arguing with," his father advised.

"*Leave it, Mikey, it's not worth it*," the stranger mimicked, his tone tinged with aggression.

Mikey clenched his fists, his father placed his hand on his son's arm and shook his head.

Meeting his father's gaze, Mikey mouthed the word 'okay' in silence.

"Forget him, bro, he's not worth arguing with. We came here to listen to what the mining corporation has to say, not idiots like him," his brother reasoned.

Laura Goodman continued to speak, unaware or oblivious to the altercation taking place.

"Here at the Tasmanian Mining Corporation, we pride ourselves on our ethical stance. Not only will the exploration site be returned to its current state but should a full mining programme be undertaken, within a year of its completion the entire site will be restocked with the same flora that exists now. The company will also make a substantial contribution to community projects to compensate for the inconvenience and upheaval our presence will cause."

"How will you do that?" Shouted a heckler sitting on the right of the hall.

Laura Goodman smiled and looked up though her lashes.

"You may well ask, sir. We have access to extensive areas of native forestry. Where one tree is felled, two of the same species are replanted. Wildlife will be protected. We will utilise local labour wherever possible. Now, may I take your questions before the head of my legal department speaks."

For a moment the hall was silent. Laura Goodman remained standing, a fixed smile on her lips.

With slow deliberation, Andrew Whitaker raised his hand.

Hugh slid down in his seat, "Gawd, what's he gonna say," he whispered to Connie.

Laura Goodman turned to face the vet.

"Yes sir, would you care to start by giving me your name?"

The strawberry blonde man removed a small black notebook from his breast pocket and started to scribble.

Whitaker stood, blushing as all eyes fell on him.

"Good evening," he paused to clear his throat. "My name is Doctor Andrew Whitaker, BVSc, PHD, DipECVIM-CA (oncology), FRCVS."

The strawberry blonde man raised his eyebrows as he scribbled Whitaker's qualifications.

"I hold a post doctorate degree in veterinary oncology and my current employment is a work placement here in Warrugul, seconded to the Devil Face Tumour Disease (DFTD) project."

Hugh thought he saw a look of concern flash across Laura Goodman's face but it was gone in an instant. She nodded as his father continued to speak.

"The continued existence of the Tasmanian devil is on a knife edge."

There was a murmur of assent from the audience.

"Even during the exploration period, the mining process could impact the local devil population."

A number of people sitting around him nodded their heads in agreement.

"This initiative could push the local population over the edge. Is that a risk we care to live with, especially when the State acted too late to save the thylacine from extinction almost a hundred years ago?"

Laura Goodman raised her eyebrows, "Well..."

"If I may interrupt," said the strawberry blonde man, standing and stepping forward.

Laura Goodman nodded and took a step back.

"Let me start by introducing myself. My name is William Appleby, I hold a Master's degree in Mining and Energy Law and I am the Head of the Legal department at Tasmanian Mining Corporation."

"Think he's trying to impress, like your Pop," Napoleon whispered, "a case of mine's bigger than yours so to speak."

Appleby continued, "Let me start by reassuring you all that a full environmental impact assessment will be undertaken in conjunction with a review of the data extracted from the exploratory bore holes."

"Ah, so are you saying the impact assessment won't take place until the mining starts?" Whitaker interrupted, "By which time the population could be decimated."

Laura Goodman glanced at Appleby as he added a note in his book before continuing.

"Any potential, and I repeat, potential impact on the Tasmanian devil population will be assessed by our team of experts and if necessary mitigations will be put in place to protect the animals."

"Experts. What experts?" Whitaker interjected, his tone tinged with aggression. He laughed, but the sound was laced with irony. "I have mentioned that I am working with the DFTD project, which is working in close association with the Save the Tasmanian Devil project as well as the Menzies Research Institute. I have not heard mention of any association with your company."

Hugh looked up at his father, his face was flushed with anger. He could see he was fighting to control his anger.

"So, can you please explain how you will determine what impact your activities will have on the devils? Perhaps you have veterinary consultants you can call on, though I am sure Ms. Goodman would have mentioned a BVSc along with the heritage officer. Or perhaps you have a third degree," he added with an air of petulant sarcasm.

Hugh sniggered behind his hand.

"Shut up, pommy. We need jobs," someone called from the back of the hall.

"You are correct, Mr?" Appleby looked at his notes to refresh his memory. "Mr. Whitaker. I am not a vet, I am a lawyer, and you have made a fair point. Rest assured *Miss* Goodman and I will take it under advisement," he replied, emphasising his colleague's title.

"Give it a rest, Whitaker. As the bloke at the back said, we need work, real work, not more protection for a few black scavengers."

The vet spun to his right to address the man speaking.

"By black scavengers I assume you mean Devils?" He fumed.

Sampi reached across and squeezed his arm. He shook his head.

"Leave it, Andrew. I know that bloke, his name is Grant Peterson, he's a local waster."

"And a racist, he's not talking about devils being scavengers," Napoleon added.

"This isn't the place, Andrew," Joe Sampi advised.

Whitaker gave the older man a curt nod of his head as he continued.

"What real assurance have you got that they will use local labour?" He said, directing his question to the heckler. "Is that a contractual obligation, or just hot air?" He glanced up at the stage and back at Peterson who seemed to be squirming in his seat under Whitaker's onslaught. "Be sensible, man. Mining is a skilled job. I can't imagine this venture will bring many opportunities for the local community. Perhaps casual labouring jobs, but my guess is that the company has its workforce they move from one site to the next."

"That's right, Andrew, you tell him," encouraged George.

"Shut your dirty mouth, *abo'*. No one was talking to you."

George jumped to his feet as his father grabbed his arm in an attempt to restrain him.

"What did you call me?"

The auditorium was in uproar. People started to shout, some in support of the mining company, others supporting Andrew Whitaker. Hugh and Connie were on their feet.

"Look," Connie pointed towards the stage.

Felicity Kameron was leading the representatives from the Tasmanian Mining Corporation towards the back of the stage where there was a fire exit out of the school.

"Looks like they are scurrying away," Sampi observed, "can't take the heat, eh? Guess we might as well go," he suggested, stepping out into the aisle.

"You're right mate," a stranger placed his hand on Whitaker's arm as he addressed him. "We need jobs, but we need the devils more, tourists do come just to see them, you know."

Hugh snuck a look at the logo on the pale blue polo shirt the man wore, it depicted a half finished pint with the words 'Thirsty Work' embroidered around it, he recognised that as the name of the saloon bar he'd seen in town.

"The only jobs this will bring will be casual, cash in hand jobs, not real work. Okay, I might pick up some bed and breakfast trade but that will be gone when the mining company moves on. I need the tourists and backpackers; this could put the kybosh on that." The stranger grinned. "You ruffled a few feathers tonight, cobber, but you did good for a pom!"

Whitaker smiled as he shepherded Hugh and Connie in front of him.

"Thanks mate."

Chapter Five

Laura Goodman slammed the door of her four by four with more force than necessary.

William Appleby looked at her. She was angry, very angry.

"I don't think that went as well as we had hoped."

Goodman turned to face him, her steel grey eyes flashing with fury.

"That's the problem with you, William. You have this annoying habit of stating the bloody obvious."

She yanked down the sun visor to check her appearance in the small mirror before rummaging in her make-up purse for her lipstick. He waited while she applied a liberal coating of the blood red cosmetic, watching as she admired her refection in the mirror.

"We, or I should say, you, are going to have to keep a close eye on that vet fellow. I'm not sure if he's someone we can use to our advantage yet, or if he's gonna become a liability we have to eliminate. He made some interesting points. We may need to engage someone local who'll be able to pacify the *good* people of Warrugul. Like many campaigners he'll be easy to manipulate once we know where his Achilles heel is. We just need to find out what it is." She glanced out of the window, wondering what on earth kept people living in a dive like this. *My God... it doesn't even have a nail bar*, she thought to herself, before returning her attention to her reflection and continuing her tirade. "We may need to tell him what he wants to know or should I say, needs to know. In return we'll pump him for information if necessary." She removed a small smudge of lipstick from the side of her mouth with the tip of her finger before pushing the visor back up against the roof of the vehicle.

Appleby placed his hand on her knee and ran it along her leg to her thigh.

"You are your father's daughter, you ruthless bitch."

"Thank you, darling," she purred, lifting his hand off her leg and dropping it into his lap. "That's a wonderful compliment. I've done my best to build on daddy's success and bring the company to where it is today. If I hadn't inherited some of his ruthlessness and business savvy, I would not have been as successful as I am."

Appleby turned the key in the ignition, revving the engine unnecessarily before shunting the gear stick into position and roaring away, ignoring Mayor Kameron who was waving them goodbye as they screeched off.

Back at their bungalow, Hugh was helping his father in the kitchen, Napoleon and his boys had returned home to collect their mongrel dog, Boy-Boy, while Joe Sampi had made a detour to the ranger's station to pick up any messages left on the answer phone before they all reconvened at the Whitaker's bungalow. There was a lot to discuss after the debacle earlier that evening.

"Do you need any help, Andrew?" Connie called from the living room.

Hugh popped his head around the kitchen door where he was helping his father make some food.

"No, you sit there and rest," he teased with a grin.

Connie lobbed a cushion at her friend, giggling as he took refuge behind the kitchen door.

"Hey that's an assault... Dad, I'm under attack!" He laughed.

A tap on the door was the starting gun for Connie and Hugh to participate in a race to see who could reach the front door first.

Connie slid to a halt, reaching the front door before Hugh had left the 'blocks'.

"Yea! Grandfather," she exclaimed in pleasure, planting a kiss on the old man's cheek.

"Hello darl, it's nice to see you too. Anyone would think I'd been gone for a week," he said, his eyes twinkling with amusement.

Connie grabbed her grandfather's arm and tried to drag him the short distance to the kitchen.

"Come on, Andrew's got the kettle on."

"Typical, you'll never take the pom out of him," he grinned. "He thinks everything can be sorted out with a cup of tea."

"And it can," the younger man laughed.

Sampi lifted a bulging carrier bag into the air, "Here, can you put these stubbies in the fridge?"

At that moment, Boy-Boy nosed open the door and bounded in, as usual his short tail wagging like a flag fluttering in the wind.

"Hiya lad," Hugh laughed, trying to fend off the dog's affections as it bounced up and down like a yo-yo in an attempt to lick his face.

"Dad, Napoleon's here," Hugh called. "Come on, you daft dog," he said, kissing the top of its scruffy head.

Eager to greet everyone in the same enthusiastic way, Boy-Boy bounded into the kitchen, his claws striking the wooden floor in a rhythmic fashion as he hurried off, no doubt to find someone else to lick.

The single story building was buzzing with animated conversation as they discussed the events of the meeting earlier that evening.

Mikey prised the top off his bottle of beer with his teeth, his actions causing Hugh to cringe. Ignoring the boy's reaction, the young man tossed a couple of packets of potato chips onto the table, almost knocking a can of soda over.

"Careful, you dill," his brother warned.

"Yeah, you could have ruined our priceless Persian rug," Hugh laughed, his voice thick with distain as he waved his hand over the rough wooden floor in an exaggerated fashion.

The Whitaker's had worked hard in the short time they had lived there to make their bungalow more of a home, the rented property still needed a lot doing to it. It hadn't been easy eradicating years of neglect and use as a drugs den by its previous occupant to change the dilapidated building into something habitable.

"Hugh, Connie, can you give me a hand?"

"Hang on, Dad, we'll be there in just a tick."

Whitaker pointed to the pile of crockery he'd just unpacked, purchased during his trip to Hobart.

"Can you take that through and put it on the table, please, Hugh? There you go, can you manage the pasta, Connie?"

Without waiting for an answer, Whitaker lifted a large saucepan of bolognaise sauce off the hob and followed the kids into the living room.

"Let's eat," Whitaker declared. Lifting a plate off the top of the pile he spooned pasta into the middle before passing it to Joe Sampi. "Help yourself to bolognaise and cutlery. I hope you are going to enjoy this wonderful *English* cuisine," he joked.

"I thought pasta was Italian?" Mikey mused.

"Na, we commandeered that, along with curry and pizza. This is now as English as roast beef and Yorkshire pud," he laughed. "Okay, not quite."

The room was filled with good natured banter while they ate. With just four chairs, to sit on, Mikey and George had joined Hugh and Connie on the floor.

"This is rather good," George complimented, reaching for his beer. "Although, can I just check, this is beef and not some road kill you picked up on the journey home, isn't it?"

Whitaker tutted, throwing the younger man a pained look.

"Of course it's beef, the kangaroo's in the freezer."

"That's alright then," George laughed.

As Connie took the last of the used crockery into the kitchen, her grandfather tapped the table in order to get everyone's attention.

"Order, order," he called before taking a swig from his beer bottle.

Hugh looked at his father and giggled as the vet raised his eyebrows in mock annoyance. *Joe can be such a laugh,* he thought to himself.

"Right it's time to be serious, no more messing around. I think we've got some idea what we are up against and how the Tasmanian Mining Corporation operate. I don't know if was just me, but I got the impression from that slick lawyer, there's a hell of a lot more to the company than meets the eye."

"Dad was brilliant though, don't you think? He got people well rattled."

The vet blushed, "That wasn't my intention, honest."

Sampi nodded, "No, I agree with Hugh. That might not have been what you intended, but you gave them a lot to think about. It was obvious the mining company hadn't done their homework. Mention of the DFTD work you are conducting was news to that Goodman woman. If they don't handle that well, what with the amount of press coverage here and around the world, their company could suffer some serious reputational damage. But that's an additional weapon in our arsenal. Let's get to the real reason for our concern, and that's protecting our Tassie tigers."

Napoleon nodded, "Agreed."

Sampi continued, "I think in the short term we need to wait and see how the situation develops."

"No!" Hugh interrupted, his face red with indignation. "We've got to do something now, we can't wait."

"What do you suggest we do?" The old man asked, deliberately keeping his tone soft so as not to embarrass the boy, they all knew how passionate he felt about protecting the thylacine.

Hugh shook his head, "Dunno," he mumbled.

"I think you have just hit the nail on the head, Hugh," his father mused.

Confused, Hugh looked up, "How?"

Joe Sampi attempted to enlighten his audience.

"We don't know what we need to do until we assess what impact the mining company has. We don't want a knee jerk reaction to a problem that may not exist. We need to discover as much as possible about the Tasmanian Mining Corporation, the exact position of the bore holes etc. When we know that, we can try and work out what dangers it may inflict on the thylacine and the devil population." He paused for a moment, it looked as if he was deciding what to say next. "I was thinking about calling in Norseman..."

Connie jumped up, "Not that traitor!"

Sampi shook his head as he sighed, "Hold on, darl, I've told you, Dick Norseman didn't betray his aboriginal heritage. You know he hacked Tate's email account. He told us that *journalist* woman, Patricia Collins had contacted him to find out what the ranger was doing. It was

Tate's subsequent actions that almost resulted in the knowledge of the thylacine being public. Norseman isn't a traitor."

They were arguing over Dick Norseman, a computer hacker engaged by Patricia Collins, a freelance journalist, to hack into the Parks and Wildlife database to verify the rumours she'd heard about genuine thylacine sightings. In particular, she had wanted access to email communications sent by the late Spencer Tate.

Although Norseman provided Patricia Collins with the information he had stolen, he returned the money she had paid him, every damn cent of it before meeting with Joe Sampi to tell him Tate was attempting to sell a thylacine. It had been a long time since he had been in touch with his ancestral heritage. In spite of the mixed blood running through his veins it was difficult to believe, when looking at his large hooked nose and sallow complexion, that he was an Aboriginal Tasmanian through and through.

Connie looked away, kissing the back of her teeth. Hugh could see she wasn't happy with this new development, her brown cheeks were flushed a deep shade of pink, tiny tears formed at the corner of her eyes as she tried to blink them away.

Sampi turned to his friend, "What do you think, Napoleon?"

The Aboriginal Tasmanian inhaled before speaking, "Well, the mining company haven't made public the research they submitted in order to obtain their licence. If we knew that, we'd have some idea what we are up against." He stole a quick glance around the room, everyone seemed to be hanging on his every word. He licked his lips before continuing. "Joe's right, perhaps we should engage Norseman to hack into the mining company's computer, access the geological data they are basing their mining applications on. It's a long shot but we could be worrying without reason."

"How can they mine in a National Park?" Hugh asked his father.

The vet shrugged.

"Dunno, big business has the habit of getting whatever it wants, son."

"That's a good point, Hugh. We could ask Norseman to check that out too," George suggested. "You've got to wonder why there are designated parks and areas of special scientific beauty or whatever they're called, if companies can just do what they like."

"Agreed. And another thing, that Laura Goodman is more than just a pretty face."

"What do you mean, Grandfather?"

"Mmm, how can I explain it? Ah I know, the way she kept looking at the floor and then up through her eyelashes, it makes her look..." he paused for a moment, as if thinking of a comparison to make. "She looked shy and vulnerable. She reminded me of the late Princess of Wales."

"Lady Di?" George asked.

Sampi nodded.

"She was a great exponent of that trick."

Connie gasped, "What do you mean, I thought you liked her?"

"I do, I mean I did. You of all people know I'm a staunch royalist, darl."

His granddaughter nodded.

"That's true, I remember you telling me how you'd waited for hours to get a glimpse of the Queen when she visited Tasmania."

"Don't get me wrong, I liked Diana but I'm not so sure there was ever a 'shy Di!' She saw her opportunity to be the next Queen of England and grabbed it. That took grit and determination. Laura Goodman looked pretty and feminine but I think she's as hard as nails."

"Yep, a right cold bitch," Mikey muttered.

"That may be a bit harsh, but she is a hardnosed business woman, she'd have to be to have achieved what she has. Let's face it, mining's a man's world," he looked at his granddaughter as a look of annoyance flashed across her face.

"I'm sorry sweetheart, but that's a fact of life, I'm sure woman are equally as good if they get the opportunity, she's an example of that, but mining is pretty much a man's world. Laura Goodman is the type who won't let anything come between her and her goal."

"Forgetting the thylacine for a moment..." Hugh interjected, holding his index finger in the air as he spoke.

Napoleon whistled.

"Wow, I never thought I'd hear Hugh Whitaker say 'forget the Tassie tiger' for a moment!" His eyes alight with amusement, "what is it you kids say - ah yes, I'm gobsmacked."

"Ahh, Napoleon, stop it. What I was going to say is, *forget the Tassie tiger for a moment,* what do you think they are after – the Tasmanian Mining Company, I mean."

A wry smile creased Sampi's face, "To be honest, I don't know. They may be legit. I've, well I've just got this feeling deep in my gut," he placed his clenched fist low on his abdomen as if to emphasise the point.

"Grandfather, I know I've made my opinion clear about Mr. Norseman."

Her grandfather cocked his head and smiled.

"But if you are sure. I mean really *certain* about him, perhaps you are right."

Her grandfather drained his bottle of beer, wiping his mouth on the back of his hand before speaking.

"Without labouring the point, I believe he didn't know what he was getting into with Patricia Collins. He didn't have to tell me Spencer Tate was trying to sell the thylacine to the highest bidder, that's for sure."

Hugh nodded in agreement.

"I don't just rate Norseman's ability as a hacker, I believe he values his aboriginal roots in spite of the fact he is of mixed race. As far as I'm concerned he can be trusted." He took a step closer to his granddaughter and engulfed her in a bear hug. "Look, I may not be able to convince you, but unlike any of us, Norseman is best placed to do some investigative work. It's illegal, we all know that, but he will be taking the risks, and he knows how to cover his tracks. I know, as a complete technophobe, I haven't got a clue what to do, and I'm sure you don't either."

"Yeah, you're right about the technophobe bit, Joe," Whitaker grinned.

Hugh laughed, "Yeah, I can remember you referring to Tate's email correspondence as e-thingy's."

"Tate was one man. These new developments mean we could be taking on a national company, maybe even the Tasmanian Government, so we need someone good enough to crack computers and such like without being found out. Dick Norseman is that good!"

Hugh leant in to whisper in Connie's ear, "You can bet this all kicks off as soon as school starts. Bloody typical, eh?"

"Yeah, too right."

Hugh continued, "I don't know about you but I'm not averse to skipping the odd day from school if needs be."

Connie glanced at her grandfather and nodded, "Me too."

"Hey, I heard that," Sampi glowered.

"He doesn't miss a trick," Hugh mumbled.

Chapter Six

Hugh's father had arranged to spend the following day at the ranger's station. He had negotiated permission to set up a small animal veterinary practice while working on secondment with the Devil Face Tumour Disease project. As with the 'local' doctor, the nearest veterinary practice prior to his arrival was over an hour's drive, so he was beginning to be popular amongst the residents of Sullivan's Creek.

He'd arranged to see a number of pets as well as neuter a kitten and a German Shepherd bitch that morning. If work continued to expand like this, he might have to consider some part time assistance. It was a pleasant thought though; he'd sold his small animal practice in London when his research career started to take off and he hadn't realised how much he'd missed it.

Whitaker smiled to himself. It was a weight off his mind to know Hugh had settled in so well, especially as before their arrival his son had been adamant he never wanted to set foot in Tasmania, or that God-forsaken-place as he'd called it. If only he and Connie didn't put themselves in peril at every opportunity, neither of them had anything to prove, but danger, it seemed, had become their constant companion.

Slowing his Land Rover as he approached the ranger's station, he reversed the vehicle in order to park under a tree, it was already hot so the shade would make the internal temperature of the vehicle more comfortable when he drove home.

Napoleon and George had already opened up and Mikey was talking to a woman clutching a cat basket. It looked as if his first patient had arrived.

Back at their cabin, Joe Sampi was getting ready for an overnight stay in Hobart. He had managed to get a message to Dick Norseman who'd agreed, if a little half-heartedly, to meet with him. Angie had pulled a few strings and arranged for a room at the nurse's hostel, no mean feat at such short notice. With luck, his battered truck would make it to Hobart and back without breaking down. Andrew had offered to cover the petrol costs, which, in spite of his pride, he was grateful to accept.

Joe called to Connie to get a move on, he'd promised he'd drop her off at the Whitaker's bungalow before leaving.

"Please, Grandfather, please let me come with you, I want to see Mum too."

"I know you do, darl. And under different circumstances you'd be more than welcome, but this is a flying visit. I have so much to do in such a short space of time. Mum'll be working too, you know that, so there's no time for sightseeing. Anyway, I need you to keep an eye on Hugh, make sure he doesn't get into too much mischief. We can't afford another accident," he said, trying to make a joke out of the situation.

Blinking back tears, Connie forced a smile.

"Yeah, even Hugh couldn't fall into another sinkhole or get involved with a thug like Spencer Tate quite so soon after the last time, eh?"

Sampi pulled the drawstring of his duffle bag holding the few bits and bobs he needed for his night away. Like so many things they owned it had seen better days, but there was no point in borrowing a suitcase for one night away.

"Yeah, I hope we never meet anyone like Spencer Tate again. I don't think I could live with the thought of someone threatening you or Hugh like he did." Joe Sampi was silent for a moment before continuing, glancing around his room to make sure he hadn't forgotten anything. "I never thought he was clever, but I guess it was a stroke of genius on Tate's part to engage two collectors in a bidding war for an animal the 'outside' world still thinks is extinct."

"Yeah, but he put the thylacine in danger, Grandfather, and," she shrugged, "it cost him his life."

Sampi slung the duffle bag over his shoulder.

"Yes it did," he said. "It did indeed. I guess the old adage 'crime doesn't pay' rang true in his case, eh? Come on, give me a hug." He opened his arms wide to embrace his granddaughter. "Right, get your bag and I'll drop you off en-route."

Connie frowned.

"I don't know why I can't stay here," she grumbled. "Napoleon's next door, oh and there's Aggi too," she added, referring to their other neighbour.

"Now you're being silly. Aggi's almost a hundred, deaf as a post and her eyesight isn't great so she wouldn't be much help in an emergency." Her grandfather's expression clouded. "I've made my decision. You are going to stay with Andrew and Hugh, and that's final."

Connie nodded, there was little point in arguing any further.

"Guess you'll still be arranging to have me baby-sat when I'm twenty," she joked.

"Na, at least thirty-five!" He teased.

Hearing the distinctive sound of Sampi's truck pulling up outside, Hugh hurried to the door. Joe Sampi waved from the cab as he approached.

"Come on darl, give us a smile before I leave."

Connie grinned, she was never able to stay angry for long, she took after her mother in that respect.

"That's better," Sampi smiled, squeezing her tight. "I'm gonna miss you. Now go on, out you get and I'll see you tomorrow."

Connie clamoured out of the cab, grabbing her bag of night clothes and went to the rear of the vehicle where Hugh was lifting her bike off the back of the truck.

"Bloody hell, I hope he makes it to Hobart and back," Hugh observed, listening to the exhaust rattle as Joe Sampi drove off. "Come on, let's stash your stuff indoors and go for a ride. Dad said he'd be back by lunchtime."

"Ha ha, knowing your dad that'll be four p.m." She laughed. "Especially if he's got stuck into something interesting at work."

"You'll be in my room, I'm gonna sleep on the sofa."

"Don't be stupid."

Hugh looked hurt, "Charming, I'm not trying to be gallant or such like."

Connie pulled a face.

"Yeah right."

"Nope, far from it. With legs like a giraffe, you'd be hanging off the end of the sofa." He grinned as he spoke. "I'm being practical, that's all. Fancy a drink before we leave?" He added, indicating the subject was closed.

Connie shook her head.

"Okay, I'll grab some water for later. Where shall we go?"

"Sullivan's Rise?"

Hugh laughed, "Snap, my thoughts exactly!"

Retrieving his bike from the side of the bungalow, Hugh paused by Titch's enclosure. The wallaby stopped grazing and hopped closer. It hadn't taken her long to learn he always had a tit-bit for her.

Spencer Tate had brought the injured animal to the surgery having 'found' her laying injured by the side of the road. Unbeknown to Hugh, the ranger had deliberately run the creature over, but thanks to his father's skill as a veterinary surgeon she was getting stronger by the day.

Hugh leant over the side of the enclosure and scratched the top of her head, before leaving her an apple to nibble on, pushing the thought of her imminent release back into the wild from his mind. He hated the idea of losing her. In spite of his father's occupation, she was the first pet he'd ever had. Mikey had given him some advice which he intended to follow, he'd convinced his father she should be released nearby, and if he continued to supplement her feeding, perhaps she'd remain in the vicinity.

As usual, Connie was streaking ahead, her long legs and natural athleticism meant she found most outdoor activities easy.

Riding to the top of the Rise, they gave the opening to the sinkhole Hugh had fallen into a wide berth. Although Joe Sampi and Napoleon had roped off the entrance to the fissure, they hadn't found the time to fence it properly, this temporary arrangement would have to do for the time being, they couldn't afford the risk of anyone else falling into it. Hugh had suffered a broken arm, but at least he'd escaped with his life, someone else might not be so lucky.

Lying in the sun, the youngsters scanned the undergrowth for sight of the magical creature, but no luck. It looked as though the thylacine had moved her pups.

Hugh was about to suggest they try elsewhere when Connie tapped his foot.

"Look, 'bout four o'clock." She pointed to a thicket of trees, it was typical of the thylacine to choose the densest area of vegetation in the immediate area.

"Damn, I can't see her."

With meticulous care he scanned the area Connie indicated, at last spotting her, curled up in the undergrowth.

"Gotcha," he whispered. "Where do you think the pups are?"

She pulled a face which said how-the-hell-do-I-know as she gazed at the sleeping creature.

"Dunno, they won't be far. In her pouch, perhaps, who knows?"

"Mmm, maybe, but judging by how big they'd got the last time we saw them, I'd say it's getting a bit crowded in there, what with three of them."

'Well why ask if you know the answer,' she fumed to herself.

A loud crash shattered the idyll.

The thylacine jumped up, disappearing into the shadows.

"What the hell!" Hugh scrambled up, grabbing Connie's arm and yanking her to her feet.

With care they crawled to the edge of the cliff and peered over the drop. From their vantage point they had a good view of the clearing below.

"Damn, damn, damn! Tell me I'm dreaming."

Connie pushed herself up onto her elbows to get a better look.

"Dunno about dreaming, I think we're both having the same nightmare." She pushed her hair back behind her ears, leaving a smudge of dirt on her brown cheek.

Hugh couldn't stop himself from shivering. For a second he relived the sight of his nemesis, Spencer Tate falling over the edge. He closed his eyes as he visualised the look of horror on the man's face and the sound of his scream as he fell. He shook his head as if the physical movement to the right and left would eradicate the image from his mind.

They could see a white van parked below, the devastation it had caused forcing its way through the vegetation evident in its wake.

Hugh pointed to the side of the vehicle. A scarlet logo dominated the side panel, it was a drawing of a digger, the words Tasmanian Mining Corporation printed in black around the circumference of the design.

"They didn't waste any time, did they?" He complained.

"And after all they said! That Goodman woman promised a period of full public consultation," Connie replied, her voice calm in an attempt to diffuse his ill humour.

"From the look of it, it was a bloody short consultative period."

"You're right," she replied. "Can you make out what they are doing?"

Hugh removed his glasses and gave them a quick polish on the edge of his tee shirt.

"Looks like those two men are removing equipment from the back of the van."

Connie nodded, "Yeah, I think you're right."

He inched closer to the edge of the cliff, disturbing some soil in the process.

"Hey, be careful," she hissed.

Hugh waved her away, "I'm fine!"

They watched in silence. One of the men erected a tripod, while the other walked a distance of several metres before turning to face his colleague, he held a long pole dissected by a series of graduations in his hand.

"I think they are surveying the area," Hugh observed. "Yep, that's what they are, they're surveyors."

"Surveyors?"

Hugh grinned.

"What's so funny now," she demanded.

"Nothing. It's, well it's you're doing your parrot impersonation. Repeating what I say... Pretty Polly... Pretty Polly."

"Oi, cut that out," she demanded, whacking him on the arm in a playful fashion. "Ouch," she laughed, shaking the sting out of her hand. "That hurt." She'd hit him harder than she intended.

He laughed, loving the way her eyes flashed with anger when he teased her.

She smiled, at least his good humour was back.

"Cut it out," she repeated. "We've gotta concentrate, this is serious," she said, shuffling into a more comfortable position.

From where they sat it was impossible to hear what the two men were saying, but it was obvious they were being meticulous in their actions as they surveyed the area. They stopped every now and again to make notes and take photographs from various different angles, as if recording every centimetre of the area below.

Two hours later, they watched as the two men packed up their equipment and drove off, managing to damage more vegetation in the process.

Hugh dragged himself to his feet before offering Connie a hand up.

"Thanks mate," she said, brushing the grass off her jeans.

Hugh smiled.

"What you grinning at now?"

"Nothing in particular, it's just, well, those are the tatty jeans you had on when I first met you. Look, there's the rip you accused me of making," he pointed to the tear in the fabric over her knee.

Connie narrowed her eyes as she spoke, "I'll have you know, these are a designer garment."

"Yeah right," he laughed.

She joined in the laughter.

"Na, you're right. I've had these for ages, and they were hand-me-downs from someone mum works with."

Hugh detected the false gaiety in her tone. The Sampi's were a proud family, even though they accepted second hand clothes with gratitude and good grace, he knew it embarrassed Connie to admit it.

"I wonder how grandfather's getting on," she asked. "Shall we head back, see if he's been in touch?"

"Sounds like a good idea to me, we'll need to tell the others what we've seen anyway."

Chapter Seven

By mid-afternoon, Joe Sampi found himself standing at the top of the stairs leading down to 'The Crypt,' the bar where he'd agreed to meet Dick Norseman.

It had been a long drive, made more arduous by the fact he'd been stuck in a traffic jam on the outskirts of Hobart for over an hour, the result of a three car pile-up. He'd parked up with a feeling of relief, there had been a couple of times when the engine of his 'beloved' truck had come very close to overheating. At least the vehicle would have time to cool down and he'd have a chance to fill the radiator with water without being engulfed in a cloud of steam before driving to meet his daughter.

It was apparent the owners of the 'The Crypt' didn't observe the ban on smoking in enclosed public areas as he peered through the gloomy layer of cigarette smoke hanging in the air. Not that he was averse to people smoking, Hadn't he been addicted to cheap durry in his youth? But with a wife he adored, a baby daughter and a low paid job, it meant he had to quit smoking, his priorities had been food, clothes and a roof over the heads of his family, it was a no brainer.

Watching the smoke swirl in the slight breeze blowing in through the open door was enough to make him think twice about descending the narrow staircase, but the folks at home were depending on him.

Turning his head, he filled his lungs with clean air and hurried down the steep stairs, his boots clumping against the wooden stairway as he descended into the bowels of the dingy building.

Joe Sampi took a few steps into the bar and looked around. A raven haired woman in a cheap red dress propped up the bar, a cigarette drooping from her lips as she hung onto every word the bald headed man she was sitting with was saying. A tall black man dressed in jeans and a checked shirt stood with his back to the staircase as he prepared to throw a dart at the board hanging on the wall opposite. To the right of the stairs, an office worker in a crumpled grey suit played the fruit machine. The contents of the glass he'd placed on top swilled in a dangerous fashion as he kicked the machine in frustration, having lost his money for the umpteenth time that day. Behind the bar, the bartender concentrated on the glass he twisted in the grubby tea-towel he held, seemingly oblivious to his clientele. Without doubt, this establishment was the pits.

The unexpected sound of snooker balls clunking together startled the old man. Twisting, he could just make out the edge of a snooker table hidden under the staircase. It was in obvious need of repair, most of the green baize was missing. The old man couldn't help wondering how anyone could line up a shot on a table like that.

Bent over the corner brace was a sallow skinned man with a large hooked nose. With undisputed skill he took aim and fired the white ball at the black, the last ball on the table, sending it cannoning towards the top corner pocket. Satisfied, he stood up and wiped his nose on the back of his hand. Sampi cringed, was it too much to expect people to use a handkerchief? Thank goodness it was his left hand and he wouldn't have to shake it!

If it wasn't from the size and shape of his nose, which had been likened to that of the Dickins character, Fagin, on more than one occasion, Joe Sampi would not have recognised the man. He was expecting someone of mixed race, scruffy in appearance with long straw-like hair. The man in front of him appeared to have undergone a radical make over, he was clean shaven, his thin hair had been cut short and his clothes were clean and tidy, he could easily pass as an office worker in that get up.

"Mr. Norseman?"

The stranger looked at Sampi, his coal black eyes made the older man shudder, they seemed to pierce right through to his soul.

Norseman nodded, "Joe Sampi?"

Sampi extended his hand.

"Is there somewhere more private we can go? I have something of the utmost importance to discuss."

"You wanna talk about the Tassie?"

The look of anger that flashed across the old man's face was enough to silence Dick Norseman in mid-sentence.

"Believe me, Mr. Sampi, what's discussed within these four walls, stays within these four walls. It's as safe as Fort Knox! There's a code of conduct adhered to by the patrons of The Crypt. The last snitch was found murdered with his tongue cut out."

Sampi raised an eyebrow.

"Okay, I was making that last bit up," Norseman confessed, "but you've no need to worry."

Sampi wasn't convinced, his expression said it all.

"Come and sit over here," Norseman pointed to a small, round wooden table. "It's opposite the stairs and you can observe the whole room, except the snooker table. You'll be able to see if anyone's ear wigging on our conversation."

Sampi nodded.

"I'll take your word for it."

He followed Norseman to the table and perched on one of the stools, tutting when he realised the one he'd chosen seemed to have a wobble.

"Drink?"

Sampi nodded, "Yes please, it's been a bloody awful trip."

Norseman whistled, producing a short, sharp sound. Sampi waited as the bartender looked up. His companion signalled for two beers. Choosing to be safe rather than sorry, the Aboriginal Tasmanian remained silent until the bartender had brought the drinks over and returned to the other side of the bar to resume his tedious job of drying the same glass.

Sampi took a sip from the cool amber fluid, it tasted good after such a long journey, while Norseman downed half the contents of his glass in a couple of gulps.

"I want to start by thanking you for giving me the heads up, about Tate's shenanigans I mean."

Norseman stared at the older man, his expression earnest.

"The tiger's safe?"

Sampi shrugged.

"We thought so."

Norseman placed his glass on the table and lent across the table, giving the older man his undivided attention.

"Go on."

"A number of licences have been granted to excavate exploratory bore holes."

Norseman nodded, he'd seen it on the telly.

"Yeah, I've heard something about that, didn't take much notice though."

Sampi nodded his understanding as he continued.

"I'm afraid one of the licences has been granted to mine Warrugul National Park."

"No shit!" Norseman exclaimed.

A wry smile sprung to Sampi's lips, "I'm afraid so."

Norseman whistled under his breath.

"Is there a way you could bring yourself to look into the mining company, the Tasmanian Mining Corporation, see what you can find out? And perhaps look into the rules and regulations for mining in a National Park, let's see if there is anything that can be done to stop it before it starts?"

Norseman was silent for a moment, picking at a dirty coaster with his fingernail as he thought.

"Gee, that causes me a problem."

Sampi's face darkened.

"I was thinking of going legit."

"What do you mean?"

"I've been looking into taking some ethical hacking courses, see about making my 'hobby' legal."

Sampi nodded, "I see. I can understand that."

"What with cybercrime so high profile, it's in the news all the time nowadays, it's getting too risky, better I go legit and get paid for what I do, than risk jail."

Sampi glanced around the room. A couple had drifted in while they were talking and were standing at the bar waiting to be served, but no one seemed to be the slightest bit interested in their conversation.

"Okay, I'll do it," Norseman whispered.

"Sorry, I missed that?"

Norseman sat up straight and looked the older man in the eye.

"I said, I'll do it. I'll make this my last illegal hack. If it means we'll ensure the Tassie tiger's safe, it's worth the risk."

Sampi nodded.

"We can't pay you very much I'm afraid. It won't be enough to compensate you for the risk you are taking."

"Let me stop you there and put you straight once and for all."

Sampi raised his eyebrows, a little taken aback by the aggression in Norseman's voice.

"I'm sorry, Dick, I didn't mean to cause offence."

Norseman shook his head, "No, I'm sorry, that was rude of me. I don't want payment. Not where the Tassi tiger's concerned. I don't know if you are aware, but I returned every cent to that journalist woman as soon as I knew I was dealing with a 'tiger', every last cent."

Sampi nodded.

"I had heard," he said, reaching into his duffle bag and retrieving the brochure he'd brought from the public meeting. "Is this of any use to you?"

Norseman flicked though the glossy pages and shook his head.

"Looks as if you are up against mega bucks here. Big business. This might be fun after all," he grinned, exposing his nicotine stained teeth.

"I've scribbled the address of the ranger's station on the back, along with the phone number and that of my friend and neighbour, Napoleon Toba. He can be trusted one hundred percent."

Norseman nodded.

"Fancy another drink?"

Sampi shook his head as he drained his glass.

"No thanks, Dick, I'm planning to spend the rest of the evening with my daughter."

"Sounds nice," Norseman said, standing to offer the older man his hand for a second time. "Don't have kids myself."

"They can be a bit of a pain at times but they're worth the hassle and heartache," Sampi grinned. "It's been a pleasure to meet you in person. Thank you for agreeing to help."

Norseman nodded as they shook hands. "It's been nice meeting you too, Mr. Sampi."

By the time Hugh and Connie arrived at Warrugul Ranger's Station, Whitaker had finished his list of routine operations and seen three patients. The tortoiseshell kitten and German Shepherd bitch he'd spayed were both recovering from their anaesthetics, along with a dwarf lop eared rabbit that needed an abscess drained from its neck, she was already up and nibbling on a dandelion leaf.

Hugh rushed up the stairs onto the veranda.

"Dad," he called.

Mikey put his finger to his lips and shushed him quiet.

"He's seeing a patient."

"Whoops, sorry," Hugh grimaced. "We'll wait outside."

Mikey nodded, "That's a good idea. You two are always rushing around as if you have a rocket stuck up your bums."

They didn't have to wait long before Whitaker's patient, a yellow Labrador, led the way out of the consulting room, dragging its owner behind her.

"She's leaving a hell of a lot quicker than when she arrived. Her owner had to carry her in, and with a dog that fat, believe me it was no mean feat," Mikey remarked as the dog skid-daddled down the stairs.

The two friends walked into the consulting room as the vet wiped the examination table with disinfection.

"G'day," he greeted as he walked to the sink to wash his hands.

"Busy?"

Whitaker looked at his son and smiled, "Yeah, I haven't stopped. It's been great. Things are picking up here, three patients and a few ops."

Hugh whistled, "That's funny. Gone are the days when you were seeing twenty or thirty animals, eh?"

His father nodded.

"What have you been up to?"

Hugh glanced at Connie, who smiled in encouragement.

Hugh rocked on his heels, "Um, don't go off on one, but we saw the mining company today."

Whitaker stopped what he was doing and turned to face his son.

"What?" He demanded. A look of exasperation on his face.

"That's it. You are about to jump to the wrong conclusion as usual." Hugh stormed out of the room, slamming the door in temper.

Whitaker looked at Connie, who blushed with embarrassment.

"I'm sorry, love. You shouldn't be in the middle of our arguments all the time. It's not fair on you," he said, opening the door to go after his son. "Hugh, stop acting like a two-year-old. I didn't jump to any conclusion, wrong or otherwise. How do you expect me to act? Angie, Joe and I are your parents and guardians." He glanced over at Connie, to include her in that statement. "What do you expect?" Glancing at his son's crestfallen expression, a wave of guilt washed over him. "I'm sorry, Hugh, okay, I'm sorry if I got it wrong."

Andrew Whitaker ran his fingers through his hair, thinking what to do next.

"No, I'm sorry, Dad. We didn't go looking for the mining company, same as we haven't endangered ourselves on purpose. It, well, it just happens."

Hugh looked across the room. Mikey stood behind the desk, pretending to be engrossed in something on the computer screen but it was obvious he was listening to every word they said.

"We went to Sullivan's Rise. You know that's where we've seen the thylacine most often. We needed to see her, check she and the pups were okay."

Whitaker nodded.

"Was she there?"

Hugh's face lit up as he spoke.

"Yeah, she was asleep, but we spotted her. Well, Connie did."

Mikey cleared his throat.

"For goodness sake, stop pussy-footing around and get on with the story," he laughed. "I can't stand here pretending to be interested in this boring website much longer," he said, flicking the monitor with his finger.

Taking the hint, Hugh continued.

"There was a crash which spooked the thylacine so we looked over the edge of the cliff."

Whitaker raised his eyes towards heaven and shook his head, "Give me strength."

"It's fine, we were careful, honest. We didn't go too close to the edge." *A little white lie won't hurt*, he thought. "There was a van in the middle of the clearing – we could see the logo for the Tasmanian Mining Corporation – the one on the front of their brochure."

Bewildered, Whitaker scratched his head.

"Are you sure?"

Connie nodded, "Yeah, we both saw it."

One glance at the kid's expressions were enough for their audience to see they were telling the truth.

"They were surveying the area."

Mikey jumped out from behind the desk, sending his chair clattering to the floor.

"You're having a laugh? They are supposed to consult with the local community before they start anything. The meeting was less than twenty-four hours ago and already they are reneging on the promises they made."

Whitaker was silent for a moment.

"I know it's not what you want to hear but we must be sensible. We can't go off half-cocked. We have to wait for Joe to get back tomorrow. When we know how his meeting with Norseman went we can decide what to do. In the meantime, we wait. *All* of us!" He emphasised, looking at his son and then at Connie.

Chapter Eight

William Appleby knocked once and entered the palatial office Laura Goodman had occupied since her appointment as CEO of the company. She covered the mouthpiece of her phone and whispered she wouldn't be long.

He wandered around the room as he waited, his eyes resting for a moment on a large piece of abstract artwork painted by an up and coming young Tasmanian artist. It seemed he was going to be the next big name to take the art world by storm, and from the price ticket he, or rather his agent, had demanded, he had started to believe what was written in his reviews.

The room commanded one of the best views of Hobart the city could offer and if he were honest it was a view he wanted for himself.

Having ended her conversation, Laura Goodman indicated he should take a seat as she instructed her personal assistant she was not to be disturbed for the next hour.

Standing, Goodman reached for the decanter of whiskey which she showed to her companion.

"Please," Appleby replied. "It must be five o'clock somewhere."

Goodman smiled at his joke, she'd lost count of the number of times she'd heard it but it kept him happy if she laughed.

Having poured two generous measures, she resumed her seat and savoured the taste of the aged golden-brown liquid.

"What did you find out?" She asked, examining a dirty mark on her glass as she spoke.

Appleby swallowed the whisky as he opened the file he had compiled on Warrugul National Park.

"The park itself has no special significance, apart, of course, for the mineral report indicating there is a substantial vein of Scandium. There is a ranger's station, again nothing special in that, but there was a recent scandal when one of the ranger's was believed to be trying to sell a rare animal to a private collector, a Tasmanian devil, I think."

Goodman pulled a face, "A Tasmanian devil, are you sure?"

Appleby scribbled a note in the margin of his report to remind himself to double check.

"I'll get back to you on that. They actually said a thylacine but I assumed it was a typo."

Goodman sniggered, "Yeah sounds like it. Either that, or we are dealing with a load of morons, the thylacine's been extinct for decades."

The lawyer continued, "There's a small community of Aboriginal Tasmanian's – they're bound to be desperate for some work, but they'll be worth keeping an eye on, you know how that sort can be trouble."

"Get the heritage chap on that," she clicked her fingers, "You know who I mean, I forget his name."

"Richard Pirlatapa?"

She nodded as he continued.

"However, as you mentioned last night, there is one name that cropped up. Someone worth watching," he tapped the page as Goodman leant over to see who he had highlighted.

"Andrew Whitaker, the vet?" She asked, cradling her glass in her hands.

Appleby nodded.

"I agree. His performance last night was spectacular. Remind me about him."

"He is a British veterinary oncologist on a year-long secondment. There is an option to make his contract permanent if both parties agree. It seems he was well respected in the UK but he gave all that up to work on the DFTD project here."

"Ah yes, he torpedoed us with that, didn't he? Right, he is the one I'm going to concentrate on." She glanced at her colleague as she sipped her drink. "Oh for goodness sake stop pouting, this is just business." She grabbed his tie and pulled him close in order to kiss him.

Goodman narrowed her eyes, "He is definitely the one to watch." She smiled, a malicious glint in her eyes, as she continued. "And, if he becomes too troublesome or pisses me off once too often, well, secondments have the habit of being shortened."

Chapter Nine

Hugh flopped down on the floor.

"Hey, shove over, you lump," Connie said to him. "You might have lost weight but you're no fairy elephant."

Hugh smiled, but the gesture masked an air of sadness.

"What's wrong, what'd I say?"

Hugh wrinkled his nose as he shook his head.

"Nothing much. It's something my mum used to say – stop charging around like a fairy elephant." He smiled at the memory.

Connie propped herself up on her elbow, "What was she like?"

Hugh was silent for a moment. His face lit up as he thought about his mother, but there was a hint of sorrow in his eyes.

"She was nice."

Connie smiled, "Wow that tells me a lot."

Hugh swivelled to face her, he could see her interest was genuine. He stared into the distance, trying to visualise a picture of his mother in his mind.

"This is gonna sound bad, but she committed suicide on my fourth birthday."

Connie gasped, her hand flying to her mouth as she groaned in shock.

"I know, I felt awful every time I thought about it until a few weeks back."

Connie looked confused.

Hugh shrugged, "I'd have never believed it if I didn't know your grandfather so well."

She was hooked, she shuffled closer.

"Go on."

Hugh sucked a mouthful of air through clenched teeth, hoping he hadn't opened a can of worms.

"Remember the day we went to see the platypus?"

Her eyes flickered with recognition.

Hugh was flushed, his skin a deep shade of scarlet as he recounted what had happened. He'd caught Sampi sitting in a trance... it had looked as if he were asleep but his eyes were open. He explained her grandfather had said he had been in touch with his mother.

"Connie, he knew everything, the fact she jumped from Blackfriars Bridge, leaving me alone. No one had told me she was suffering from a terminal brain tumour, something my dad didn't know until the post-mortem."

Connie shook her head.

"Wow, I'd been told he was good. Spiritual, I mean, but that's, that's way out," she moved her arm in a horizontal plane at head height, "way out," she repeated.

"We'd spend hours playing hide and seek, and she would read a story to me every night. That's, well, that was until she got sick. I was too young to realise, but in hindsight she started to change, but what can I say, she was my mum," he gushed, "Dad refused to talk about her. For a long time, he stayed silent and that hurt. That was the time when I needed to talk about her, to remind myself what she was like, to keep her memory alive. We were at loggerheads. He couldn't move on from his grief, and I needed to learn as much as I could about her."

Connie shuffled even closer to her friend.

"You can talk to me about her anytime. I'd love to get to know her," she smiled.

"That would be great." Hugh smiled.

"And you're sure you're okay about Andrew dating my mum? It's obvious how close you were to your mum."

"Of course, I said I was fine about it and I meant it."

"Good. I'm glad, as far as I'm concerned it's a no brainer. You know that my dad, or should I say *sperm donor* did a bunk before I was born."

Hugh nodded, she'd told him ages ago.

"So apart from Grandfather, I've never had a male figure in my life. I'm pleased they are spending time together, if something comes of it, great."

"Yeah, but we won't make plans for a wedding yet. As soon as something nice happens, something else goes wrong – take the thylacine," he mused, changing the subject. "I can't believe she's in danger again."

"Yeah, I know, but it was great to see them again, eh?"

"I still get a thrill every time; I hope that never changes. Though she's in danger from two fronts now."

Connie looked puzzled.

"A confirmed sighting from a member of the public, for instance. There has always been a risk from people charging around trying to claim the bounty for proof of life, but more important than that, now there's the harm to the environment the mining company will cause."

Connie nodded.

"The million-dollar bounty has been around for so long, it's never caused much of an issue, but judging by the damage one van did, the mining is gonna be a nightmare. The trees and vegetation give protection and shelter, places for her to hide and it's gonna get ripped up. You know it will strengthen the case for calling in the Government. Telling them our secret."

Hugh lowered his eyes, "Yep, they'll come in with all guns blazing. Order some population protection initiative, run tests, take blood etc. etc." he speculated. "On the other hand, I suppose there's a chance they'll get it right, this time. Remember, back in the nineteen thirties, they didn't protect the thylacine until it was too late. They left it until they had one specimen left, or so they thought. Perhaps they could create an 'ark project' like they are doing for the devils, you know, capture and move the thylacine to a designated sanctuary?" He suggested, his expression questioning.

"The New Zealand Government did something like that with the Kakapo."

"What's a Kakupooh?"

"Ka-ka-po, not pooh! It's a flightless parrot – a dumpy looking bird too heavy to fly. I believe New Zealand was down to the last fifteen or so birds, but they were moved to an island free from predators, Kakapo can't fly so they nest on the ground, their eggs were easy pickings for rats. Moving them in the nick of time has made a difference, their numbers are still critical, but they are holding their own."

"Kakapo," Hugh repeated.

"Yeah, you've got it."

"Maybe that's the answer. At least the thylacine would be safe from the likes of Spencer Tate and the Tasmanian Mining Corporation. But it'll leave them at the mercy of scientists and such like."

They were startled by the sound of a vehicle backfiring.

"Grandfather."

"Joe."

They shouted in unison.

"Dad, Napoleon... Joe's back," Hugh shouted, following Connie out of the office.

They ran towards the on-coming vehicle as Sampi slowed to a crawl allowing the kids to jump onto the back. Checking they were sitting, he accelerated the short distance back to the ranger's station, reversing the truck to park up alongside the station's Land Rovers.

Whitaker and Napoleon waited on the veranda to greet the arrival.

"Didn't think that heap of rust would make it to Hobart and back, fair dinkum," Napoleon observed.

Whitaker nodded, "I offered him the Land Rover, but you know Joe."

"Yep," Napoleon replied, "that's Joe."

Hugh and Connie leapt from the truck before it had come to a complete standstill.

"Hey, don't let me see you do that again!" Whitaker shouted.

Napoleon shook his old friend's hand as he stepped onto the veranda.

"How did you get on," Hugh demanded. "Is Norseman gonna help?"

"Is he, Grandfather?"

"Hey you two, let him at least get inside the door before you start on him."

Sampi raised his hand.

"It's fine, Andrew. I was expecting the Spanish Inquisition and before you ask, young lady, your mother sends her love," he added, his eyes sparkling as he spoke. "I'll tell you everything before these two burst. Where's Mikey and George?"

"They wanted to get in some tracking practice. They've taken Boy-Boy off somewhere."

"Okay," Sampi perched on the corner of the desk.

"Dick Norseman has agreed to help."

Hugh relaxed, in spite of his reservations, he felt as is a ton of weight had been lifted from his shoulders.

"He wasn't happy to begin with, but he's on board now."

"I hope we can trust him," Connie interrupted.

Sampi raised an eyebrow, the small gesture was enough to push Connie into silence but not before she had muttered an apology.

It wasn't that Sampi was a tyrant, or over strict, indeed Connie could wrap him around her little finger with one of her smiles but he insisted on good manners, in particular when in company. Even when the company were friends as close as these.

Sampi cleared his throat as Connie, blushing a deep shade of pink, stared at the floor.

"Norseman's first instinct was to walk away. He's planning to become legitimate, take some ethical hacking courses, whatever that means."

"Companies will pay him to break into their computer systems, Grandfather. Tell them where they are vulnerable."

Sampi nodded, "I see. Anyway, when I explained about the Tasmanian Mining Corporation and Ms. Goodman, he agreed to undertake some research into the legal niceties of mining in national parks and nature reserves."

"Any idea when he'll be able to get back to us?"

Sampi looked at the vet and shook his head.

"Are you going to tell your Grandfather what you've been doing today?" Napoleon asked.

Connie nodded. It was her turn to tell their audience what they had seen earlier that day, which she did with relish.

"So, in light of the glorious promise for co-operation and consultation, it looks as though the Tasmanian Mining Corporation is jumping the gun and its full steam ahead as far as they are concerned," Whitaker commented. "Why is nothing simple or above board," he added, his question thick with irony.

"For the same reason we had problems with Spencer Tate. We know where money's involved – big money – scruples and ethics go out of the window."

"Connie and I have decided that we're going to keep an eye on their activities from Sullivan's Rise."

"No!" The adults in the room chimed together as if on cue.

Napoleon laughed.

"Your faces are a picture. This is what you look like." He raised his eyebrows, opened his eyes as wide as he could and formed the letter 'O' with his mouth.

"Yeah right," Hugh retorted, irritated at being the butt of everyone's joke again.

"It is rather a good impression," his father teased.

"Wow, if looks could kill, you'd be a puff of smoke, Andrew," Joe Sampi observed.

Chapter Ten

With danger surrounding the future of the thylacine, Hugh and Connie were not prepared to sit back and let the adults dictate the situation. The start of the school term was fast approaching, and they were running out of time and options.

In spite of frequent trips to the top of Sullivan's Rise there were no further sightings of the thylacine and her pups. It was obvious the disturbance was too much for her and she had moved her den.

On the flip side, there were no further sightings of employees from the mining company either. Not that they believed they had seen the last of the Tasmanian Mining Corporation.

Racing one another to the small aboriginal community where Connie lived with her grandfather, they skidded to a halt, catching sight of a battered car parked outside the cabins.

"That's in as bad a nick as Joe's truck," Hugh joked as they walked towards the yellow vehicle. The front bumper was held in place with red plastic string, the type often used to bind agricultural feed bales such as hay and straw. The wing mirror on the passenger's side of the vehicle was missing and there was a crack radiating from a chip in middle of the rear window.

"There's no way that would pass its MOT back home."

"Ha, I doubt the blue heelers would consider it road worthy if they catch sight of it."

"Let's see who the driver is."

Leaving their bikes in a tangled heap, they pushed the corrugated iron door of Connie's cabin, cringing as it slammed against the wooden wall.

"Grandfather, Andrew."

Hugh followed her into the one storey building. A quick glance around the small living area was enough to tell them the building was empty; it wasn't as if there were many places to hide.

"Napoleon's?"

Connie shrugged.

"Worth a look. Come on," she said, leading the way. "Ouch!" She exclaimed, her elbow colliding with the door as they rushed out.

"You ok?"

Connie nodded, blinking away the tears of pain stinging her eyes.

"I've never been able to understand why they call it the funny bone," she grumbled. "There's nothing funny about it when you bash it," she continued, rubbing her arm.

The door to the Toba's cabin stood ajar. Connie knocked once before entering, not waiting to be asked.

Mikey looked up from the note he was writing.

"G'day, young'uns."

Connie smiled.

"Whose car is that outside?"

"What, the yellow one?"

Hugh raised his eyes to the ceiling, "Nooo, the pink Rolls Royce," he retorted, his tone laced with sarcasm.

"Oh, I didn't know Lady Penelope was coming for tea today, I thought that was next week," Mikey replied, calling Hugh's bluff and expanding on the inadvertent joke the boy had made.

"Sorry," Hugh muttered.

"Forget it," Mikey said, exposing his perfect, white teeth which would not have been out of place in a toothpaste advert. "It belongs to Dick Norseman."

"What's it doing here then... where is he... has he found anything out?" Hugh demanded with a string of questions.

"Whoa, one question at a time. No, he isn't here, he's at the ranger's station, and no, I don't know what he's found out. I volunteered to let Boy-Boy out for a pee, he's been cooped up all day as none of us could take him to work with us. I was writing you a note in case you didn't call into the ranger's station. If you want a lift, climb into the back and I'll drive you over with me," he said, holding up a key-ring and rattling it.

"But you can't drive."

Mikey threw Connie a hurt look.

"Let me correct you there, miss," his expression serious. "I can drive, I just haven't *passed* my test, yet."

"Oh how stupid of me," she replied, with a wink. "Do you really expect us to get into that death trap?"

Mikey opened his hands, his palms uppermost.

"Up to you, it's that, or make your own way over."

"Come on, don't be a wuss," Hugh goaded.

"Bagsy I'm in the front."

"Dick's a good guy. I think you'll like him."

Mikey's comments were directed at Connie, but Hugh couldn't help thinking he'd make his own mind up about that.

Boy-Boy was waiting outside, as usual his stubby tail wagging ten to the dozen.

"Is he coming?" Hugh asked, bending to pat the dog.

"Looks as if he's invited himself," Mikey grinned, concertinaing his bulk behind the wheel.

"You insured?"

Mikey grinned and looked at the boy in the rear-view mirror.

"For goodness sake, Hugh, I'm not going to go fast. And I don't intend to hit anything."

Hugh smiled back, as usual Mikey's good nature was infectious.

"Mind you, I think there's the contents of a dustbin on the floor. Boy-Boy's having a field day sniffing though it," he said raising his voice above the revving engine and holding up a greasy fast food bag between his finger and thumb.

Minutes later, Mikey brought the vehicle to a stuttering halt.

"G'day," George waved from the shade of the veranda. "Yo, the prodigals have returned," he called over his shoulder as he hurried down the steps, heralding their arrival to those inside the building. He slapped his brother on the back as he emerged from the vehicle. They had always been close, inseparable, more like twins than older and younger brothers.

He side-stepped Mikey, who was easing the stiffness out of his back, having squashed himself into the small car, in order to hold the front seat forward to enable Hugh to escape from the back while Boy-Boy seized the opportunity to lick the boy's face while he tried to scramble out of the car.

Hugh stretched, he felt a little nauseous. It had been a short, but uncomfortable journey. Mikey may have driven Joe Sampi's truck a few times but his driving prowess left a lot to be desired. That, and the obnoxious smell permeating from the pile of rubbish littering the floor left him feeling more than a little queasy.

"Dunno what you're grinning at," he said, pushing past Connie, "It was fine for you in the front. I was sitting on a soda can, goodness knows what was hidden on the floor."

"Oooer," Connie replied in his wake. She looked across at George and laughed, "Poms moan a lot don't they?"

"Yeah, pommy drama queen," he teased.

"Hey! I heard that."

"Heard what?" She grinned, poking her tongue out at her friend's back.

George slung his arm around Hugh's shoulders, "Don't mind her, she's just teasing."

Feeling nervous, Hugh followed the others into the building. He wanted, no, he needed to know what Dick Norseman had managed to find out, but at the same time he was frightened to learn how much danger the thylacine, his thylacine was in.

"G'day. You must be Connie and Hugh?" Norseman stood as they entered the room.

Hugh was about to retort ten out of ten for observation but thought better of it. Not only would it have been rude but he'd promised himself he would stop making snap judgements about people, and anyway, Joe had vouched for the guy so he couldn't be all bad.

"G'day," he replied, shaking Norseman's hand, looking the man square in the eye, un-nerved as the stranger held his gaze without blinking. It was almost as if he were being hypnotised. Hugh was the first to pull away, a little annoyed to see the look of amusement in Joe Sampi's eyes.

"It's a real pleasure to meet you both." Norseman spoke with sincerity. "Your father and grandfather have been telling me about your adventures," he nodded towards the two men as he spoke. "I've been blown away. Many people a great deal older than you wouldn't have achieved so much. Well done. Well done to both of you."

"Anyway," Sampi interrupted. "Dick has to return this evening so we can't hold him up too much longer."

"It's no problem, Joe. I wanted to meet the young 'un's before I left."

Sampi nodded.

"Okay, we've been waiting for you to get back so Dick didn't have to keep repeating his story."

Connie smiled her thanks, accepting the chair Mikey brought for her as Hugh perched on the desk.

"Dick, whenever you're ready."

Norseman smiled at the elderly man as he picked up a pile of printed paper. He blushed as everyone turned their attention to focus on him, shuffling the paper as he cleared his throat.

"When Joe," he nodded towards the older man, who smiled in acknowledgement, "came to see me, I was, well, I was more than a little reluctant to get involved, err, to accept the challenge, but I'm glad I did."

Sounds ominous, Hugh thought. He glanced across at Connie, but she was concentrating on Norseman.

"Anyway, moving on to what I've found out. The Tasmanian Mining Corporation was formed about six years ago."

"That's interesting, a new company, eh?" Whitaker interrupted.

Norseman angled his head, "Yes and no."

Sampi raised an eyebrow as the younger man continued.

"In this guise, the Tasmanian Mining Corporation is just six years old."

"Guise?" Hugh questioned.

Norseman smiled, it looked as if he was beginning to enjoy himself.

"The Tasmanian Mining Corporation was formed following the demise of Townsend Mines."

Sampi tapped Napoleon's arm, "That sounds familiar."

His friend and neighbour nodded, "Sure does, can't remember why though."

"Okay, I'll enlighten you. Some seven years ago Townsend Mines suffered a tragedy. There was a massive landslide, about a hundred miners were trapped and only fifteen got out alive."

Sampi nodded, "I remember now."

"The company were fined for utilising unsafe practices, their third violation in ten years. In an effort to get out of paying the fines and compensation, Townsend Mines went bust. Craig Townsend filed for bankruptcy and did a runner, leaving the Tasmanian Government to foot the compo. bill."

"What's that got to do with the Tasmanian Mining Corporation?" Connie asked.

"You may well ask, little miss."

Connie blushed.

Hugh shook his head; he knew it was irrational but he felt jealous. *She's flirting*, he thought to himself, *wasn't she grizzling before how Norseman had betrayed his aboriginal roots?*

"The Tasmanian Mining Corporation was like a phoenix rising from the ashes of Townsend Mines. Laura Goodman is the daughter of the CEO, Craig Townsend. Goodman is her mother's maiden name."

Sampi and Napoleon exchanged worried glances.

"Is that legal?" Connie asked.

Mikey shook his head, "Sounds a bit crook to me."

"It's legal. The Tasmanian Mining Corporation is a new company. I'm still looking into where it got its start up funds from. I'm certain the money trail will lead right back to Craig Townsend."

"I'm sure I remember the demise of Townsend Mines led to a change in legislation," Napoleon said. "And as an un-discharged bankrupt I'm positive Townsend shouldn't be trading."

"Right on," Norseman pointed at Napoleon, he'd hit the nail on the head. "If I can prove he financed the Tasmanian Mining Corporation we might get the licence revoked. But Laura Goodman is no pushover, it's not a compliment but she's a chip off the old block, that's for sure." Norseman was silent for a moment, allowing the others to absorb what he had said.

Whitaker took the opportunity to retrieve a pack of cold stubbies from the fridge, they could all do with a drink. He offered one to Norseman who shook his head, asking for a soda instead. He had a long drive back and he didn't want to smell of alcohol if the cops, or blue heelers, as Connie had called them, pulled him over.

As the vet took his seat, Norseman continued.

"I've looked into their recent mining activities. It's bad news I'm afraid." In an instant he had their full attention once again, all thoughts of beer and sodas forgotten.

"They are not the ethical mining company they claim to be, if there is such a thing."

"What do you mean, Dick?"

Norseman turned to face Hugh and shrugged.

"Maybe I'm simplistic, but if you mine and pillage the planet's resources, how can it be done in an ethical manner? Don't get me wrong, I know mining is a necessary evil, given the technological age we live in."

"Can you be more specific, regarding the ethicality?" Sampi challenged.

Norseman nodded, flicking through the bundle of printed pages he'd brought with him and extracted some photos from the pile of paperwork which he passed around.

"That's how they left a project a few years back, and there's the photo before they started. I know they ask for twelve months to allow them to return the mined areas back to the same condition as before excavations started but three years have elapsed and the site still looks like a bomb has hit it. I'd say the photograph says it all."

"Bloody hell," Hugh muttered, looking over his father's shoulder.

Whitaker studied the photo before handing it to Napoleon. Mikey whistled under his breath, the once pristine forest had been devastated. There had been a little replanting but the vegetation was nowhere as dense as before the mining started.

"Can we keep this?"

Norseman nodded, "You can keep the lot, there's some information around mining in protected areas too," he said passing his research to the vet. He snatched a look at this watch, "Bloody hell is that the time. I've gotta head back."

Sampi placed a hand on the younger man's shoulder, and shook his hand with a firm grasp. "Thanks, Dick, you've been invaluable."

"Yeah, thanks, Dick," Napoleon echoed, tipping his beer bottle towards him in salute.

"I hope you keep in touch," Whitaker added, "perhaps find the time for a proper visit."

"Maybe you'll let me see the thylacine?" Norseman asked, directing his question towards Joe Sampi.

The Aboriginal Tasmanian nodded.

Dick Norseman grinned, his eyes twinkling with delight.

"I'll hold you to that. With luck I'll be accepted to study in Devonport, that's just around the corner, so to speak, so I can pop over."

Sampi nodded, "No problem. We'll walk you out to your car." He retrieved a battered pouch from his back pocket – it had been patched on more than one occasion but it was one of his most treasured possessions, Angie had made it when she was a little younger than Connie and presented it to him for Christmas. He went to pull out some crumpled notes.

Norseman shook his head.

"Joe, I said it wasn't necessary. I didn't do this for the money."

"Looks like you misjudged him," Hugh hissed.

"Eh?"

Hugh nodded towards Dick Norseman as he stood by his car, "Joe's just offered him some money and he's refused. I think you, err, I mean, we, misjudged him."

Chapter Eleven

Although Dick Norseman was a skilled hacker, the Tasmanian Mining Corporation was one step ahead. Laura Goodman was well aware of the Government legislation she was breaching by using her father's money to finance the company. She had engaged one of the most prestigious corporate legal firms in Australia to keep her inside the law – just!

Within a short space of his engagement on her personal account, her lawyer had proved his loyalty. William Appleby moved to become her right hand man and part time boyfriend within months of his appointment.

Appleby spent a lot of his time hiding the money trail. Laundering the proceeds from Townsend Mines through placement in a number of companies and off shore accounts to guarantee the Tasmanian Mining Corporation and in particular, Laura Goodman, were squeaky clean.

To ensure their business activities and financial records were kept secret, at Goodman's insistence, he had overseen the installation of state of the art intrusion detection software.

William Appleby looked up from the document he was reviewing as the computer screen started to flash a warning message. He'd been working late, looking forward to meeting Laura for drinks before an intimate dinner for two in his apartment. His housekeeper had done all the hard work, leaving him with the task of heating the food in the microwave. The vintage champagne would be chilled to perfection by the time they got home, all in all, it was set to be a special evening.

"Shit!" He grumbled before taking a sip of the wine he'd been drinking while catching up on his paperwork.

He clicked on the warning message and scanned the report that filled the screen.

Reaching for his mobile, he punched in a number, his fingers drumming against his glass as he waited for his call to be answered.

"Parker, g'day mate. I'm sorry to be calling so late but I need you to get your arse back here as soon as you can. I'll fill you in when you arrive, I don't trust phones when it comes to confidential information, but I think, no I know we've been hacked. See you in ten?"

A voice at the end of the phone said that would be cutting it fine. He could be back within a quarter of an hour.

Appleby took a sip of wine and smacked his lips together, grimacing as the woody flavour hit the back of his throat as he swallowed. He pushed Laura's number on speed dial, downing the contents of his glass while he waited.

"Laura, sweetheart. I'm gonna be a little late for drinks. We've, we've had a bit of an incident."

"Incident?" Goodman repeated in her succinct way. "What do you mean, an incident?"

"The intrusion detection software the Board grizzled over purchasing has come up trumps, but for the wrong reasons. We have been hacked."

"Fuck. Tell me you are joking?"

"It's okay, sweetheart. I've called Parker Briggs back to work. He'll be here within the next fifteen minutes. I'll get back to you as soon as he's had a chance to assess the situation."

"No, I'm coming over."

Appleby closed his eyes, that was the last thing he needed.

"Okay, good idea," he lied. "See you in a while."

"Don't do anything until I get there," she commanded, the call disconnecting as she hung up.

"No sweetheart, yes sweetheart, three bags bloody full sweetheart," he muttered as he reached for the wine bottle. "It looks like dinner's out of the question."

Twenty minutes later Parker Briggs and William Appleby were interrupted by the sound of stiletto heels clicking against the white marble floor.

"Hello darling," Appleby half turned to kiss Goodman's cheek as he felt her arm slip around his waist. "The hacker is gonna wonder what hit him if we get hold of him," he said. "I'm sorry this has ruined our evening."

"Forget it. I'd have been more pissed off if you didn't tell me and kept me in the dark."

Appleby nodded his head, no one crossed Laura Goodman and hung onto their job for long. He had learnt that within a week of joining her when she'd had a car valet sacked because he'd left a smudge on the rear view mirror of her four by four.

"No fear of that, my sweet," he murmured.

"Right, what do we know?"

Briggs looked up at the lawyer who nodded for him to explain. It was better not to keep her waiting.

"Well, 'John Doe' is good. Very good."

Goodman glanced at the IT specialist, a look of annoyance flashing across her face.

"Don't tell me that," she retorted. "I don't pay you the sort of salary you demanded to be told how good the hacker is. I want to know what he's been looking at, where he's located, who he is working for and last but not least, who the hell he is! Then and only then can we think about damage limitation." She snapped her fingers close to his face, "now get on with it."

Briggs returned his attention to the screen in front of him as Laura Goodman stomped towards her office.

"God help the poor bastard if she gets hold of him," Appleby muttered as he followed her.

Two hours later, Parker Briggs knocked on the door to Laura Goodman's office.

"Come!"

He pushed open the frosted glass door in time to see Laura Goodman, her back towards him, adjusting her skirt.

Briggs cleared his throat.

"I'm sorry to disturb you."

"What have you found out?"

Briggs looked at Appleby and smiled to himself, he could see Goodman's reflection in the window as she buttoned her blouse.

"I've traced the hacker via a number of servers. It was a bit of a spaghetti maze, bounced via Poland and China, but I managed to trace him to an internet cafe just outside Geilston Bay."

"That's about five kilometres from here," she mused.

Briggs nodded, "Yes, not far eh?"

"What was he looking at?"

Briggs moistened his lips.

"That's the funny thing. Nothing."

"What do you mean, *nothing,*" she snapped.

"Perhaps, I should have phrased it better." He shrugged, "when I said nothing, I meant nothing important. He was reviewing the company archives, looking at previous projects, that sort of thing."

Goodman looked puzzled.

"Are you sure."

"It's possible, I guess, that he's discovered the link between Townsend Mines and your good self, but I can't be sure."

Goodman spun round, her eyes blazing, "I don't pay you to guess." She was silent for a moment. "Anyway, Daddy lives in the Dominican Republic, there's no extradition there so I doubt anyone will be going after him. That's not important at the moment. If he didn't want money or intellectual property rights, what was the bastard after?"

Appleby shook his head.

"I've gotta be honest, I'd be more worried if he had stolen something. I think it was a kid flexing his muscles."

Goodman nodded, "It's possible. I expect you to monitor the situation, check whatever it is you need to check to ensure the network is secure, I don't want another repercussion, do you understand?" She said, directing her statement towards Parker Briggs. "And while you think on that, I don't need to remind you about the confidentiality agreement you signed. Do not mention this to anyone. I don't want it recorded in the logs or discussed at any of your governance groups. Do you understand?"

"Yes, Miss Goodman. Any further developments will be reported to Mr. Appleby, no one else."

Briggs turned to go, it was obvious the matter was closed.

Goodman waited until the IT specialist had left the room.

"Check he's gone."

Appleby looked at her.

"Do it!"

Tutting, he crossed the room and opened the door. The outer office was empty. He held the door wide in order that she could see.

"Satisfied... getting a little paranoid aren't we, sweetheart?"

She shook her head.

"I don't buy it. No one goes to this much trouble for nothing. I want you to monitor the press, news streams, social media, anything that could throw some light on this, but do it with caution. I don't want to draw attention to ourselves. Oh, and double the security at the mine sites, in particular that awful place we visited last."

"Warrugul?"

She nodded, "Yes, Warrugul," she repeated, "I've got a gut feeling that place is going to be a whole heap of trouble." She pushed him down into her chair and sat astride his lap. "I don't know about you, but I'm starving."

Chapter Twelve

George looked up from his book, his concentration broken by the sound of footsteps on the veranda. A man, similar to height to him, dressed in a grease-stained tee shirt under a worn leather waistcoat and sweat pants sniffed in an uncouth fashion, regurgitating a mouthful of phlegm, which he spat on the floor.

George's stomach lurched, "Charming," he muttered to himself as he noticed a crude skull and crossbones tattoo scratched into his forearm. "Can I help you?"

The man stepped closer to the desk, his eyes roaming the office as he started to speak. "I've just moved back to the area, and I've been trying to look up a mate?"

George stood up as the stranger balanced on tip-toe and tried to peer into Whitaker's consulting room. The young man reached over and closed the door.

"I'm not sure I can help with that," he said, "unless he's missing."

Realising he may have misunderstood, and the stranger was here to report a disappearance, his attention heightened in an instant.

The stranger shook his head, "Na, I don't think it's anything like that. I've just lost contact with him."

George looked puzzled.

"I'm sorry this isn't a lost and found. Unless your friend is missing in the park, may I suggest the police or perhaps the Salvation Army. I hear they are great for putting people in touch with lost folk."

The stranger seemed to baulk at the suggestion of contacting the police. George's skills at tracking and reading signs was not as adept as his brother's yet, but he didn't miss the change in the stranger's body language.

The stranger seemed to pull himself together, "I'm sorry, I didn't make myself clear. My mate, he works here. Spencer... Spencer Tate. You must know him?"

A shudder ran down George's spine.

"Um, Spencer used to be a park ranger here."

"Yes, that's right, the park ranger." A look of confusion clouded the stranger's expression, "hang on, mate, what do you mean, 'used to be'?"

George licked his lips, he'd never had to inform anyone of a death before.

"I'm sorry to have to inform you that Spencer Tate passed away a couple of weeks ago, Mister?"

The stranger shuffled on the spot. He seemed indecisive, as if wondering what to do next, ignoring the question about his name.

"Aw, he was looking after some of my gear. Did Spencer leave anything here? Belongings, I mean, I know he hasn't got any family, local like so perhaps he left my gear with you?"

Napoleon pulled the door of the consulting room open and walked out into the office.

"I thought I recognised your voice. G'day, Lennie."

The stranger curled his top lip into the semblance of a smile, which in truth looked more like a sneer.

"Napoleon," Lennie nodded towards the older man.

"When did you get out?"

"Yesterday."

Napoleon nodded, "I see. Sorry, we've had to tell you like this, but my son is correct, Tate suffered a serious accident and died from complications. Anything he left here was confiscated by the police as part of their investigation into his activities and suspected involvement in the murder of a local vagrant. Perhaps you should call into the station, see if you can identify anything that belongs to you?"

Lennie looked startled by the additional information Napoleon disclosed.

"Um, okay," he sniffed, "sorry if I've wasted your time."

"No, don't worry about that, please accept our condolences for your loss."

The Toba's watched as Lennie shuffled out of the building.

"Bloody liar!" Napoleon cursed under his breath.

George threw his father a surprised look, it was unusual for him to curse.

"What makes you say that, Pop?"

Napoleon looked at his son. He was proud of both his lads. With work so hard to come by, it would have been easy for them to have been drawn into the shady dealings of drugs and violence, but in spite of the hardships they'd had to endure, along with the Sampi's and other members of their local community, none of them had strayed off the straight and narrow. The same could not be said of Lennie Watts.

"As soon as he heard Tate was dead, Lennie said he'd been holding onto some of his gear. It's my guess he knew Spencer was dealing and was making a ridiculous attempt to claim his stock - as if it would still be here!" Napoleon tidied a pile of trail leaflets as he continued. "Lennie Watts was in Mikey' year at school."

George tried to think if his brother had mentioned the name, he was a couple of years older but most of their friends were mutual.

"Poor sod never stood a chance, his father was in prison for most of Lennie's life. When he was out he took it in turn to use his missus and the kids as punch bags to take his frustrations out on. No, that's making excuses for him. Trevor Watts wasn't frustrated; he was plain evil. Anyway, Trevor was shanked during his last spell inside, bled out before the screws could get to him."

"What about Lennie? You asked him when he got out so I assume he's been inside."

Napoleon nodded, "Yeah, that's right. I'm surprised you don't remember. Lennie was convicted for the attempted rape and robbery of an old woman in Devonport."

George couldn't hide a look of horrified disgust.

"*Nice* – not!"

His father watched as he filled a bucket with water and stepped outside, swilling away the mucus Lennie had spat onto the veranda.

"Don't want his disgusting germs in here," he muttered.

Back at the Whitaker's bungalow, Hugh looked up from his computer, disturbed by a knock on the door. He'd been researching Gordon Sullivan, the Scottish explorer whom the town and everything around it seemed to be named after. He had discovered Sullivan had spent his life mapping the State, but, born the fourth son of a Scottish Laird who, with little or no expectation of inheriting any of the family's dwindling fortune, had set out for Australia. Here, while on a visit to Tasmania, he'd met and married a local aboriginal girl of Palawar descent.

Hugh opened the door to Connie standing on the doorstep, "g'day," he grinned. "You're late."

Connie stepped inside, "It's nice to see you too, Hugh," she laughed. "I've been out tracking."

"What! Without me, that's not fair," he whinged. "Why couldn't I come?"

Connie pulled a strained expression, "You, a tracker? Next you'll be telling me that you are related to Crocodile Dundee, some cousin twenty-six times removed," she exaggerated.

"That's not fair, and you know it," he grizzled, "I include you in everything."

A look of guilt hounded her eyes, "You're right, I'm sorry. Don't get all huffy. I promise I'll let you know next time."

"Okay," his response was grudging, but he conceded she always kept her word.

"Anyway, it's no big deal, I got lost."

Hugh roared with laughter, the guttural sound reverberating around the room.

"The granddaughter of the great Joe Sampi got lost. How come?"

Connie was furious.

"It's not that funny," she spat the words as if she were a wild she-cat."

"Come off it, you have to see the funny side. Joe's reputation is State wide. Still I suppose even he had to start somewhere."

A pink tinge flecked Connie's cheeks.

"Yeah, I guess it's a bit funny. I was following a trail grandfather left this morning and I took a wrong turn. He double backed on himself and I missed it."

"Wait till I tell Mikey."

"Oh don't, please don't. You know I'll never live it down."

Hugh stopped laughing.

"Don't be daft, I'm not gonna tell anyone, okay?"

She nodded, clenching her fist and raising it.

"Cool?"

Hugh knocked knuckles with hers, "Always. Come on, let's not waste our last day of freedom. Shall we make sure the mining company hasn't come back?"

"Sullivan's Rise?"

Hugh nodded, "It's as good a place to start as any. And..."

"We might see the thylacine," she grinned, finishing his sentence.

The past few days had been hot and dry and as a result the undergrowth was beginning to die back. Connie was obscured by a cloud of dust thrown up by her wheels as she pedalled at speed. As usual she was streaking ahead, not that Hugh was bothered, it gave him the opportunity to immerse himself in his own thoughts. He felt sick. Apart from the fact tomorrow was the first day of the school term, which was always daunting, it was the first day at a new school, in a new country.

Having emigrated with his father a few weeks before Christmas, by the time he enrolled, he'd have been off school for almost three months. He'd gotten to like the idea of his freedom.

"Hugh!"

Connie's screech dragged him out of his daydream of wallowing self-pity.

"Look!"

He braked hard, his back wheel skidding from under him as he pulled up alongside her.

Bloody hell, that was close, he thought, repositioning himself on his bike as he checked his back wheel.

Connie was silent. Blinking back tears of frustration, her hand covered her mouth as she stared in shock at the sight in front of her.

The ground at the foot of Sullivan's Rise was an area of devastation. What had happened in such a short space of time? The Blackwood tree where they used to hide their bikes had been pulled up, it was lying on its side, its white roots exposed to the air. A wide corridor had been cut through the undergrowth, a raw scar dissecting the vegetation.

Hugh placed his arm around Connie's shoulders and hugged, her.

"Come on," he urged, "let's get a closer look."

Dismounting, they wheeled their bikes forward, making their way towards the cliff face.

"Can you hear that?"

Connie nodded. The sound of someone shouting was just audible, but too faint to make out what was being said.

In silence they made their way towards the sound.

"Oh my goodness," disbelief seeped through his words as Hugh pointed ahead of them.

Parked up in front of the hidden cave entrance was a yellow and black Ergo Harvester machine, a sapling clenched between its mechanical teeth.

"What do you think that is?"

"My guess it's some sort of logging machine, judging by the tree it's holding," he said. "If there is anything positive, at least they haven't touched the vegetation attached to the cliff face, the vines and foliage still hide the entrance to the cave at the bottom of the sink hole."

"Yeah, that's something."

Voices carried on the wind.

"No, that's unacceptable."

"I suggest you take it up with the boss then!"

Hugh tapped his friend on the arm and pointed. Doug Langdon, Warrugul's senior park ranger, followed by Connie's grandfather stormed towards them. He could see the Aboriginal Tasmanian was furious. He'd only seen him this angry on one previous occasion, when he told him Tate was holding Connie captive. The brown skin of his forehead was furrowed with anger, his jaw jutted with determination and his fists clenched into tight balls at his side.

Connie waved towards the men and jumped on her bike to make her way across.

"Grandfather, what's going on?"

His eyes were black with fury, Sampi shouted at the kids.

"What are you doing here?"

"We were out for a ride, it's our last day of hols," Hugh heard himself explain.

The old man nodded.

"I'll catch you later, Joe, I've got some calls to make back at the office. G'day, kids."

"Bye Doug," Hugh waved as the ranger stomped off.

Sampi waited until his boss was out of earshot.

"Langdon's fuming," he said, stating the obvious. "The illustrious Tasmanian Mining Corporation are going to start drilling their bore holes."

"No way," Hugh cried. "What about the consultation. There's got to be legislation?"

Sampi nodded.

"To a point, but that's on the back burner for the moment as it would mean exposing the thylacine. Dick Norseman advised us to consult the 'Environmental Law Handbook'. It's an easy to read guide produced by the Environmental Defenders Office for citizens, business owners, councils etc."

"A guide for numpty's," Hugh quipped, blushing as Connie silenced him with a glare.

Ignoring the interruption, Joe Sampi continued.

"First the flora and fauna," he moved in close in spite of the fact they were on their own, "for example, the thylacine falls into that category," he whispered, "and is covered by three acts. These are, The Parks and Wildlife Acts, The Threatened Species Protection Act and The Environment Protection and Biodiversity Conservation Act, so as I say, we have that to fall back on if there is any impact to either the thylacine or the devils. However, it seems mining can take place in National Parks under certain conditions. In a nutshell it has to be compatible with the management objectives of the Park, focusing on natural heritage and landscape values."

"Joe, it's all a contradiction in terms," implored Hugh. "The mining company can get away with what they like provided they tidy up afterwards. It's not fair."

"I know, son. Langdon's gone off to see if he can stop them in their tracks as they are reneging on their promise to undertake a full public consultation, but if I'm honest with you, I don't think he'll get much joy."

"At least they haven't found the entrance to the cave," Connie observed.

Her grandfather shushed her quiet, looking around to make sure no one was walking up to them. Happy they were still alone, he nodded.

"Yes, that's a small blessing. But the pair of you must be careful. I know you are both riled up, but you can't go shouting your mouths off."

"But we're alone, Joe."

Sampi pointed towards a man leaning against the huge wheel of the logging machine, smoking a cigarette, his eyes focused on them as they talked.

Sampi shouted at the man, "Make sure you put that out when you've finished. We don't need a fire on top of everything else your company's doing!" He opened his arms wide as if to embrace the devastated landscape as he spoke.

"It'll clear it a damn site quicker," came the reply.

"Ha bloody ha, you are so funny!" Hugh snapped.

"Leave it, Hugh. He isn't worth wasting your breath on. At the end of the day he's nothing but a puppet doing just what the puppet master wants him to do when he pulls his strings."

"If they are gonna start drilling, what about the thylacine and her pups? We haven't seen them for a day or so."

"I'm going out with Napoleon and the boys tonight, see if we can locate them. They'll stay with their mum for about nine months or so, but it won't be long before they are weaned, that's when they'll be in greater danger, as they start to become more and more independent."

"Can we come, Joe?"

Sampi looked at the kids as he shook his head.

"I'm sorry, no, not this time." His tone was adamant, "you've got to get up early tomorrow, what with it being the first day of school. And we need to make sure we aren't seen. It seems with all this equipment they're transporting into the area; the mining company will be bringing in additional security staff. That's all we need, a load of mediocre patrol men, running around gung- ho so to speak."

Chapter Thirteen

Andrew Whitaker looked up from reading his copy of the Australian Veterinary Journal. He was writing a paper, which, he hoped they would publish, something he had done on an occasional basis at home. He'd received a number of excellent reviews for his published work in the Veterinary Record, the official journal of the British Veterinary Association.

"Who are you, and what have you done with my son?"

"Dad, cut it out!" Hugh cried, feeling self-conscious in his new uniform. He pushed his glasses back off the end of his nose. "I feel sick."

With a look of understanding in his eyes, Whitaker pulled a chair out from under the table.

"That'll be first day nerves," he said. "Come on, have a little breakfast, it'll help settle your stomach."

Hugh shook his head.

"I'll puke up if I eat anything."

Whitaker pursed his lips.

"At least have a cup of tea. I'll make you a sandwich, which you can eat at break if you feel hungry. Have you got everything you need?" He asked, walking towards the kitchen, removing the cheese and butter from the fridge.

Hugh nodded, "I think so. Have you forgotten we spent ages getting the things on the list provided by the school?"

"Ah yes, my credit card remembers it well," his father laughed. "Okay, I know you haven't seen your schedule yet, but just remember you fractured your arm a few weeks ago, be careful, the hospital may have discharged you but it is still healing. I can write a note if you like, explain to the sports master you need to take it easy for a few more weeks."

Hugh tutted as he rolled his eyes to the ceiling, "No thanks!"

"Okay, okay, I get the message," his father laughed. "Come on," he said placing a paper bag on the table, "that's for break time, in the meantime try a slice of dry toast."

Half an hour later, Whitaker was stowing Connie's bike alongside Hugh's in the back of the Land Rover while she said goodbye to her grandfather.

"Hi," Hugh greeted his friend with a broad smile.

"Wow, I almost didn't recognise you," she said, sliding onto the seat alongside him.

"You look nice too," he complimented, "is that new?" He asked, nodding at her dress.

Connie wrinkled her face, "New to me at least, I've grown so much over the hols I needed new school uniform. We picked these up at the op shop. Grandfather still hasn't been paid for the work he's been doing for Doug Langdon so we were short of money. We are always short of money," she said, her voice little more than a whisper. "Mum's wages go straight on bills."

Hugh nodded, "Op shop or not, you still look pretty," he complimented.

Blushing a deep shade of pink, Connie stared out of the window, refusing to look at him.

"Don't drive too fast, Dad, I think I'll be sick."

"No chance of him breaking any speed limits, Hugh, you know that," Connie teased, whispering from behind her hand.

Hugh responded with an easy grin, she was getting to know his father a little too well.

"I'll park up after I've dropped you off, come in and see the head with you, then leave your bikes at the bus stop if you like? I don't have any appointments so I can spare the time as I'm planning to check my traps, I'm after a juvenile male devil for quarantine," Whitaker explained.

The 'Insurance Population project' was developing ahead of schedule. The first disease free devils had completed the quarantine period and were due to be released on Maria Island, six kilometres off Tasmania's east coast. In addition, some specimens were being moved to selected zoos across the mainland of Australia. The plan was to reintroduce the animals, where the local population had died out sometime in the future, hopefully to repopulate the State.

"Nah, it's fine, Dad, I don't need you to come in with me, I think you forget I'm not six anymore."

Dropping the kids outside The Academy, Whitaker went to tousle his son's hair as he turned to enter the school.

"Dad, why do you keep trying to do that," Hugh demanded, fighting to keep the annoyance out of his voice. "You know I don't like it."

"Sorry son," his father grinned. "It makes me smile. Okay how 'bout I promise not to do it again?"

His son nodded, knowing full well that was a hollow statement.

"Have a good day, see you tonight."

"Bye, Andrew."

"Bye," Hugh threw his father a casual wave before turning on his heel and walking towards the school building. He felt terrible.

Connie linked arms and stole a crafty look at her friend. His skin was pale and blotchy; he really did look awful.

"Come on, I'll show you to reception."

Hugh swallowed hard as they weaved their way through the throng of students making their way to their classrooms. They were surrounded by a meandering sea of blue and white gingham dresses and grey polo shirts as everyone jostled one another in the corridor.

With seven hundred students, The Sullivan Academy was small in comparison to the High School he had attended in England. It was a vibrant hive of anticipation as the start of the new term meant new friendships to forge, new sporting achievements, victories to attain and battles to be won and lost.

The school secretary looked up from the note she was scribbling inside a class register, her bee hive hairdo and cat's eye spectacles would have been more in place in nineteen fifties London than modern Tasmania.

"Good morning, Connie. Did you have a good break?"

"Yes, thank you, Mrs Dean. It was fine, if a little uneventful," she lied.

"I hope you've kept up your athletics training. We're counting on you for the 400 m again this season," the receptionist trilled.

Connie smiled, "I'll give it my best shot," she replied. "This is my friend, Hugh Whitaker, he's starting today. Hugh, this is Mrs Dean, school secretary, assembly pianist and miracle worker."

Mrs Dean tutted, but her expression was enough to let them know she was pleased with Connie's introduction.

"Nice to meet you, Mrs Dean."

"And you, Hugh. You'll be pleased to know that we are expecting you," she said, running her finger down a list of names in her notebook. "Yes, there you are," she added, pointing at his name.

Hugh smiled, *that's a start*, he thought.

"Your father has completed all the enrolment forms so there is nothing for you to do."

Surprised, Hugh raised his eyebrows, it was unlike his father to be this organised with anything that wasn't work related.

Mrs Dean continued, "Well young man, I'm sure you will be happy to learn you are in Connie's tutor group," she flicked through a pile of timetables, looking for the sheet with Hugh's name on the top. "Ah, here we go. Connie will show you the way to your form room. There's a pile of maps at the end of the desk, please take one as we don't want you getting lost. The head will send for you at some time during the next day or so. She tries to see every new pupil on their first day, but I'm afraid she won't be able to do that with you − circumstances beyond her control, I'm afraid." The secretary said in a matter-of-fact way.

"Right, thank you, Mrs Dean," Hugh said, but his words went unheard, she had already turned her attention to the next child in the queue who had lost his lunch money on the way to school and needed to call his parents.

"Come on," Connie urged, snatching a map off the pile as directed.

The school always left out a stack of maps on the first day of a new term to help orientate new students and members of staff around the two storey building. It was a bit of a maze when it came to finding the correct room, the naming nomenclature in use was less than straight forward.

He followed his friend along a labyrinth of corridors until they arrived at their form room. Each passageway was identical to the one before, only differentiated by the student's artwork and posters on display. He had no idea how long it would take him to familiarise himself with the building.

"This is us, 2H. That's second floor, and H being the eighth letter of the alphabet corresponds to this being the eighth room along," she explained.

Two boys, deep in conversation, pushed past, knocking Connie's bag as they entered the room.

"Hey, watch out!"

The taller one spun round, the swift movement causing the crucifix suspended on the ring through his ear to dance.

"Wassup, Sampi?"

Hugh didn't like the way the boy's eyes seemed to travel over Connie's body in a lascivious way as the youth looked her up and down, resting a little too long on her chest.

"Just watch where you are going, Nigel," she growled, pulling her navy blue cardigan closed.

The boy dismissed her with a curt nod of his head. He whispered something to his friend as he glanced at her over his shoulder, blowing her a kiss before bursting into laughter.

"Come on, Hugh. Let me introduce you to Mrs. Beal, she's our form tutor."

Hugh gazed through the open doorway. The form tutor was busy unpacking her bag, ignoring the disruption in the classroom, he guessed she couldn't have many years left before retirement, her salt and pepper hair was pulled into a stark bun, but her expression was soft, belying her apparent age.

Connie waited until she had finished what she was doing.

"Ah, good morning, Connie, I'm sorry I didn't notice you there." Her hazel eyes turned to focus on Hugh. "Mr. Whitaker, I presume?" She asked, extending her hand for him to shake.

Hugh smiled as he shook her hand.

"Nice to meet you, Mrs Beal."

"I was reading your file last night, you're from England, is that right?"

Hugh nodded.

"Wonderful place, went there for my honeymoon. Err, it rained every day if I remember correctly," she smiled. "I don't know if Connie has explained, but I like my classes to sit in alphabetical order." She pointed to an empty desk which was one row over from Connie. "I think it prevents cliques developing, there's plenty of time for that in the playground. You're here to study when in my class, not chat to your latest bezzie mate."

Mrs Beal may be one of the oldest members of staff on the teaching faculty but on the whole her students respected her authority. They knew she was fair but took no quarter.

As Hugh took his seat, the teacher clapped her hands to call the class to order. She waited for a moment, it was the first day of term and students were busy exchanging stories and hot gossip. She clapped her hands a little louder as she glanced at the clock, lessons were almost due to start.

"Class!"

The cacophony petered out as the students turned to face her. She looked around the room, "Welcome back. I hope you all had a good vacation."

A murmur of assent rippled around the room.

She smiled as she continued to address them, "I'm sure you will have every opportunity to catch up with one another at the end of your lessons. Before you go I have one announcement to make and that is to welcome a new member to our form. Stand up please, Hugh."

Shock evident in his eyes, Hugh stood up, his face burning with embarrassment at being the centre of attention, as everyone swivelled to face him.

"This is Hugh Whitaker. Welcome to the Sullivan Academy, Hugh."

Hugh nodded, "Thank you, Mrs Beal."

"Connie, you know Hugh already, so timetables permitting, I'd like you to escort him around the building for the next day or so."

Mrs Beal took the register, ticking the last name on the list as the school bell announced the start of lessons. The classroom erupted once more in a cacophony of sound as chairs were pushed back, scraping across the tiled floors and conversations picked up where they had left off.

"Oh, one more thing. The caretaker has asked me to remind you that chewing gum is not to be stuck to the underside of the desks." She shouted to the throng of students as they made their way towards the door, heading to their first lesson.

Hugh glared at Nigel as they jostled one another to get out of the room. His 'adversary' pointed two fingers at his eyes and then at Hugh before pointing back at his own. Hugh sighed, he knew he'd pledged not to judge by first impressions but he had the distinct feeling he and Nigel Watts were not going to get on.

With the exception of maths lessons, where Connie was in a higher group than he was, their timetables were the same. It was good to have someone to show him around the building as the map provided by the school left a lot to be desired when it came to detail.

He knew, in time, he would make friends other than Connie, but he couldn't help feeling a little jealous when he was left alone for the duration of the lunch break. The athletics coach wanted the teams, of which Connie was their star member, to get back into their regular training routines as soon as possible. The first track and field meet was scheduled for three weeks so there was no time to loose.

Having survived his first day at school, Hugh carried a bowl of mixed salad to the dining table, he was starving. His father had arrived home an hour later than expected and had then spent ages on the phone catching up with a colleague at the Animal Health Laboratories in Launceston. They were both due to attend a seminar the following week to be delivered by a team from the Menzies Research Centre, updating attendees on the progress of the development of a vaccine for DFTD and they had been busy planning their route and deciding where to meet.

"How was school?" Whitaker asked when, at last, he was able to join his son for dinner.

Hugh looked up from spooning a second helping of salad onto his plate. He licked his fingers as he shrugged.

"Okay, I guess."

His father nodded, "That good, huh?"

Hugh sighed, he knew he'd have to elaborate otherwise he'd never get his father off his back.

"It was fine, honest. Connie is my designated 'school-buddy'. She's supposed to help me settle in, it's something they do with all new students.

His father nodded, that was pretty standard practice nowadays.

"I'm in all the same classes as her, apart from maths."

"Are you going to take up any extracurricular activities, sport, chess or something?"

"Eek, I doubt it," his son grimaced in pretend disgust. "I think you're having a laugh. Though I might look for something to do at lunch time, Connie's part of the athletics team and that's when they tend to practice."

Whitaker smiled to himself, it was still Connie this and Connie that almost every time his son opened his mouth. It would be interesting to see if their relationship deepened into anything other than friendship down the line, err, much further down the line. Connie took after her mother in so many ways, and her mother wasn't just smart she was one good looking girl.

Chapter Fourteen

At last the long school week was over. Having knuckled down and completed the homework set for the weekend as soon as he got home, Hugh could look forward to actioning the plans he and Connie had made during the ride home.

The first thing on their list was to check the progress of the exploratory bore holes. Connie had overheard a conversation between her grandfather and Napoleon the night before. The mining company had announced plans to drill an additional exploratory bore hole, thus extending the area they needed to requisition for the potential mine as projected in the original application. She had heard Napoleon suggest the company must have bribed some faceless Government official to allow them to push the legislation to the limit, and from his tone it was obvious he wasn't joking.

Hugh made his way toward the aboriginal community where he planned to meet Connie. Ahead of him he spotted two young men messing about with a ball. Slamming on his brakes he squinted, trying to work out who it was, but the sun was causing his eyes to water.

Is that Mikey and George? He wondered.

He was about to call out to his friends when one of them spun round, sticking his foot out in an attempt to control the ball.

"That's Nigel what's-his-name," he said to himself, recognising the tall frame of the boy he'd had the run-in with at the beginning of the week.

Not wanting to draw attention to himself, Hugh started to turn his bike around in order to make a detour when the 'ball' seemed to squeal. He narrowed his eyes as he tried to focus, tutting as he decided he needed to get some prescription sunnies as he shaded his eyes from the bright morning sun. That wasn't a ball those thugs were kicking to one another, it was an animal, though from this distance he couldn't make out what it was. It looked as if, no, he was sure, they were torturing a Tasmanian devil.

Flushed with anger, Hugh rode a bit closer. Yes, it was definitely a devil.

"Oi!"

The youths stopped what they were doing. A look of recognition evident on Nigel Watts' face as he leant over and muttered something to the other lad who nodded.

"What do you want, Whitaker? What makes you think you can stick your nose into other people's business?"

"Leave that animal alone."

The older youth laughed, "Why, what you gonna do about it?"

Hugh tightened his grip on the handlebars of his bike as he tried to control his anger. He held back, no doubt, Connie would call him a wimp but he was being realistic, there were two of them and one of him.

"Just leave it alone. You've had your fun."

Growling, the devil tried to push past it's tormenters but they yanked it off its feet, the poor creature was tied to a rope, it didn't have a chance to escape.

"Oi, leave it alone. That's cruel."

The older of the two youths was someone Hugh didn't recognise, he stuck two fingers up at Hugh, exposing a skull and crossbones tattoo on his arm. From the bleeding of colour around the outline, it was a poor quality piece of body art, maybe even a do-it-yourself job.

"Don't know why you are so worried about it. Devils are vermin, everyone knows that," the older lad drawled. "They need to be exterminated, I know, I read it somewhere, so it's okay to kill them because they've got a disease... a contagious cancer."

Hugh got off his bike and took a step forward.

"Bloody hell, you can read. What a surprise!" He retorted, regretting his rash words in an instant. *That was a bloody stupid thing to say.*

"Wass that? You saying I'm thick or something?"

"Um, I wouldn't go quite that far," *shut up, Hugh, for goodness sake shut up!* He told himself.

The older youth, who, unbeknown to Hugh, was Nigel's brother, placed his hands on his hips, "You must have a death wish, kid," he snarled, his top lip curled in such a way it looked as though he had a nasty smell under his nose.

"Come on, Lennie, there's two of us," said Nigel Watts. "It'll be a swizz taking that fat bastard out."

The older youth lurched towards Hugh as Nigel Watts lunged forward with the prowess of a rugby hooker, tacking Hugh's legs from under him, the devil forgotten for a moment.

Hugh fell to the ground as they both pounced at the same time, yelping as his fall was broken by his recently fractured arm. He closed his eyes, and with clenched fists hit out in any direction in an uncoordinated fashion, at the same time his legs flaying, grimacing as he made contact with soft flesh.

Lennie landed a punch to Hugh's stomach, knocking the breath out of him. Winded, he lay on the ground, it was a cliché but he was gasping for air like the proverbial fish out of water.

"Come on Nige," his brother called, "fat boy's had enough."

With Lennie leading the retreat, Nigel landed a well-aimed kick at the wounded devil as he ran past.

Pulling himself up onto all fours, Hugh tried to drag air into his burning lungs. He squinted through his watering eyes, the devil didn't appear to be moving, those bastards had killed it.

He crawled over to the injured animal, wincing as a sharp pain shot down his damaged arm. *Please God, don't let it be broken again*, he prayed.

Peering at the bundle of black fur, he could see its chest was moving. The devil was still breathing, but only just. For a second, Hugh was paralysed with indecision, he wondered what to do. Should he try and get the animal to the ranger's station where his father could examine it, or take it to Joe Sampi? *What should I do... think, Hugh... what should I do?*

With caution, as he knew what a vicious bite a devil could inflict, more so when it was frightened and in pain, Hugh examined the injured animal. Its eyes were closed, its breathing shallow and sporadic. To his untrained eye it looked unconscious. His mind was made up. The Sampi cabin was closer than his father, that's where he had to go. He removed his shirt and placed the furry creature into the centre of the garment. With care, he tied the four corners together to create a sort of sack. It wasn't ideal, he didn't think it was in a fit state to attack, but he couldn't take that risk, suspended from the handlebars of his bike it wouldn't be able to bite him.

Tasting blood, Hugh ran his hand over his face. His nose was bleeding; he hadn't come off unscathed but that was nothing in comparison to the injuries the devil had received.

He pushed his glasses back from their usual position on the end of his nose and lifted the devil, clenching his teeth as another spasm shot through his arm, the animal was a lot heavier than he had expected.

Hanging the home made sack from the handlebars, Hugh pushed his bicycle towards Joe Sampi's cabin.

Progress was slow and awkward. He was finding it difficult to stop the injured animal swinging against the bike frame, he hoped he wasn't compounding its injuries.

"Oh my goodness! Grandfather! Grandpappy, come quickly," Connie screamed, dropping the washing basket she was carrying and running towards Hugh. "What the bloody hell..."

Hugh pulled a wry smile, "I've got an injured devil. I need Joe to look at it, it's in a pretty bad way."

"Here, let me take the bike, you take the devil."

Hugh nodded, "Yeah, I think it'll be more comfortable to carry the bundle, I keep jarring my arm."

At the sound of Connie's scream, Sampi came running, he charged out of the cabin, his face still covered in foam from where he was about to shave.

The old man's eyes took in the sight of the blood stained boy walking towards him. He hurried forward and took the bundle out of his arms.

"It's an injured devil, Joe," he explained.

"What happened?" Connie demanded.

"Let's get the lad indoors, darl," her grandfather said. "There'll be time for stories later. Can you run and get Napoleon, ask him to leave Boy-Boy indoors please? The dog won't fare well if he gets into a scrap with a devil, injured or otherwise!"

Moments later, Hugh followed Joe Sampi into the one storey building which had become so familiar over the last couple of months.

"Go get yourself cleaned up, lad, there are towels and such in the bathroom. I'll check you over later."

"I'd rather stay and help."

Sampi lowered his eyes as he placed the devil onto the table, "As you wish." This attitude, when it came to wildlife, was something he had come to expect of Hugh. He had known the Whitaker's for such a short space of time, but over the past few weeks he had watched Hugh mature from a gawky, chubby boy to a young man who knew his own mind.

Sampi untied the shirt to reveal the contents. He gasped, as he cast his expert eye over the animal, assessing it with skill.

"What's wrong?" Napoleon demanded, crashing through the doorway. Seeing Hugh standing there bloodstained and bare chested he swore under his breath.

"Not again?" He muttered.

He spun the lad round to face the light and angled his head. His nose had stopped bleeding. Napoleon looked into the lad's eyes. The pupils were normal. What looked like a boot print was turning into a beautiful bruise in the middle of his abdomen, its blue and purple hues would be a delight to behold in a few hours.

"I can report there's no serious damage," Toba announced to no one in particular.

Hugh dragged his eyes back to the dining table, smiling to himself as Connie placed her hand on his arm for a fleeting moment.

They stood side by side, watching as Joe checked each of the devil's short legs in turn.

Sampi pursed his lips as he thought for a moment.

"I can't feel any broken bones but we'll need Andrew to check that. There's a nasty cut on its left flank and it looks as if it's been half strangled. See here, see where the fur's damaged around the neck."

Connie and Hugh lent in for a closer look.

"They had a rope tied around its throat."

Sampi probed the area with care.

"They?"

"Nigel Watts and some other bloke a few years older were torturing the animal. Yanking it about on a rope and kicking it as it if was a football."

Napoleon turned away, "Cruel bastards, there's no need to do that."

"The other kid said devils were vermin and needed to be exterminated because they were carrying a contagious cancer. Imbeciles must have thought they could catch it. Guess they were too stupid to know the animals in this area are disease free too."

"Or the fact they are an endangered species," Connie added.

"What did the other lad look like?"

Hugh shrugged, "There's not a lot to tell. I'd say he was a bit taller than Nigel, oh and he had a bad skull and crossbones 'tat' here," he pointed to his forearm.

Sampi and Napoleon exchanged glances.

"Lennie Watts," they said together.

"Nigel's brother?" Connie asked.

Napoleon nodded, "Yes, Lennie Watts is Nigel's older brother."

"He's been in prison, hasn't he?" Joe Sampi asked.

Napoleon nodded, "Yes, he's just been released. He came into the ranger's station looking for Tate."

Sampi's expression darkened as Napoleon continued.

"He seemed surprised to learn Tate was dead, or at least that's what it looked like. Then he makes up some cock and bull story about Tate looking after some of his gear when he was inside, he didn't elaborate. It's my guess he was gonna pretend Tate's drug stash was his if it was still there and perhaps try and muscle in on the drugs trade."

"He must think we were born yesterday. Even if Tate was looking after Lennie's belongings, everything was taken away by the police, not that I can imagine Tate doing a favour for anyone. One thing's for sure, if Lennie's involved in this he's gonna be in big trouble. Langdon will have to report it to the authorities. But first things first, right now we need to get this little chap over to your father. I suggest you clean yourself up while I look for a box," said Joe, his instruction directed to Hugh. "If Andrew sees you like that he'll have a fit. Connie can you get the lad one of my shirts. It'll be a bit big, but he can't wear this one," he said, rolling up the blood stained garment. "Napoleon and I will run this little critter over to the station in the truck, meet you there?"

Connie nodded.

"Yeah, we'll bike over in a bit." She nudged Hugh, "Come on, I'll get you a towel."

Half an hour later, they were slowing up outside the ranger's station. Leaving their bikes in the usual place, they made their way into the building. Joe Sampi was on the phone reporting the incident to Doug Langdon, the Park's Head Ranger. With the Tasmanian devil's population so low, any incident like this had to be followed up. He waved the kids through to the examination room. Whitaker was asking Mikey to place a saline drip in warm water. The devil was dehydrated and in shock, a cold intravenous drip could kill it.

"How's it doing, Dad?"

The vet glanced at his son, raising an eyebrow.

"Not good. Joe was right when he said its limbs weren't broken, but she's..."

"It's female?"

His father nodded.

"She's suffered a severe beating. I'm sure she has internal injuries. I've taken some x-rays and can't see anything obvious but she is far from out of the woods. I'll start her on antibiotics, keep her warm and calm. If she survives, I'll see about putting her in quarantine and move her somewhere safe. I'm not going to risk an anaesthetic to suture the wound, it's not life threatening, I can do that when she's stronger."

Hugh stroked the semi-conscious animal. It's course black fur rippling under his hand. Surprised at how muscular she felt, for the first time he could appreciate the strength of these formidable little creatures.

"Thanks Mikey," Whitaker nodded as he hung the warm bag on a hook on the wall. "If you raise the vein like I showed you, I'll insert the cannula and we can connect her up. Watch your hand, it looks as if she's coming round a little."

"That's a good sign, eh, Andrew?"

"Maybe, Connie. 'Fraid it's a waiting game, but I'm not giving up hope."

As soon as he was happy with the flow of the drip, Whitaker helped Mikey place the semi-conscious creature into a cage, a plastic cone around her head to stop her from gnawing at the drip and cannula. He positioned a heat lamp over her as an added precaution.

Sampi peered around the door, "How's she doing?" He asked, his hand covering the mouthpiece of the phone.

"Too soon to say, Joe, I'm a little more optimistic though."

They listened as Sampi repeated the information to Doug Langdon at the other end of the line.

"Right, thanks, Doug. I'll sort out the paperwork and have it ready for you next time you call in. Bye."

"What did he say?"

"He's fuming." The short answer said it all.

"I'll need to inform the 'Save the Tasmanian Devil project' too," Whitaker said. "Joe was telling me these idiots seemed to think the cancer was contagious, which it is, but only if you're a devil. We, along with all other species are safe. It's not transmissible to us. The project may have to release more information about the disease, to explain that, we can't have this happening again, idiots killing devils in case they can pass on cancer.

"Ah, it's that allo-thingy," Hugh said, remembering his father mentioning it before.

"Yes, that's right, an allograft disease. I thought there were two contagious cancers, but when I researched it a little, I discovered there are four."

"Four," Hugh repeated. "Yuk, how awful."

His father nodded.

"I'm afraid so. There's one which affects dogs, one that affects Syrian hamsters, another that affects some marine bivalves such as soft shelled clams and now DFTD."

"In what way is it contagious?" Mikey asked.

Whitaker pulled a face, "I don't want to go into some long winded medical explanation. But."

"That's good," High giggled, interrupting his father and pretending to roll his eyes.

His father threw him a pained look, "Ever the comedian, eh son? So Mikey, as I was saying, allograft diseases or perhaps a more accurate term is clonally transmitted cancers are usually spread by physical contact. In the case of the devils, when they jaw wrestle they transfer cancer cells to one another, and we know that's correct because the cells are genetically identical."

"Oh, that's nasty. Thank God it's not airborne or something, we'd never stand a chance at keeping it under control."

"It would make it a hell of a lot more difficult," Whitaker agreed, "a hell of a lot more difficult."

Chapter Fifteen

Somewhere in the distance, Hugh could hear banging. Groaning, he rolled over.

Outside, Connie pummelled on the door, "Come on, come on," she grumbled under her breath. She stepped off the porch and hurried around the side of the building. Thank goodness it was a bungalow.

She tapped on the window of Hugh's bedroom and waited. Tutting she rapped on the glass with her knuckles, this time a little harder.

Startled, Hugh sat bolt upright. For a moment he was confused. What was going on?

Connie knocked on the window for a third time.

Reaching for his glasses, he kicked the bed clothes off and whipped the curtains back. Light streamed into the gloomy room, blinding him for a second.

"Connie."

He looked at his friend as she stood on the other side of the glass, her hands on her hips, her angry expression was not to be argued with.

"Hang on, I'll let you in."

Connie tutted and strode round to the front door.

"At last, I was thinking of crawling along the secret tunnel. Or better still, if I was Harry Houdini I'd break in."

"He was an escapologist, he broke out of things, not into them!" Hugh retorted, as she flounced into the living room. "And good morning to you too," he said to her back. He tied the cord of his dressing gown as he kicked the front door shut. "What's got you so riled up?"

Connie opened her arms, the palms of her hands facing upper most.

"You are not gonna believe this."

"That's for sure, unless you tell me," he grumbled. "You had breakfast?

"What?" Connie shook her head, her curly hair flying around her shoulders with the sharp movement. "Sorry, no I haven't. I came straight over as soon as I woke up."

"Toast 'n' tea?"

Connie relaxed, "Yeah that sounds great, thanks."

Hugh pointed towards the kitchen, "Come on, tell me what's got you so fired up."

"I heard Grandfather talking to Napoleon last night. They thought I was doing my homework."

"You're turning into a regular little Secret Squirrel."

"Err?"

Hugh stared at his friend. From her expression it was clear she had no idea what he was talking about.

He smiled, his eyes shining as he remembered.

"I had a DVD of the Secret Squirrel television shows when I was little, they were broadcast in the sixties, I think. The main characters were a spy, a squirrel, hence the name Secret Squirrel and his sidekick, Morocco Mole," he laughed out loud. "The little mole wore a red fez and was as blind as a bat. Secret Squirrel, well he," he looked at her face; he could tell she wasn't in the least bit interested. "What I meant was that you're becoming a good little spy, eavesdropping on conversations, that's all."

Connie smiled, "Okay, I understand what you are going on about now. Grandfather has been in contact with Dick Norseman."

Hugh stopped what he was doing, his eyes wide as he listened.

"The Tasmanian Mining Company isn't just going to drill a bore hole where we've seen the camp, at the bottom of Sullivan's Rise. Their geological results, or whatever they're called show the stuff they are after is much more widespread. They are seeking permission to mine in a number of sites across the Park. It could be decimated. The Park as we know it will be gone."

"And with it the thylacine!"

"I wanted to come over and tell you last night, but Grandfather wouldn't let me, he can be mean like that, and then he told me off for eaves dropping."

Hugh shook his head as he placed four slices of bread under the grill.

"He's not mean, you know that."

Connie pursed her lips.

"I suppose not, but it felt like it last night."

"Yeah, 'cause you couldn't get your own way. Which is unusual when it comes to your grandfather. We both know you've got him wrapped around your little finger. But he was right to stop you charging over here in the dark. That was a hair-brained idea."

"I know, but it seemed sensible at the time."

"Right, this throws the plans we made yesterday out of the window. Let's talk about it over breakfast."

"Where's your dad?"

"Dunno, his room's empty, look the door's open. He must have gone to work earlier than usual, strange for a Sunday. Do you mind looking after the toast while I have a quick shower?"

Connie kissed the back of her teeth.

"Charming, invite a girl to breakfast and she has to cook it herself! And I wondered what that pong was," she added, holding her nose between her first finger and thumb.

Hugh looked at her, not sure if she was messing around or not.

"For goodness sake, I'm joking. Go on, it's fine, I'll keep an eye on it. And before you remind me... *again*, I know you like toast burnt and cold," she grinned as she reached for the kettle and started to fill it under the cold tap.

Ten minutes later, Hugh had re-joined Connie in the living room. Picking his specs up off the table, he pulled out a chair and sat down.

Connie inhaled deeply.

"You smell better," she joked.

"Now who's being charming?" He rebuffed. "Here, this is the map we used when we were trying to work out where I'd seen the thylacine for the first time, remember?" Hugh placed the tatty chart he'd retrieved from his bedroom onto the table. He stood the jar of jam on one edge and the tea pot on the other to keep it from curling up.

He reached for a slice of toast and spread it with a thin layer of butter before biting off the corner, wiping away a shower of crumbs from the table with a subconscious swish of his hand.

"Here's the exploratory drill site, look, next to Sullivan's Rise," Connie traced an approximate diamond outline with the tip of her finger.

Hugh nodded.

"According to grandfather, Norseman says this site is going to be extended to here, and these could be the new sites," she pointed to the lake where Joe Sampi had shown them the platypus and the clearing where the body of Tate's murder victim, Floyd Jackson was found.

Jackson had been a respectable shopkeeper the citizens of Sullivan's Rise could turn to when they were in dire straits. He ran a general convenience store where the unisex hair salon now stood. Community spirited, he was always willing to extend credit to his regular customers if they fell on hard times. That was until he lost his wife and developed a drug habit which cost him his business, and with it, his reputation and respectability. All too quickly his former customers ostracised him, forgetting the good turns he had done them in the past.

Down on his luck, he had struck up an arrangement with Spencer Tate to distribute some of his cocaine for him. The crooked ranger had killed Jackson during a row over money, he'd accused the older man of stealing from him, and Jackson had paid with his life.

"Bloody hells bells."

Connie pulled a face.

"What's the matter?"

She smiled, "I've never heard that expression before, that's all... and before you say it again, yes, I do speak English," she groaned. "Hells bells, bloody hells bells. Yep, I like it."

Amused, Hugh tapped the map, "Come on, this is serious." He fell silent for a moment as he chewed. He chuckled to himself, he'd had a brilliant idea.

"What's funny?"

"How do you fancy a bit of subversive behaviour? A spot of sabotage?"

"Err, I'm not sure I know what you mean."

Hugh took a swig of his tea, pulling a face, "Yuk," it was luke warm. "Okay, let me explain. We have to stop the mining company. Make them think it's not worth their while to continue."

"You aren't suggesting terrorism, blowing them up or anything?"

Shocked, Hugh shook his head.

"No way, that's terrible. No, I mean, small acts of sabotage to hold them up a bit, until we can think of a better plan. What'd you think?"

"Fine."

Disappointed, Hugh reached for another slice of toast.

"You don't sound convinced."

Connie shrugged.

"It's not that, Hugh. It's a better idea than I've come up with." She stole a quick look at his face, "Okay, I mean it's the only idea we've come up with, but it isn't going to be easy. This is a big corporation we'll be taking on. They operate State wide; they aren't gonna put up with a couple of kids getting in the way of their plans for long."

"But that's the beauty of it. Don't you see? All we need to do is buy some time. A little time to formulate a proper plan. I don't know what that is yet, but I'll think of something, you know I always do."

Connie nodded.

"Agreed, we've got to do something. We all know there's too much at stake here. The thylacine, the devils, environmental damage, the whole caboodle." She was silent for moment, her expression pensive. "Ok, I'm in. What do you think we should do first?"

Hugh concentrated on buttering another slice of toast. He looked up, his eyes blazing with the same excitement she'd seen when he told her about the thylacine for the first time.

"Let's go to Sullivan's Rise after we've finished here. I'll explain when we get there."

From their usual vantage point at the top of the Rise, Hugh and Connie surveyed the damage developing below. In the short time the Tasmanian Mining Corporation had been in the area they had cleared the thick vegetation which had flourished beyond the cliff face. Although they didn't have a clear view, it looked as though the vegetation clinging to the monolith was undamaged. Not that there was much chance the thylacine would be using the cave as a den in the near future, what with the on-going disturbance in the immediate vicinity.

A pre-fabricated warehouse type building had been erected, alongside a couple of portable toilets, a portacabin and a number of heavy plant vehicles.

Hugh whistled, "It's far worse than we expected, eh?"

Connie peeped at her friend, his face was set, his jaw jutted as he stared ahead.

"Much worse. Okay, what's your plan?"

Hugh pointed at the vehicles.

"Those tyres look mighty expensive, eh? We could find something to puncture them. That'll hold them up for a wee while, what do you think?"

A faint smile flickered across Connie's face, but her eyes were black with anger.

"It's a start. If you'd have said earlier, I'd have brought a screw driver or something." She fiddled in her pocket for a moment. "Will this do?" She opened her hand to reveal a small penknife.

"Where did you get that?"

Connie shrugged, "Mum gave it to me before she left, what with Tate beating me up and all that."

"Almost killing you, you mean."

"Whatever. It's not big enough to cause the authorities any headaches, it's more peace of mind for mum. I can say I use it for fishing or something if anyone asks."

Hugh took the knife out of her hand and pulled out the blade. He ran his thumb along the edge, it wasn't the sharpest thing he'd ever encountered but he was sure it would be sharp enough to puncture the tyres.

"Perfect," he said. "Right, now we need somewhere to hide the bikes. The Blackwood tree's gone so we have to find a new spot. But close, we might need to make a quick getaway if we're spotted."

"That's fine, but I'm gonna take the lead on this."

Hugh looked aghast.

"Don't look at me like that," she demanded, her eyes blazing. "I've done everything you've asked up to now, and more," she snapped.

He'd never seen her so adamant. He nodded, "That's true," he said. "What do you suggest?"

Connie inhaled through clenched teeth, "I've done a bit of tracking. I'm not brilliant, but I can track."

Hugh nodded.

"And I was watching you when you moved in, remember?"

An image of the faded red sweatshirt he had seen when he and his father first moved into the bungalow flashed into his mind. He remembered how annoyed he had been at the thought of a peeping tom spying on him.

"But I saw you!" He sniggered.

"Not all the time!" She retorted. She held her hand up, "let's not argue."

"Agreed," Hugh muttered, not meeting her eyes. She was talking sense, not that he would admit it to her.

Connie softened her tone, "We'll do as you suggest, hide the bikes and take a closer look at the vehicles. If we can puncture the tyres, we will." She looked up at the sky. From the position of the sun it was past noon, the workers, at least those who hadn't knocked off yesterday would have left for home for what was left of the weekend by now.

"I think we'll be pretty safe, but we need to act as if people will still be around the site. We can't let our guard down. Not for a second."

Hugh nodded.

"Fair point."

"Listen, Hugh. I'm not taking over here. We're a team. A damn good team. I'm just better than you are at this - at least at the moment," she added as an afterthought.

Hugh was silent. *You're right*, he thought. *You found the tunnel leading from the bungalow, your grandfather's the best tracker in the territory, you are better at this than I am.*

"Well?" She asked, interrupting his thoughts.

He forced a smile, "Okay." He made a fist and lifted his arm. "Friends?"

She knocked knuckles with his.

"Always, you dill, always."

Half an hour later they had stashed their bikes under a bush, placing a branch on the ground as an indicator to where they were hidden. Taking the lead, Connie skirted the edge of the clearing. They hid between two tall celery topped pine trees. Hugh pointed to the rock face.

"We were right, that's something, I guess. They haven't torn down the foliage covering the entrance to the cave."

"Yeah, but close up the devastation is worse than it looked from the top of the Rise. If this is anything to go by, the thylacine will die. She can't survive."

Hugh turned to face Connie, the colour had drained from her brown cheeks.

"It'll be fine. We'll save her and the pups, I promise."

Connie smiled, "I know, even if we are killed in the process. Come on, follow me."

She got on her hands and knees and crawled forward. She swivelled to take a peek over her shoulder. Stopping, she placed her hand over her mouth to smother her giggles.

"Shush!" Hugh hissed.

"I'm, I'm sorry, but you need to get your bum down, it's sticking up in the air."

"What? Oh my God!" Hugh flopped to the floor, "sorry."

"No harm done this time. Crawl along like me, instead of scuttling like a crab. Ready to try again?"

"Yep, lead on."

With caution, they crawled around the perimeter of the camp. Stopping every few metres or so to check they were alone. As they had anticipated, the camp was deserted.

Reaching the first vehicle, the van used by the surveyors, Connie opened the blade and pushed it into the rubber. She hit the hilt of the small knife with the heel of her hand.

"Argh, it's no good."

"Here, let me have a go. I'm not implying you're a wimp or anything like that, I've got my weight behind me," he suggested.

Connie's eyes travelled over Hugh's frame. He was heavier than she was, there was no denying that, but he'd lost a shed load of weight since the first time she'd seen him. Perhaps he wasn't as strong as he thought he was.

Without raising an argument, she passed the knife to him, shuffling out of the way.

"Go for it."

He wiped his sweaty palm down the front of his tee shirt. Gripping the knife, he placed the tip of the blade against the tyre and shoved. He twisted the small knife to the right and left as he pushed his weight against it, falling against the side of the vehicle as the rubber gave way. The pressurised air started to hiss from the hole which he made bigger by wiggling the knife round and round.

"Nice one. Shall we move on to the next?" She asked, her eyes scanning the area, "the coast is clear."

They crawled from behind the van, crouching beside a JCB digger. This tyre was going to be much harder to puncture.

Hugh pushed the blade into the rubber with his full weight behind it, but the blade didn't make an impression in the material. He gritted his teeth and adjusted his grip.

"Grrr," he growled. Again he pushed, he shuffled his feet in order to get a better hold as he shoved. "Argh!"

It was useless. The rubber was too thick. He dropped the blade and shook his hand before turning it over to inspect the damage. In the middle of his palm was a perfect imprint of the hilt of the knife.

"We're gonna need something stronger and sharper."

Hugh nodded, "Perhaps we should use a screwdriver and a hammer to hit it with?" He suggested. "We'll need to be extra careful. If we are stopped by the cops we could be arrested, tooled up for a job so to speak."

Connie threw him a quizzical look.

"I think your imagination's running away with you!"

"Maybe, but we'll play it by ear."

"Shall we have a scout around? We might find some tools or something sharper."

"It's a bit risky."

Connie winked, "Don't be a wuss," she teased.

"Hey, that's not fair!"

"Shush," she put a finger to her lips. "I was joking!"

Hugh nodded, *sometimes I'm not so sure,* he thought.

"Come on, let's head back."

"Wanna go first?" Connie asked.

Hugh stole a glimpse at her face, not sure if she meant it.

"Go on then!" She said, opening her eyes wide to emphasise she wasn't joking.

Hugh took a fleeting look around. Nothing moved. Keeping his butt low to the ground, he started to crawl back the way they had come. Reaching the edge of the clearing, he stood up.

"Hey, what are you kids up to?"

Clamouring to her feet, Connie spun round on the ball of her foot.

"Bugger, we didn't check the toilets," she hissed as one of the men they had seen surveying the area came out of the blue and white cubicle, a newspaper under his arm, holding a mug in his hand.

"Do you think he saw what we were doing?"

"Hang on," Hugh hissed through clenched teeth. "We wanted to get a closer look at the machines, mate. That's all," he called, keeping his tone and expression as neutral as possible. "Can we come over?"

"No, clear off, the equipment's dangerous!"

"Please?"

"I said no. Now get out of here," the surveyor shouted.

Hugh raised his hand in acknowledgement.

"Start walking, but don't rush," he whispered.

He led the way, fighting the urge to look back. Reaching their bikes, they dragged them from out of the bush.

"Hey, get back here you little shits!"

"Come on, Connie, quick. He must have noticed the tyre." Hugh jumped astride his machine and started to pedal, while she ran beside him, pushing her bike before jumping on. "Don't look back."

They pedalled as fast as they could for several minutes before Connie risked a quick glance over her shoulder, slowing her bike to a more comfortable pace.

"The coast's clear, no one's following," she called as he continued to charge along. "Hugh. Hugh!" She shouted. "No one's following us."

Hugh whooped with relief, "Phew, that was close." he screamed, braking to match her pace. "Do you think he'll be able to recognise us?"

"You maybe, because of your accent," replied Connie. "I'm not so sure about me, being aboriginal, many people say you've seen one of us... you've seen us all!"

"That's bloody rude."

Connie agreed, "But it's a fact of life."

"I'd have loved to have seen his expression when he saw the wheel."

"I don't think I would have," said Connie, being sensible. "If we had been any closer he's have caught us. He ran pretty damn fast. Nah, we've got to be much more careful next time," she warned.

Ah, at least there will be a next time, he mused.

"Are you going to tell the others?"

An expression of horror crept over his face.

"Don't be daft. Can you imagine what my old man would say?" He shook his head to dismiss the image of his father's disappointed face. "No way, this is our secret."

Chapter Sixteen

William Appleby knocked once and strode into the office without waiting to be asked.

"And g'day to you too," Laura Goodman looked up at her lawyer cum part-time boyfriend and smiled.

Appleby returned the smile.

"I'm sorry, sweetheart, good morning." He lent over the desk and brushed his lips against hers. "I hope I'm not going to ruin your day but we have a problem at Warrugul."

"Another one?" She asked, watching him over the top of her coffee cup.

Appleby dipped his head in acknowledgement, "I'm afraid so."

"Go on," she said, warming her hands against the sides of her cup.

"We have had an incident of vandalism."

Laura Goodman raised her eyebrows, it wasn't the first time her property had been damaged, she often had to endure the antics of eco warriors and general do-gooders. They might be a fact of life but they were an irritation she could do without.

"Tell me the damage."

"A tyre was punctured."

Goodman tutted.

"Why are you bothering me with that, it's nothing more than a triviality? It's possible it was an accident, we've both seen the area, it's hardly a cricket pitch."

"I agree, and I wouldn't bother you, except one of the lads saw a couple of kids hanging about. Their behaviour was suspicious and they ran off when challenged. Apparently they wanted to look at the diggers but he said they'd hidden their bikes, that's not how a kid behaves if they just want to look at the machines, is it?"

She positioned the bone china cup in the middle of its saucer as she thought for a moment.

"What's the profit margin for this one?"

Appleby scratched his head.

"I'll need to check to be exact, but..."

"You do that and let me know," she said, her tone dismissive as she returned her attention to the commodities page of the newspaper she was reading. Her eyes scanned the list of companies and their prices as she tried to assess how her competitors were faring before the start of the new trading week.

Moments later, Appleby slipped a printed page in front of her. She reviewed the document which listed the geological projections, proposed margins of error and predicted profits verses expenses. To the untrained eye this information would mean nothing, but to Laura Goodman it made perfect sense. She had spent many an hour sat alongside her father, training to take over the company one day. Training to become the son he never had but always wanted. She reviewed the bottom line. As she thought, Warrugul was not a site she could afford to lose.

"What security presence do we have?"

"Well, I've asked for additional patrols, like you requested. The site manager will be camping at the location during the initial development phase. With work at such an early stage we don't factor in that expense, it's not until mining begins full swing we'll take on some security guards."

Goodman shook her head.

"No, not for this one, William. I suggest we rectify these niggles once and for all. This is the place where that vet made all the commotion about the devils isn't it? And there's an abo community if I'm correct in my thinking, I can recall some black faces in the audience. No, I want you to engage the security presence straight away. If you don't think it warrants using the normal company yet, take on some casual workers."

Appleby was about to interrupt but she continued to talk over him.

"I know you are going to start whinging about licensed patrolmen, that's not what I'm saying. During the development stage take on some of the locals as casuals and have a couple of full time security chaps to oversee them, how's that?"

Appleby was thoughtful, "I think we can live with that."

"Right, I also want to see the heritage chap," she clicked her fingers, "you know the one, I can never remember his name. Check my diary for an opening."

Appleby scribbled a note as he walked across the room, he'd get onto that right away.

"William."

He stopped, his hand on the door handle.

"I mean what I say about using local casual labour. They'll have their ear to the ground." She was interrupted by the trill of her phone. Glancing at the display she dismissed him with a curt nod. "I've got to get this." She spun her chair round and stared out of the window, "Daddy, how wonderful to hear from you."

Appleby pulled the door to his office closed behind him and slumped into his chair. He sighed, she might be easy on the eye, and yep she paid well, very well, but hell she was hard work, especially when she treated him like an office junior.

Reaching for his diary he ran this finger down his list of contacts, smiling when he recognised the name he was after. He dialled the number and started to review his boss's forth coming engagements while he waited.

"Canton."

"Dave, it's William Appleby."

"Hi Bill, G'day."

Appleby cringed, he detested it when anyone shortened his name. He hated to be reminded of his poor childhood. He'd worked too long to eliminate the friends and family tying him to those memories, he didn't need reminders such as his childhood name to ruin his day.

He explained what they were looking for, local casual labour who wouldn't mind turning a blind eye when corners needed to be cut, but who could be dispensed with when the full operation got underway.

Canton sighed at the other end of the phone.

"Warrugul's the back of beyond, Bill. It isn't gonna be easy."

"I don't pay you for excuses, Dave. I pay top dollar and I expect you to come up with the goods."

"Yes boss, leave it with me."

"And don't forget I want local heavies. I'm not saying we are expecting more trouble, but I'm not taking any chances. This way if they break a few bones or bloody a few noses the shit stops with them, and we can wash our hands of them."

"Got it under control."

The day had dawned with grey skies and drizzle, a welcome relief after the hot temperatures of the last couple of days and with the rain came a reduction in the threat from forest fire, a constant risk at this time of year, not just from natural causes such as a lightning strike but more and more often from accidental or even deliberate fire setting.

At least the inhabitants of Sullivan's Creek were not complaining. So far the activities of the Tasmanian Mining Corporation hadn't impacted their businesses. Workers from the mine site were expected to make up the shortfall if the tourist numbers fell in the immediate future, whether that continued throughout the whole season remained to be seen.

To save time, Hugh and Connie had agreed to meet en-route to Sullivan's Rise. He was pedalling as fast as he could but he was tired. He'd had a bad night suffering the reoccurring nightmare of Tate falling from the top of the cliff and as a consequence he'd overslept by half an hour.

"Good, at least she doesn't look cross," he muttered to himself, spotting Connie waiting at the agreed meeting point. "G'day," he smiled.

Connie beamed back, she looked happier than he'd see her if several days.

"I got to speak to mum last night," she gushed.

"Did she call Napoleon's number?" He could tell from her face that's what happened.

"She's coming home for the weekend. She managed to swap a few shifts with a colleague who needs time off in the week for a minor op or something."

"Bummer for her, but great news for Angie. And of course for you and Joe," he added as an afterthought. "I wonder if dad knows?" he laughed. "I'm sure he'll be itching to take her out."

"Dunno, forgot to ask."

"How long is she off for?"

Connie grinned, "Friday afternoon and doesn't have to be back at work until Tuesday. It means she'll have worked ten days without a break but she's done it before. I can't wait."

"I'm being selfish here, but it may mean you can't get away, you'll want to spend time with your mum."

Connie dismissed the suggestion.

"I'll be fine; I'll do some juggling."

Hugh smiled, it was clear nothing was going to dampen her spirits. It was good to see.

"Come on, I'll race you."

"Hey, I'm not ready," he shouted at her back as she pulled away. Not that it would have made much of a difference even if they had started neck and neck, she was still faster than him.

He sighed as he started to pedal, he didn't care, he knew how much she and her grandfather both missed Angie. Absorbed in his thoughts he wasn't looking where he was going.

"Damn!" He braked as he tried to regain control of the bike, he'd hit a stone and the front wheel was wobbling in an ominous fashion as it started to deflate.

"Hold up, Connie. Connie, Connie!"

Hearing his yell, she rode in a circle without reducing her speed and headed back.

"I've got a puncture. I don't suppose you've got a pump in your bag?"

"Hang on."

He waited as she rummaged in the bag, wondering what on earth girls found to carry around with them.

She dragged out a small telescopic pump.

Though at times like this, he conceded, it was good to carry everything apart from the kitchen sink with you.

"There you go."

Hugh unscrewed the cap and started to pump air in the softening wheel. He squeezed the tyre and waited.

"I hope it holds, I don't have a repair kit on me," she said.

"Me neither."

He waited a couple of minutes more before squeezing the tyre to check the pressure.

"Can I hang onto this, looks like I'm gonna have to keep pumping it up."

"Want to head back?"

"Hell no. I'm sure it'll be fine if I take it steady, sorry."

"It's not your fault."

Hugh inflated the tyre up as much as he dare, over pump it and he ran the risk of it splitting if he hit anything else, under inflate and he'd have to stop every couple of minutes."

Satisfied, he went to hand her the pump.

"No, do as you said and hang onto it, save me the trouble of keep fishing it out of my bag."

Hugh slipped the pump into his pocket as he mounted his bike, "Come on, let's take it steady."

Progress was slow as they had to stop every ten minutes or so for him to pump up the tyre. At last they reached the bush they had hidden their bikes in the day before, the branch was still lying where they had left it.

"Before we go any further we need to sort a few things out. This is decision time."

Connie stared at her friend, a look of confusion on her face.

"Decisions?"

Hugh ran his hand over his face while he thought, licking his lips before speaking.

"There were times when Joe, your grandfather."

Connie tutted as she tapped the toe of her plimsoll on the ground.

"Okay, okay, I know I'm rambling."

"And stating the obvious," she said with a huff.

Hugh inhaled, "There have been times when I'm sure Joe has regarded me as a bad influence."

Connie shook her head, "Not true."

Smiling at her loyalty, Hugh continued, "We should examine the evidence as he'd see it, we keep getting into danger and having accidents."

"True," Connie conceded.

"What the two of us have done to date has been legal and above board, all we have been guilty of is trying to keep the thylacine a secret."

"To protect her and her pups."

Hugh continued, ignoring the interruption, "If we carry on as we plan. With the sabotage, I mean, we will be breaking the law."

A look of apprehension clouded Connie's eyes. Hugh stared at her, scrutinising her expression. He had to be sure, no, she had to be sure she wanted to do this.

"We could go to prison. If we are found out I mean."

Hugh smirked, "Yeah, but that's if we are found out. Are you sure you are up for this?"

Connie's eyes sparked, "Hell yes!"

Hugh beamed, she was even beginning to sound like him.

They hid the bikes before retracing their steps from the previous day. Crouching between the celery topped pines they waited. They didn't want to be caught out like yesterday.

They waited for an eternity. Nothing moved except a few tufts of grass swaying in the breeze.

"Come on, I think the coast is clear. No one could be in the dunny that long."

Hugh frowned, sometimes she could be so unladylike.

"Do you want to go first?"

Connie shook her head, "Your turn, but keep your butt down."

Hugh feigned a look of hurt, "Are you saying my bum looks big in this?" He joked, slipping the screwdriver up his sleeve she had retrieved from the depths of her bag.

"Connie slapped his backside as he passed, "Never."

After a quick scout around the area, Hugh headed towards the JCB, with Connie close behind him. He ran his hand around the rim of the tyre, it was huge, pushing his thumb against the rubber it didn't make any impression. This wasn't going to be easy. Connie watched in silence as he twisted the tip of the screwdriver to the right and left, applying as much pressure as he could. A trickle of sweat ran down his face as he pushed against the tool.

At last the blade punctured the rubber, emitting a satisfying hiss as the pressurised air started to escape.

"Come on, let's do the back one too."

Scuttling the length of the machine, Hugh repositioned the screwdriver and shoved.

"Hey!"

Connie started at Hugh, "Shit. Quick, run."

Keeping as low as they could they doubled back to towards the trees.

"Get back here you little bastards."

Ignoring the shouting behind them, they kept running, Hugh could hear his heart pounding inside his chest.

A shot rang out.

He stopped dead. He shook his head in disbelief, that *sounded like a gunshot, nah, it couldn't be?*

Connie shoved him in the back, "For goodness sake keep running, you dill!"

"This isn't the way to the bikes."

"I know, we don't have time to pump up your tyre, we need to hide." She leapt over a bush, skirting around a tree, her natural athleticism allowing her to move with the grace and speed of a gazelle.

Hugh charged after her, desperate to keep up. His breath was becoming laboured as he forced one foot in front of the other.

"Hold up," he gasped.

Connie glanced over her shoulder. She could see he was struggling, his feet were dragging along the ground as he moved, his face a shocking shade of pink.

Pausing, she stared back the way they had come. Nothing moved. Hugh bent over, filling his burning lungs as he tried to steady his breathing.

"B, bloody hell that was close."

"I think it's okay. We aren't being followed."

She patted the sweat from her top lip with the back of her hand as she watched Hugh flop to the ground. At least he was returning to a more normal colour.

"That idiot could have killed us," she fumed.

Hugh shook her head, "He shot way above our heads."

"That's comforting," she snapped.

"Don't take it out on me," he barked, "neither of us was expecting to see anyone, let alone to be shot at. A reaction like that, could be described as overkill."

Connie smiled, amused he hadn't realised he had made such an appalling joke.

"What?" He demanded.

"That was one bloody awful joke," she teased.

Realising what he had said, he grinned, diffusing the tension between them.

"Yeah, something isn't right for a company sinking a few bore holes." She slumped down beside her friend, "the trouble is, how do we tell anyone what's happened without getting into trouble ourselves? Grandfather would kill me."

Hugh pulled a face, "I can't imagine dad would be too pleased with me either. You know he doesn't even go above the speed limit, he's so square."

"Yeah, tell me about it," she teased, nudging his arm.

"Hey, are you dissing my dad?"

"Nope, just agreeing with you."

"Come on, let's go back and collect the bikes," he suggested.

Chapter Seventeen

Laura Goodman loved her job. She was a Machiavellian control freak and a manipulator. Her father had called her a user but she'd taken that as a compliment.

She stared out of her office window. It was a clear day and the view was spectacular. She couldn't help wishing he was here to enjoy it with her.

A light rap on the office door disturbed her thoughts. She didn't bother to respond, she recognised the knock. This, like so many things about him, was predictable. She sighed, predicable he may be, but William Appleby did have his uses.

"More trouble at Warrugul."

Goodman raised an eyebrow, but continued to stare out of the window, in actuality it was a beautiful day, was he going to ruin it for her?

Appleby paused for a moment before continuing.

"The site manager says the same kids have been back. They punctured the wheel of a JCB. And before you ask, no he didn't see them do it, but it's no coincidence, this time the little shits left a screwdriver behind when they ran off."

"I assume he ran after them. But then I'm not surprised, after all kids will be kids - the little larrikins."

Appleby cleared his throat. She smiled to herself, detecting his nerves.

"Well?"

"I'm afraid he fired a warning shot at them."

She uncrossed her elegant legs and spun round, the movement so violent it caused her leather chair to sway.

"Please tell me you are joking," she whispered. She glared at the man standing in front of her as if he were the one wielding the gun.

Appleby shook his head.

She looked up at the ceiling, "Give me strength," she muttered to herself. She tapped the table with her manicured nail while she thought. "Right, we need a damage limitation exercise. Whoever fired the gun is gone. Do you hear me, gone today!"

"We can't do that. The unions won't allow it."

She waved away his protests, "Unions! Unions! Do you think I give a rat's arse about unions? William, stop behaving like a wimp. It's your job to sort this out, so get it sorted".

Appleby held up his hand, "Laura, sweetheart, the union can shut us down."

Goodman narrowed her eyes as she fought to control her temper.

"Yes, you're right. Okay, he's still gone." She raised a finger to silence the protest she knew would be coming. "He is gone from Warrugul today. Move him, move him wherever you like, to the back of beyond for all I care, but he is gone by close of business tonight. I told you to increase the security presence, I want it tripled. At least until full production is underway. And where's that heritage chap? I want him in my office within the next half an hour."

"It's Sunday afternoon, Laura."

She raised an eyebrow.

"Not everyone is a workaholic sweetheart. I managed to get hold of him first thing this morning but he was taking his family out for the day."

She waved away his explanation.

"Nine a.m. sharp. No excuses."

Chapter Eighteen

Richard Pirlatapa fingered his tie. He was so nervous he felt sick. This was the first time he's been summoned to Laura Goodman's office and he was worried. The frosted glass door opened and Appleby beckoned him in.

Laura Goodman was bent over a pile of papers. She signed the one on top with a flourish before looking up. Without uttering a word, she pointed to the empty chair on the other side of her desk. Pirlatapa shuffled forward, he was a tall man but walked with a stoop, making him look several centimetres shorter than his full height. He perched on the seat, he was uncomfortable but he daren't move.

Goodman reached across her desk for a blue file which she opened and re-read the first page. From where he sat, Pirlatapa could see the name, 'Warrugul National Park', printed across the front.

She looked up and smiled, but there was no friendliness in the gesture.

"Richard, can I offer you a drink, tea, err, coffee perhaps?"

Pirlatapa didn't have a chance to respond before she continued.

"Warrugul National Park − is there anything special about it?"

Pirlatapa looked confused, "Warrugul?" The name meant nothing to him.

"Yes, Warrugul. It's south of Devonport." She looked over the head of the heritage officer, her eyes questioning as she glanced at William Appleby, was he really the calibre of her middle management employees?

She returned her attention to the file in front of her.

"Apart from a small abo..." She cleared her throat, "I beg your pardon, a slip of the tongue. Apart from a small Aboriginal Tasmanian community," she tipped the page, "consisting of five families, a couple of kilometres from the proposed development I can't see anything that makes it special."

Richard Pirlatapa shook his head.

"I'm sorry, Miss Goodman, my investigations into all of the proposed sites revealed nothing of significance."

"So no aboriginal hunting grounds, meeting places," she lowered her voice as she continued under her breath, "the usual claptrap that holds me up?"

Pirlatapa shook his head.

"No, nothing. I understand a couple of the families are helping out the Parks and Wildlife service, but that's on a temporary basis," he added as an afterthought. "No, I can assure you there is nothing special about the area."

Goodman nodded.

"What about the Tasmanian devil problem?" She asked, but the question wasn't directed at either of them in particular.

Appleby and Pirlatapa glanced at one another, neither sure who should answer.

"Well?"

"The area is free from any recorded instances of Devil Face Tumour Disease," Appleby replied.

"Is that good or bad for us?"

The lawyer shrugged.

"I don't think it will have any impact on us."

"I want that vet," she snapped her fingers.

"Andrew Whitaker."

"Yes, Andrew Whitaker, I want him brought on board. I don't care what it takes."

Back in Warrugul, Whitaker was engrossed in a post mortem. The Tasmanian devil, Hugh had fought so hard to save, had died overnight. He dropped his bloodied scalpel into the instrument tray. The sound of metal against metal reverberated around the quiet room.

Post-mortems were often an unsatisfactory job, resulting in more questions than answers but this one was conclusive. He finished his task by suturing the incision with a long running stitch.

Hugh watched from the doorway, his father hadn't noticed him standing there. Turning round, Whitaker took in a sharp intake of breath, his son had startled him.

"Hugh, hi, I didn't hear you come in."

"What happened, Dad? I thought she was doing well?"

Whitaker pulled the gloves off his hands, the latex flicking back on itself with a satisfying thwack.

"So did I, son. She'd suffered extensive bruising and when I went in, I found a small tear in the hepatic vein. So, in spite of the drips and medication, she died from internal bleeding, caused by the kicking she got. It's a real shame, what with the population in steep decline. No animal deserves to die like that, through cruelty, pure ignorance and stupidity." He paused for a moment, "ah, that's the phone. Excuse me, I'll clear up in a moment."

Hugh watched as his father walked towards the front desk. *I might as well get started on these,* he thought, picking up the instrument tray and carrying it to the sink.

He knew how to clean the instruments before they were packaged and sterilised in the autoclave which stood in the corner of the room, he done it dozens of times before.

"That was an interesting conversation."

"Err?"

"Oh thanks, son. That's saved me a job. That was Laura Goodman's lawyer."

Hugh felt his skin bristle as it erupted in goose bumps. His body stiffened at the sound of her name. He didn't know if it was guilt over his subversive activities over the last couple of days or because she and her company were a threat to the thylacine.

"What, err, um, what did he want?"

Whitaker removed a black body bag from the cupboard and placed the devil inside, he'd incinerate the poor creature when he'd finished clearing up.

"Oh, he wanted to arrange an appointment for me to meet with Laura Goodman. She wants to discuss the disruption to the local devils. I suggested Doug should attend. That way I can give my professional opinion as a vet and I'll consult the Save the Tasmanian Devil project, but Langdon will have the authority of the Parks and Wildlife Service behind him."

"Fat lot of good they've been till now."

"Hugh," his father rebuked. "I suggested Friday morning, that way I can bring Angie home when she finishes her shift. Joe told me she was back for the weekend."

Hugh's mood brightened.

"That's a great idea. Connie told me she was coming home. We weren't sure if you knew or not."

His father smiled, his expression was a dead giveaway.

"You'll be careful, won't you, Dad?"

His father looked surprised, "What with Angie you mean? Safe sex, that sort of thing?"

A look of shock flashed across his son's face.

"Dad!" He exclaimed. "I was talking about the Tasmanian Mining Corporation and Laura Goodman. I've got a bad feeling about her," he said.

His father laughed, "Oh dear, that's a bad omen."

"Dad!"

His father held his hands up in surrender.

"Okay, son. I'll finish clearing up here, and then I need to drive over and see Joe."

"Don't worry, you go. I'll finish this off."

"Brilliant, thanks." His father scooped the bag containing the body of the devil off the table in order to take it to the incinerator.

"On second thoughts, can I come with you, to Joe's I mean?"

"Is your homework done?"

Hugh tutted, "Y-e-s! I finished it on Friday."

"Fine, lets finish up and drive over together."

Some fifty minutes later they were standing outside Sampi's cabin.

"G'day," Connie smiled in greeting as she opened the door. "Grandfather, Andrew and Hugh are here."

"I can see that, darl," said the old man, looking up from where he was sitting. "Come on in, both of you. Wasn't expecting to see you this evening, Andrew. Is there a problem?" He asked, standing to shake the younger man's hand in greeting.

"Not sure, is Napoleon in? Perhaps he should hear this too?"

"Yes, as far as I know, he is."

"I'll go and check, Grandfather."

"Shall I come?"

"It's next door, Hugh."

Whitaker and Sampi exchanged amused glances. Hugh blushed, he'd noticed the look they shared.

"Come and sit down. Cold beer, Andrew?"

"Sounds good. Yes, please."

"Hugh, I can offer you juice or water?"

"Water please, Joe. Need some help?"

Sampi waved his offer away, "I'll be fine, Hugh, thanks."

Moments later, it was standing room only in the small living room as Connie returned with Napoleon and his sons, as usual Boy-Boy made it his duty to greet each of them in turn with enthusiastic licks.

Hugh laughed as he tried to fend the scruffy mongrel off as he jumped up and down in an attempt to lick his face.

"Down, Boy-Boy, get down, you daft mutt."

"Come on, Hugh, let's go into my room, at least we can sit down in there."

"Leave the door open," he whispered, "I want to hear what they're talking about." Hugh perched on Connie's bed as he watched his father prise the cap off his beer bottle. "Oi, for goodness sake stop fidgeting," he hissed.

Connie bounced up and down a couple of times for good measure, just to annoy him. The springs of her old bed groaning in protest.

Hugh tutted, licking the water that had spilt onto his hand.

"Keep that up and you'll be sleeping on a water bed," he grumbled.

Connie poked her tongue out.

"Stop being a misery," she laughed.

"Laura Goodman's lawyer called me earlier," Whitaker announced. That one sentence was enough to command the attention of everyone in the room.

"What did that pretentious young man have to say?"

Whitaker smiled at Napoleon.

"He invited me to meet with Laura Goodman to discuss the impact of the mining on the devil population. I suggested Doug Langdon should come along too."

Sampi nodded, "Good move, Andrew."

"Do you think it's a legitimate interest, or are they just trying to butter you up by asking for your advice?" George asked.

The vet shrugged, "I've got to assume it is. I'm going to speak to the co-ordinator of the Save the Tasmanian Devil project tomorrow, see if there is any information I should share with the mining corporation."

"Could it be enough to call a halt to the drilling of the bore holes?" Hugh called from Connie's room.

Whitaker pulled face, "If I'm honest, I doubt it, son. I bet we are told to monitor the population, review the impact and report back."

"We know it's already impacting the thylacine."

"How come, Hugh?"

Hugh glanced at Connie, but her expression was one of complete innocence, he wasn't going to get any support there. He looked back at Napoleon.

"We've been to Sullivan's Rise a couple of times. We haven't seen any sign of her or her pups."

"Hugh, Connie," Sampi narrowed his eyes, "you just happened to be looking for the thylacine in the same vicinity as the designated mining area?"

Hugh felt his face redden.

"Mmm, I see."

Mikey threw the kids an understanding look.

"We saw the thylacine and her pups, all of them, last night."

"Where?" Hugh demanded, before muttering an apology, he hadn't meant to sound quite so abrupt.

"We were about two miles south of Sullivan's Rise, way off the tourist trail."

"She's safe for the moment?"

Mikey nodded, "Yeah, she's safe for the moment. Don't worry, Hugh, We'll keep her that way."

Chapter Nineteen

Once Laura Goodman issued an instruction, it was a brave man who failed to act on it. By mid-week a number of local men had been taken on as casual labour to supplement the professional security services employed to patrol the exploration area. The damaged equipment had been repaired and was now parked up behind portable fencing. The site manager had been replaced and removed to another development.

In order to give Angie a lift home, Andrew Whitaker had turned down an invitation to travel to Hobart with Doug Langdon. He hovered in the lobby of the impressive building used by the Tasmanian Mining Corporation as its headquarters, waiting for his colleague to arrive. Staring up at the glass and steel façade, he couldn't help thinking it reminded him of the Shard, a building which dominated the London sky line.

Spotting the ginger hair of the head ranger as he entered the motion activated revolving doorway, Whitaker walked towards his colleague.

"G'day, Doug."

"Andrew, g'day mate. It's nice to see you again." Their handshake was cordial. In the few weeks they had worked together both men had developed a mutual respect for one another.

Whitaker pointed to the reception desk, they were a little early but catching the eye of the male receptionist they explained who they were and that they were here for an appointment. The receptionist checked his monitor before asking them to take a seat as he dialled the extension number for Laura Goodman's personal assistant.

Minutes later they were ushered into the CEO's panoramic office. Langdon whistled under his breath.

"Bloody hell," he mumbled, "this is bigger than the floor space of my whole apartment," he observed, turning a full circle to take in the magnificence of the expansive room.

"Laura will be with us in a couple of minutes," William Appleby announced, following them into the room.

Laura Goodman blotted the lipstick she'd just applied on a tissue, leaving it screwed up on the side of the basin, after all when you pay for a cleaner why clear up yourself?

"Good morning, Andrew, Doug... I hope you don't mind me using your first names?" She said with a familiarity neither man felt comfortable with, but neither of whom felt happy to voice their disapproval.

"*Ms.* Goodman," Langdon highlighted her title with formality as he returned her handshake.

Whitaker shook her hand, surprised at the firmness of her grip, it wouldn't have been out of place if she'd have been a two-metre-tall bloke!

"Please take a seat." She indicated they were to sit on the huge leather Chesterfield couch. "May I offer you something to drink?"

Langdon and Appleby refused, but Whitaker asked for tea.

"How English," she smiled, "Do you mind if I join you?"

They waited while she poured the steaming amber liquid into two bone china cups.

"Help yourself to milk and sugar," she said, slipping a slice of lemon into hers.

She settled back in her chair and crossed her legs, her short tailored skirt rising above her knee.

"Let me start by thanking you both for accepting my invitation. I want to begin by reassuring you that the Tasmanian Mining Corporation is serious about its environmental responsibility. It is of paramount importance to us that the flora and fauna is protected, and remains as unaffected as possible." She looked straight at the vet as she spoke, almost ignoring the park ranger. "Correct me if I'm wrong." She moistened her lips before continuing, running the tip of her tongue over the bright red lipstick she had applied moments before. "But having consulted with our indigenous heritage officer, Richard Pirlatapa, I believe Warrugul National Park has little or no indigenous native significance."

"Mmm, I doubt the local aboriginal community, small though it is, would agree with that statement," Langdon interrupted.

A faint smile played on her lips as Goodman continued addressing her comments to the vet.

"I didn't mean to suggest the aboriginal community had no significance, what I meant was that there are no aboriginal burial grounds or areas of indigenous cultural heritage we need to avoid."

Whitaker nodded his understanding focusing on his cup, a little uncomfortable under her gaze.

Appleby stared out of the window, he'd seen her operate like this before, he knew they would be putty in her hands by the time she'd finished with them.

"Perhaps you can enlighten us to the potential impact on the Tasmanian devil population, Andrew."

Whitaker placed his cup and saucer on the low coffee table which filled the space between them. At last he was on a more comfortable footing.

"I have contacted the Save the Tasmanian Devil project, as well as the Menzies Institute for Medical Research."

Laura Goodman nodded, her head held on one side as she hung on his every word, her eyes never leaving his face as he spoke, her tea untouched in the cup she held.

"It's our conclusion that the bore holes will have little or no impact on the population, um," he cleared his throat, once again uncomfortable as she continued to stare at him. "However, we reserve the right to review the situation if the mine goes into full production. At the moment the disease has not reached Warrugul. Our devil population remains healthy, but that could change at any moment."

Laura Goodman nodded.

"May I ask a question?"

Relived, Whitaker turned his attention to the lawyer.

"Playing 'devil's advocate', no pun intended. As a bull-nosed lawyer for a commercial business enterprise, can I ask if there would there be more of an impact if the disease reached the park?"

Whitaker looked at his colleague, "Shall I answer?"

Langdon nodded, "Please."

"From the project's perspective, if the disease breached the boundary of the Park, we will be approaching the Government to ensure there is no further damage to the environment. I expect that would mean the mining would be stopped."

Appleby looked at Goodman and raised his eyebrows.

"I'm not sure you appreciate the seriousness of the disease," Whitaker said. "At the moment it has a one hundred percent mortality rate. That in itself is very unusual."

Goodman looked surprised, "I wasn't aware of that." She threw her colleague a withering look, yet again she had been let down, this was the sort of information she expected to be briefed on prior to a meeting to prevent from being broadsided.

Whitaker continued, "The project is mapping the genome of the disease in order to develop a vaccine. I'm afraid it's still a long way off. That's why we are capturing healthy animals and moving them to unaffected areas such as Maria Island as well as zoos here and on the mainland. Once the disease is eradicated we can think about reintroducing healthy animals back into the wild."

"I see, that is very commendable work, Andrew. Thank you for the explanation."

Whitaker glanced at his colleague before responding to her praise. He looked straight at the chief executive officer of the Tasmanian Mining Corporation.

"I think it only fair to warn you, Miss Goodman."

"Laura, please. We are all friends here, Andrew."

"Err, um, yes, Laura, I have to warn you that the Tasmanian Government, no, it's fairer to say the world will not allow another avoidable mistake to occur on Tasmanian soil such as occurred with the extinction of the thylacine. Some things are beyond our control, but we are doing our damnedest to save the devil, and its continued existence will override any mining project."

"Here, here," she said. "And to support your fantastic work the Tasmanian Mining Corporation will make an immediate donation to the project."

Chapter Twenty

Joe Sampi had spent the last hour watching the progress of the Tasmanian Mining Corporation from the vantage point at the top of Sullivan's Rise. With a sigh he started to trek down to where he had left the Land Rover. Nearing the parked vehicle, he noticed two youths watching him, they were lent against a tall blue gum tree, one of them slouched with his hands deep in his pockets, the other, a little shorter than his friend, was lighting a cigarette. Had they been waiting on the corner of a street in Sullivan's Creek they might not have looked out of place, but here they stood out like a boil on the end of a nose, their actions nothing short of suspicious.

Sampi nodded in their direction, "Hey lads, g'day. Can you make sure you extinguish that cigarette when you've finished smoking? Even with the recent light rain there's still the threat of fire at this time of year and we can't take that risk."

The youths remained silent, the one with the cigarette flicked the ash in a deliberate haphazard fashion.

"Am I speaking gobble-de-gook?" Sampi muttered to himself as he walked towards them. "Look lads, all I'm asking is for you to show a little common sense, no big deal, eh? Hang on, I know you, don't I?" Sampi said, addressing the taller of the two men.

The younger man wrinkled his nose as he looked the Aboriginal Tasmanian up and down, a look of disgust on his face.

"Nope, don't think so, old man."

"Is he saying once you've seen one of us, you've seen us all ah, eh... we all look alike, us white guys, Lennie?" His companion whispered.

Lennie scooped to pluck a long blade of grass, allowing Sampi a glimpse of his tattoo poking out from under the edge of his sleeve, a skull and crossbones tattoo.

"I wasn't talking to you, son," Sampi replied without taking his eyes off Lennie's face as he spoke.

"Don't you ignore me you..."

The sentence went unfinished as Sampi turned his attention to the other lad.

"What you looking at, you black bastard."

Sampi remained silent, he'd heard similar comments and worse before. The youth dropped his eyes, cursing under his breath,

"I've been looking for you, Lennie," Sampi said, returning his gaze to the older of the two youths.

Lennie shuffled, repositioning his weight.

"I wasn't lost," he retorted, smiling as his friend roared with laughter at his puerile joke.

Sampi nodded, he was all too familiar with kids like this.

"I have some questions I'd like to ask you. Questions about a report stating you were seen torturing a Tasmanian devil with your brother, Nigel, and then I'd like to ask you about an assault on a young boy."

Lennie snorted, "What, that chubby pom? What about it?"

"Ah, so you are admitting you know about the incidents I'm referring to?" Sampi asked, catching Lennie unawares with his accusation. "In addition to that, the Tasmanian devil is an endangered animal, therefore it is protected. What you did was illegal and the chubby pom, as you described him, happens to be a very good friend of my granddaughter, come to think of it a very good friend of mine as well."

Watts pursed his lips, "Soooo, what do you want me to do about it?"

"I'd like you to accompany me to the ranger's station where I'll ask you some questions. At that stage I'll consider if the police need to be informed."

"Dunno about you, Tom," said Lennie addressing his friend, "but I aint going anywhere with this stinking abo."

Sampi turned his back on the youths, he intended to return to his vehicle and call for help, but he was taken by surprise. Lennie yelled as he charged towards the elderly man. Sampi was bent double, winded by the force of the impact. He wheezed as he tried to drag air into his lungs as Watts hooked his foot around the old man's left leg, yanking him off his feet.

The Aboriginal Tasmanian hit the ground with an agonising thud. Although he had the stamina and physique of a man at least twenty years his junior the impact sent a searing pain shooting through his body. Winded, he lay on the ground gasping for breath.

Taking his cue from his friend, Tom Connaught started to rain sharp kicks to the prostrate body in front of him, a badly aimed blow to the head caused the old man to become unconscious

"Oh Christ," Connaught sank to his knees, a feeling of panic overwhelming him. "I think he's dead. We've killed him."

"Good riddance," Lennie snarled.

"Come off it, Len, I think he's a goner. He might just be an abo. but that's a heap of trouble."

Lennie peered at the prostrate figure, staring at his chest to see if he was breathing.

"Nah, the bludger's not dead, he's still taking in air."

"Thank goodness for that," Connaught grabbed his friend's arm, "let's go, Lennie, come on, make a run for it."

"Sod that, Tom, stop being a dick. Let's get him to the Land Rover and dump him somewhere. We don't know who else has seen us here."

Like most bullies, Tom started to panic at the thought of being caught. He had no idea if they had been seen by anyone else. He liked a bit of fun, but there was no way he had planned on anything like this. He turned and walked away, his head in his hands.

"What have we done, Len? What have we done?"

"Cut that out. I've done nothing, we're in this together, right up to our necks. Get your arse back here this instant."

Tom Connaught paused, he didn't know whether to do as Lennie said or make a run for it.

"For fucks sake, Tom, I mean it; get back here or I'll hunt you down and kill you. You know I will."

Connaught stayed where he was, but made no attempt to run. Lennie hurried to the Land Rover and checked the doors. *Damn*, they were locked.

"Tom, Tom! Check his pockets for keys."

Connaught's complexion was ashen.

"You've got to be joking, me touch a stiff?"

"He's not dead, I told you that!" Fuming, Lennie stomped back to where the Aboriginal Tasmanian lay unconscious.

"Do I have to do everything for you?" He screamed, "next you'll be getting me to hold it when you take a piddle!"

He patted the body down, smirking when he located the keys in Joe Sampi's trouser pocket.

"Come on take the legs."

Connaught didn't move.

Lennie stared at his friend.

"Take hold of his fucking legs."

Connaught was rooted to the spot, he'd never seen a *dead* man before and this was freaking him out. Lennie grabbed the front of Tom's shirt and yanked him over to where Sampi lay.

With his face centimetres away from his friend he started to goad him.

"He's not friggin' dead. If you don't want to get banged up, take his legs and I'll get us out of this, okay?"

Shocked, Tom moved like an automaton, his movements jerky and uncoordinated, his heart pounding in his chest. Reaching for Sampi's legs, he gagged, vomiting up the remnants of his breakfast.

Lennie closed his eyes, "Give me strength," he muttered.

"What?" Connaught demanded, "what?" He shook his head, "I aint never seen a dead man before."

"Pull yourself together, Tom. He's not dead, let's dump him where we know no one's seen us. I'm not gonna spend the next twenty years banged up because you're behaving like a Shelia, a bloody ugly one at that. Now take hold of those blasted legs."

With reluctance, Connaught grabbed Joe Sampi's legs, while Lennie placed his arms under the old man's shoulders.

"On three. One, two, three!" Lennie groaned as he took the strain, he might as well have carried the body on his own for all the help Connaught was providing.

By more luck than co-ordinated skill they half carried, half dragged the body over to the Land Rover.

"Here, take the keys and get the back of the vehicle open."

Connaught dropped the legs without needing to be asked a second time and fished the keys out of Lennie's trouser pocket.

Watts man-handled the unconscious man into the back of the Land Rover before slamming the door shut.

Making a final sweep of the area to ensure they weren't being watched, Lennie Watts hissed an instruction to Connaught to get into the vehicle as he switched on the ignition. With one angry movement, he thrust the vehicle into gear and accelerated, the wheels spinning on the grass for an inordinate moment before leaping forward.

With his foot jammed down on the pedal, Watts drove the car as if he were fleeing from the four horseman of the apocalypse. He drove for about ten minutes, swerving to avoid a variety of obstacles before losing control and hitting a tree.

Stunned, the youths scrambled from the vehicle and ran off in opposite directions, leaving the doors of the Land Rover open, steam billowing from the fractured radiator and Joe Sampi unconscious on the floor.

Chapter Twenty-One

Pulling up outside Joe's cabin, Andrew Whitaker leant across and kissed Angie.

"It's great to have you back."

"It's great to be back, even if it's only for a few days," she said, placing her hand on his cheek.

"Hey, where is everyone," Whitaker tooted the horn, "I was kinda expecting a welcoming committee."

"Me too, if I'm honest. It was as much as Connie could do to contain herself last night when I spoke to her, she was so excited."

"Let's see if Napoleon's at home."

Walking around the cabin to their neighbours, Boy-Boy appeared, he wagged his tail but without the usual exuberance. Her intuitive senses bristling, Angie grabbed Whitaker's arm.

"Something's not right." She pushed the door open and hurried into the cabin. Napoleon was trying to comfort Connie who was sobbing against his shoulder.

"Dad!" Hugh cried, "we've been trying to get hold of you, where's your mobile? Was the radio turned off?"

"What on earth's the matter?" Whitaker looked at the faces staring at them as Angie knelt beside her daughter. She pushed Connie's hair back and looked into her daughter's distraught face, her eyes were red and swollen from crying.

Connie sniffed, she was so choked with emotion she couldn't speak.

"Joe's missing, Dad."

"What!"

Angie held her daughter at arm's length and looked deep into her eyes.

"Is this true, darl? Is your Grandpappy missing?"

Connie's face creased in agony as she started to cry again.

"What's going on, Napoleon?"

The Aboriginal Tasmanian shook his head, "Me and the boys, we got home about ten minutes ago. As we got here, the kids came charging round. They were here waiting for you. It seems Joe went to Sullivan's Rise hours ago. He was going to check on the drilling. No one's seen him since. We were just about to go and search for him."

Whitaker stole a look at the clock. Five p.m.

Napoleon noticed where he was looking.

"We've got at least four hours of light; I think we should leave at once."

"I'm, I'm not staying here," Connie stuttered.

"Neither am I," Hugh said with steely determination.

Whitaker glanced at the other men, "I guess we knew that was coming," he observed with a wry smile.

Mikey laughed, "Yeah, guess so."

"Give me two minutes to change out of my uniform," said Angie, from her tone, it was a statement rather than a request for permission to join them.

Whitaker followed her to the door, "We'll find him, sweetheart, you know we will, the Toba's are almost as good at tracking as Joe, we're in good hands."

"Go wash your face and dry your eyes, little Connie," said Napoleon with uncommon kindness. "No one is going to leave without you."

The vet returned with a map he had retrieved from the glove compartment of the Land Rover which Hugh spread on the table.

"I'm gonna call Doug Langdon, tell him what's happened."

Napoleon nodded, "We'll mark up the search areas."

Whitaker punched in Langdon's number, kicking the floor in irritation while he waited.

"Come on, Langdon, what's keeping you? Come on, come on, come - ah, Doug, it's Andrew."

"Hi Andrew, what's..."

Whitaker cut him off in mid-sentence, "Joe's missing."

"What!"

"No one's seen him since about lunch time."

"Are you sure he hasn't got caught up somewhere, you know how thorough he is?"

Whitaker shook his head, "Na, something's wrong, Doug, he'd be here to meet Angie."

Doug swore under his breath, "Yep, you're right. Who have you got there for a search party?"

"Napoleon, his boys, Angie and the kids."

"Great, after Sampi, Napoleon and his boys are the best trackers in the territory."

Whitaker nodded, the gesture unseen by the man on the end of the line.

"Where are you heading, I can be with you in about forty-five minutes, perhaps thirty if I really toe it."

"Might be a good idea if you stay there, Doug, we might need you to pull a few strings."

Napoleon nodded, "Good idea," he mouthed.

"Right, but make sure you stay in touch!" Langdon instructed.

"Will do. Call you as soon as we've got news." Andrew disconnected and pocketed his phone.

"Okay, Angie's ready. Let's head out to Sullivan's Rise, we can start there as we know he was making for the drilling site," Napoleon instructed, taking command of the situation. "If there's no obvious trail we'll split up into two groups. I'll take George and Hugh. Mikey'll take you, Andrew along with Angie and Connie. Okay, equipment check. Mikey have you got your gear?"

Mikey held up a battered backpack.

"George?"

His younger son lifted his backpack

"Andrew, where's your vet's bag?"

"In the Land Rover, Napoleon. And there's a first aid kit there too."

"Beaut. Joe had the spare Land Rover so we'll take your vehicle and Joe's truck, if that's alright with you, Angie."

She opened her hand to reveal the keys to the truck.

"Way ahead of you, Napoleon. Right, can we get going, please?" She implored.

"Hang on a minute longer, darl, we have to make sure we've got everything, you know that, you've been on enough search parties. We have to be prepared, we don't know what we are going to find."

"What do you mean, *prepared*?" Connie demanded.

Napoleon looked at the young girl, "Your grandfather could have had a fall, anything, we don't know until we find him. But he's a tough old fox, he'll be fine," he said, with more conviction than he felt. "Right, a couple of last things, Mikey, grab a blanket out of the cupboard and, Angie, something of Joe's with his scent on, for Boy-Boy."

"Crikey, I forgot that, sorry, Napoleon." She hurried to find an article of clothing as Napoleon ushered them outside.

While Hugh and Boy-Boy scrambled onto the back of Joe's battered truck, Napoleon coaxed the reluctant engine into life. He turned the key once, the engine backfired and died.

"Come on, come on," he cajoled through gritted teeth. "Don't let me down now, girl." He waited a moment before turning the key, he didn't want to flood the engine.

Tapping the steering wheel with the palm of his right hand as if encouraging the vehicle, he turned the key.

"Come on," he whispered. The engine turned over before spluttering into life. "Good girl, I knew you'd come up trumps."

He pushed the gear stick and applied the gas as he rammed the accelerator pedal down on the floor.

As the truck leapt forward, Whitaker followed behind, his view, all but obscured by the cloud of dust thrown up by the truck as Napoleon drove at breakneck speed towards the last place they knew Joe was heading, Sullivan's Rise.

Pulling up on the edge of the exploration site, Napoleon applied the brakes and turned off the ignition. In one leap, Hugh and Boy-Boy landed on the ground, causing his father to swerve as he went to park alongside the truck.

"Hugh!"

The boy spun round, Napoleon was pointing at the dog, "hold onto him, you know why."

For a moment, Hugh had no idea what Napoleon was on about, Boy-Boy always ran loose. Connie hurried up and grabbed the excited dog.

"The thylacine's scent is all around here," she hissed.

Shaking his head at his own stupidity, he reached for a length of rope from the back of the truck which he tied around the mongrel's scruffy neck.

Whitaker grabbed his son's arm and called Connie back.

"I want you both to remain here. Napoleon and I will go and see if there's anyone about, with a bit of luck they may have seen Joe."

Hugh was about to complain, but his father walked off. He was in no mood for a discussion.

If Hugh was in a rational frame of mind he would have realised that this was good advice, although his father didn't know it, they had been spotted twice while undertaking their acts of sabotage. There was every possibility they would be recognised.

They watched as the two men strode over to the portacabin and knocked. The door was opened by a man neither Hugh or Connie recognised. He was dressed in a white shirt with a logo printed over the left breast pocket, which they guessed was the same design they had seen on the van.

"G'day, mate," Napoleon greeted the man who stood with one hand on the doorframe. "We're looking for a colleague of ours, an aboriginal man like myself, we were wondering if you'd seen him. He'd have been in a Parks and Wildlife Land Rover like that one," he said, pointing towards the vet's vehicle.

"Yeah, I saw him, oh must have been around lunch time. He drove by," he waved in a vague direction over Whitaker's head, "and started up the Rise."

"He didn't come into the camp?"

The man looked at the vet and shook his head.

"If he did, I didn't see him. Hey Pat, have you seen an aboriginal man today?"

"What, playing a didgeridoo or throwing a boomerang?" A voice shouted from inside the office.

"Sorry about him," the new site manager apologised. "Look, do you need some help? I had a cousin who went missing once. If it wasn't for people like you," he looked at Napoleon as he spoke, "tracking him, he'd be dead."

Surprised at the offer, Napoleon shook his head.

"Thanks, but there's enough of us at the moment, but we may call back. Is that alright?"

"Fine by me, mate. I'm not going anywhere. I'll be making a sweep of the perimeter in a few minutes, I'll keep an eye open for you."

Napoleon touched his forehead with his finger, "Thanks."

"Hang on a minute, there was a couple of casuals hanging around earlier."

"Casuals?"

"Yeah, the Corporation wanted some additional help on the cheap. They were walking the perimeter, simple stuff."

"Where are they now?" Napoleon asked.

The site manager shrugged.

"Come to think of it, I haven't seen them all afternoon."

Napoleon thanked the man again as they turned and made their way back to the others.

"No joy?"

Whitaker looked at his son and shrugged, "The bloke said he'd seen Joe heading up the Rise, which is what we thought, but at least that's been confirmed now. He also said the Corporation's started to take on casual labour. He didn't know much about it, other than a couple of lads had been employed to walk the site perimeter, that sort of thing, but he hasn't seen them this afternoon."

Connie gasped, "That's not good."

"Don't let your imagination run away with you, darl," her mother said, hugging her. "Casual labour isn't always reliable, they could have got bored and headed home. We mustn't jump to conclusions."

"Okay, let's get cracking," Hugh urged.

His father squeezed his shoulder.

"We'll find him, Hugh. You know how good Napoleon and the boys are."

"But they aren't as good as Joe."

"May be not, son, but there's three of them. We will find him."

"Promise."

"I promise, son."

"Right." Napoleon clapped his hands to get everyone's attention. "We know Joe was here," he said as he tapped the map. "We'll make a thorough search before heading to the top of the Rise, and then we'll break into groups if we have to. The four of us will spread out and form a line."

"Four?" Connie asked.

Napoleon nodded, "Your mama's a good little tracker," he looked at Angie and smiled as she blushed. "She may be a little rusty, but she's good."

Hugh looked at Connie, who shrugged, this was news to both of them.

"As I was saying, the four of us will form a line, I'm sorry but I'm gonna have to ask you kids, and you too, Andrew, to follow us. We can't have you walking on any of the tracks Joe may have left."

Disappointed, Hugh and Connie hung back a couple of paces as the four Aboriginal Tasmanians formed a line.

"Angie, can you let Boy-Boy smell Joe's jacket, yes that's right, hold it over his nose. Let him have a good long sniff."

"Good job Joe doesn't wear perfume, Boy-Boy would be charging off to the drug store," Hugh said in a poor attempt to cheer Connie up.

Connie forced a smile, "Don't be daft."

Hugh tilted his head, "Made you smile though, huh?"

George took hold of Boy-Boy's rope and lengthened it to allow him to track Joe's scent unheeded. Although the thylacine had been seen some distance away, they couldn't take the chance that she wasn't back.

"Give him his head a little more," Napoleon urged.

Boy-Boy, his nose to the ground, sniffed as he made his way forward, pulling at the end of his tether.

"Look," Mikey shouted, pointing to an area of flattened grass the dog was trying to drag him to.

Napoleon held his hand up to stop Whitaker and the kids moving too far forward as his sons examined the area. They couldn't afford for the slightest clue to be damaged by their own footprints.

With deliberation, Mikey and George skirted the area of flattened grass, pointing things out to one another, while Napoleon looked on, pride evident on his face.

He knelt down and observed the grass from a different perspective.

"Look there's two, no, three sets of foot prints.

Mikey pointed to the ground, his expression animated, "These are Joe's."

Angie inhaled sharply, bending for a closer look.

"Yep, they are Joe's. Right on, bro," George smiled, complimenting his brother. "See here, Joe's got a split in the side of his shoe, he was complaining about it the other day," he explained to those of the group who were less skilled. Hugh stared at where George was pointing. He wasn't sure if it was wishful thinking on his part but he was convinced he could see a different mark in the ground, indicating the damage to the shoe to which George referred.

Mikey pointed to some bruised grass.

"Here's the second set of prints, and there's the third."

Hugh nodded, it was obvious when you know what you're looking at.

Napoleon stood up, and started to walk backwards a few paces, his eyes trained on the ground.

"See here, this is where Joe walked down from the top of the Rise, so at least we know he came back this way."

"That's good, huh?"

"Yes, Connie," he smiled, "that's very good."

"And see here, Andrew, here's Pop's footprints," Angie said, pointing to the ground for the vet's benefit.

Mikey followed the trail.

"Yes, Dad, you're right, Joe stood here for a moment. And then headed off over here," Mikey half walked, half ran towards a tree. "Whoa!" He pulled up, almost slipping as he stopped in haste, "something's going on here." He crept in a large circle, before edging towards a tree. "The other two were hanging around here. Look there's a cigarette." He went to pick it up.

"Hold on, Mikey."

The young man jerked his hand away, a look of annoyance flashing across his face as he turned.

"It could be evidence. We need to put it in a bag, it may need to be tested for DNA. Is it okay to walk over?" He glanced at Napoleon for confirmation.

Napoleon nodded, pointing to where it was safe to walk. They watched in silence as Whitaker placed a small plastic bag over his hand and collected the cigarette end without touching it

"I didn't mean to snap, Mikey. I didn't want it contaminated, sorry."

Mikey grinned, "No worries."

"Go on, son," Napoleon urged, "you were about to point something out."

Mikey scanned the area of grass between them as George inched his way towards his brother.

"Looks like a fight, eh?"

"Grandpappy might be old, but he's as strong as an ox."

"Yes, darl, he is as strong as an ox, but he was out numbered, it wasn't a fair fight."

Mikey nodded, "See here, someone's fallen to the ground," he waved the palm of his hand over an area of grass, "and here, you can see some heel marks, as if someone's scrabbling to get a foothold. Look at the damaged grass. Perhaps trying to get up, or maybe kick out at his assailants."

"Is it Joe?"

Mikey ignored the vet as he moved to the left, Napoleon joined him and crouched, placing a hand on the ground to steady himself. He looked at his son, and nodded.

"Yep, we think it was Joe on the ground."

Connie's hand flew to her mouth as she uttered a cry. Her mother moved closer, placing a protective arm around her daughter's shoulders.

"See here, this is the last full print from Joe's damaged shoe," Mikey pointed at the ground. "Someone charges, they are running on their toes, not walking with flat feet. They knock Joe to the ground and then there's a mass of prints all over one another."

Tightening his grip on Boy-Boy's rope, Hugh watched as George shuffled around, a few paces to the left of where his father and brother were studying the ground.

"You're right, but see here. There's two sets of prints, but the grass is squashed flat, their weight has increased. It looks as if they were carrying something. Pop, they're carrying Joe."

Angie gasped. "If they are carrying my dad they must have hurt him."

"Hey Pop," Mikey called, pointing to the vomit. "Looks like someone didn't have the stomach for what they were doing."

Whitaker placed his arm around her waist.

"Don't panic just yet. We don't know that's what happened."

"I think we do," Mikey objected.

The vet threw him a scathing look.

"Let's try and remain upbeat eh?"

Mikey stared at his feet.

"Andrew, we can't avoid the truth," Napoleon observed.

Mikey threw his father a grateful look.

"Our expertise has been called upon to find our friend. The signs indicate Joe's assailants, for want of a better description, are carrying something. It's right to assume at this stage it's Joe. The tracks where they were standing around and then leading away from the blue gums don't indicate they were carrying anything at that point, however, they show something heavy was being carried away from here."

The vet was silent for a moment before muttering an apology.

"It's, well I can't stand seeing the worry on the faces of the ones I love."

Hugh tried hard not to show the surprise he felt at hearing his father's statement. Things seemed to have moved on a lot faster with Angie than he had realised.

Angie shook her head, "I'm finding this hard to take in. Who could have attacked Dad? He hasn't got any enemies?"

Chapter Twenty-Two

For a moment they stood in silence. Angie's words reverberated around Hugh's head like a bullet ricocheting in an enclosed space. He couldn't think of anyone who would want to hurt Joe. Spencer Tate was gone, but in reality he had made an enemy of him, actually, both Connie and him, not Joe. If anything, Tate was *frightened* of Joe, not the other way around. Hugh shook his head. *Nah, Joe was too well respected, both by most of the citizens of Sullivan's Rise and the wider aboriginal community.* He shook his head as he thought. *Whoever was dumb enough to take on Joe would be taking on him as well as Connie.* He glanced at the group around him, d*amn it, they'd be taking on the whole lot of them.*

"Hugh! Hey, Hugh!" Connie startled him out of his daydream with a jog to his arm.

"From the look on your face you were about to step into the ring with the heavyweight champion of the world," she said. She stole a glance at the others but they were engrossed in conversations amongst themselves. "I've never seen you look like that," she observed, flicking her hair out of her eyes.

"I was thinking. Trying to work out who'd be stupid enough to hurt Joe, they must know that hurt him and they've got to deal with all of us?"

Connie pulled a face, "I know, I've been thinking about that too. Look how the cavalry came to the rescue when Tate attacked me."

Hugh's eyes twinkled as he spoke, "That's the precise point I was trying to make," he replied, remembering how angry the 'gang' had been when he told them Tate was holding Connie hostage.

Angie stepped into the centre of the ring they had formed around the disturbed grass.

"Are we gonna stand here all night engrossed in our own thoughts or are we gonna find Joe Sampi?" She asked, her eyes blazing.

"Find Joe, of course."

Angie smiled at George. She held out her hand to her daughter.

"In spite of your praise, I'm still a beginner, just like Connie here. Yes, your grandfather told me he's taken you tracking," she smiled at her daughter. Joe relayed his granddaughter's progress with pride to her mother whenever they caught up on the phone. "So we are in your hands. You've been brilliant so far, all three of you," she said, looking at Napoleon and his sons. "But now I've got one word for you, and that's track!"

Napoleon clapped his hands.

"You heard the lady, let's get on with it. George, Mikey, lead the way. Come on, show us in which direction they carried Joe."

The boy's continued to study the ground, pointing out things to one another as they moved further apart. Napoleon followed, his eyes making a second sweep as they edged forward.

Standing at a distance of five or six metres, George beckoned the others over.

"Dad, Mikey. This is where they were heading."

The group hurried over.

"Good work son."

"See here, this is where Joe parked the Land Rover," George continued.

Mikey held his two thumbs up in recognition of his brother's success.

"Way to go, bro! Come and look at this," he waved Hugh and Connie over. "Can you see four depressions?" He pointed to four flattened areas of grass.

Connie knelt down, "Oh yeah, I see it."

"And here," George pointed to a patch of grass. "This is where the footprints stop for a while, Pop, look, I think one of them placed Joe's feet to the ground, here's his heel imprints."

Napoleon grinned.

"Yes, son, I agree."

"Soooo, are you saying, they man-handled Joe into the back of the Land Rover?"

"That's how it looks, Hugh," Mikey confirmed as he continued to examine the area where the Land Rover had been parked. "See here, this is where Joe got out of the vehicle, there are his tracks, heading away from the vehicle."

George concurred.

"So from what we know, Joe walked up to the ridge, to the top of Sullivan's Rise, we can assume, to see the progress of the mining company. We know from Hugh and Connie that's the perfect vantage point." The irony of his tone wasn't lost on the other's, they all knew the kids had been up to the top of the Rise to spy on the Corporation.

Mikey picked up from where George left off, "We know the fight occurred over there," he pointed over Angie's shoulder, "and they carried Joe here, to the vehicle." He walked to the area where the front of the Land Rover would have been positioned and showed the others where it had accelerated away. "Looks like they tried to accelerate quickly, you can see where the vehicle lurched forward. They went in this direction," he indicated with a wave of his hand.

Napoleon nodded.

"I agree, son. It's clear they left in a hurry." He rubbed his hands together, once again taking command of the situation. "Mikey, George, you'll continue on foot. I'll take Joe's truck, Andrew, you'll bring your Land Rover."

No one argued.

"Wait here until we come back with the vehicles."

With the vet trying desperately to keep up with the older man, they ran to where they had left their vehicles and drove back to the rest of the waiting group.

"Hugh, give Boy-Boy back to George, please."

Angie climbed in beside Andrew Whitaker, while Hugh and Connie sat alongside Napoleon.

Mikey and George were able to follow the trail with ease, the Land Rover had been driven at speed and without skill. It was clear it had skidded on the grass as the driver had attempted to avoid the obstacles in his path.

"This is like taking candy from a baby," George quipped, "eh, bro?"

"Yeah, but we shouldn't talk too soon."

With Boy-Boy pulling at the end of his rope, the two young men ran ahead of the following vehicles.

"I've got a bad feeling," Hugh said to no one in particular.

"Don't, Hugh, please don't."

"It's gonna be fine, little Connie. Don't you worry, you're gonna make yourself sick. We know your grandfather is strong. He'll get through this. After all, when have we ever let you down?"

"Never," she whispered.

"And we aren't going to start now."

"Unlike the rest of us, Boy-Boy's having a good time, look at him, his tail's going ten to the dozen as usual and he's barking his head off," Hugh observed.

Mikey raised his arm, sliding to a halt.

"Whoa, looks like the boys have spotted something."

Boy-Boy's barks changed from excitement to short sharp yaps as he strained at the rope in an attempt to get free.

"Quick, the Land Rover's wrapped around a tree," Mikey shouted, waving towards a thicket of trees.

The boys started to run towards the crashed vehicle as the others disembarked and followed at speed.

"Dad!" Angie screamed.

Whitaker grabbed her arm and held her back.

"Hang on, love. Let the boys check it out first. Connie, Hugh, wait here."

"Dad!" Hugh exclaimed.

"Hugh, for once in your life do as your bloody well told!"

Connie reached for his arm.

"Your dad's right, Hugh. I want to see too, but I'm frightened what they'll find." She turned her back on him for a moment, blinking back the tears welling in her eyes before turning to stare at the crashed Land Rover.

With reluctance, Hugh did as he was told, straining to see what was going on in front of him.

"I can see him. I can see Joe," George shouted, reaching the Land Rover first.

Angie pulled herself free from Whitaker's arms and started to run towards the vehicle. The vet caught hold of Connie and his son.

"Wait a minute kids, let them check it out first."

Napoleon pushed his son out of his way with more force than he intended and yanked open the back door of the Land Rover, cringing as it crashed against the side of the car.

"Bloody hell, he's in a bad way," he muttered as he reached in and felt Sampi's neck. "He's alive. I've got a pulse. It's weak, but he's alive. Joe's alive!"

Connie sank to her knees, sobbing. Hugh crouched beside her.

"Don't cry, he's alive," he said. "Joe's alive."

"Dad!" Angie screamed.

"Stand back, Angie, the boys will help me lift him out and then you can examine him, okay?"

She was a nurse, not a doctor. She wasn't as skilled as her father in homeopathic and traditional aboriginal medicine, but along with Whitaker's skills as a vet, at that moment she knew they were her father's best chance of survival.

Angie stared into the back of the vehicle, her hands clasped to her chest.

"Yes, but hurry, Napoleon, please hurry."

"Now you know better than anyone, we can't hurry it, darl. Take a step back and give us some room to work. Here, Andrew, while we get Joe out, can you call Doug?" He tossed the radio to the vet as he spoke. "You won't get a phone signal out here, but you should get through on the radio."

Whitaker caught the radio and nodded, twisting the dial in an attempt to get a signal.

"Whitaker to Langdon, can you hear me?"

The air was filled with the hiss of static as the vet twiddled the knob.

"Ah that's better. Whitaker to Langdon, Doug, can you hear me?"

"Andrew, it's Doug. What's the situation?"

Whitaker explained they'd found the Aboriginal Tasmanian, and were about to remove him from the Land Rover. As yet they didn't know the extent of his injuries, except he appeared to be unconscious.

"Right, call me back as soon as you've appraised his medical condition. I'm not gonna move from the radio."

As the smallest of the three Aboriginal Tasmanian's, George squeezed into the Land Rover, alongside Joe's crumpled body.

"Check his legs, George, make sure they aren't broken and then can you straighten them as best you can," Napoleon instructed. "I'll hold his head to make sure his neck isn't moved."

They watched in silence as George ran his hands down each of Sampi's legs in turn, applying sufficient pressure to determine if any of the bones were broken. Satisfied, he straightened them as best he could, one at a time.

"Why don't we use the trick Joe came up with to prevent Tate's neck moving, you know, use some bark as a make-do neck brace?" Mikey suggested.

His father nodded, "Good idea."

"We don't have time to waste," Angie shouted with a petulant stamp of her foot.

"No, Angie, there's little point in saving Joe's life if he ends up paralysed, you know he'd never forgive us," Napoleon rebuked. "It'll take a couple of minutes, and it'll be time well spent. Go for it, son."

Mikey hurried over to a saplings and peeled back a strip of bark. It had worked for Tate, it had to work for Joe.

"Have we got anything we can wrap around it to cushion it against Joe's neck?"

"Hang on a minute," Whitaker dropped to one knee and opened his veterinary bag, pulling out a roll of cotton wool. "This should do."

With a layer of cotton wool between the bark and his friend's neck, Napoleon tied the make-shift brace in place with a length of twine he'd found on the floor of the Land Rover. Satisfied there was nothing more they could do while Joe was in the vehicle he nodded to Mikey to take Joe's shoulders, he'd hold his head and George would hang onto his legs.

"On three I want us to lift him out, making it as smooth as we can. Andrew be ready to help George till he gets out of the vehicle. Right if everyone's ready," he paused for a moment, everyone was waiting for his command. "One, two, three..."

Taking the strain, they lifted the old man out of the vehicle, carrying him a few paces before placing him on the grass.

Connie gasped at the sight of her grandfather lying unconscious on the ground in front of her. He had always been so strong, he was the one constant in her life, what with her mother having to work away from home. He was her rock.

Whitaker ripped open Sampi's shirt, the buttons flying in all directions with the force of his actions. He parted the fabric to reveal an array of blue and purple hues where the kicking Joe had been given had bruised his body.

Angie gasped, "Oh my goodness."

She hurried to her father's side and watched as Whitaker placed his stethoscope on the old man's chest. He moved it to the right and left, listening to his heart and lungs.

"His heart sounds strong, but his breathing is laboured," Whitaker explained. He offered her the ear pieces so she could listen for herself but she shook her head, instead reaching for the pen light torch she could see in his bag. Moving closer she lifted each of her father's eyelids in turn and shone the light into his eyes. The pupils were reacting, if a little sluggish.

"I don't like the look of this," Whitaker observed, pointing to the old man's swollen and bruised abdomen. "I think he might have some internal bleeding."

"That sounds serious, Dad."

Whitaker looked over at his son.

"It can be, Hugh, but we'll have to wait and see."

Angie sat back on her heels to allow the vet more room, watching as he palpated the swollen abdomen.

"It doesn't feel good," he whispered, his voice low so as not to alarm the kids.

She nodded her understanding.

"Everything's fine," she lied, calling over her shoulder.

Hugh bit his lip as he watched them examine his friend. He reached for Connie's hand and squeezed it. Ordinarily she would have slapped him away with a laugh, but she didn't react, her eyes were fixed on her grandfather.

"He needs medical attention, and he needs it now. Napoleon. Can you call Langdon, see if the air ambulance can get here? There's enough space for it to land."

Napoleon took the radio and called through, getting an immediate response from the head ranger.

"Langdon's gonna call right back."

Hugh tutted, he felt useless, everything was taking so long. His thoughts were interrupted by the radio crackling.

"Napoleon, it's Doug. The air ambulance is on another call; it will be quicker for you to transport him yourself. I'm sorry. I'll meet you at the hospital."

Angie and Connie started to cry. Devonport Community Hospital was two hours away.

"It's not your fault, Doug. Thanks for trying, we'll see you there."

Chapter Twenty-Three

Ignoring the speed limit, Whitaker had driven like a bat out of hell in order to get his friend and colleague to the hospital as fast as possible.

In spite of his best efforts, it had taken some ninety minutes to complete the journey to Devonport Community Hospital, Connie sat beside him, while her mother travelled in the back of the Land Rover, monitoring her father's condition.

Hugh followed behind, travelling with the Toba's in Joe Sampi's old truck. He sat in silence, wrapped in his own thoughts, oblivious to the banter Mikey and George exchanged between themselves from the back of the truck.

Not wanting to waste time dropping Boy-Boy home, the two young men offered to sit with him. It was too dangerous to leave him on his own, in the back of the truck, daft creature would no doubt try and jump out if he saw something worth chasing, ending up with a broken leg or hanging from the side of the vehicle by the rope they had used as a leash.

While Napoleon reversed into a parking bay, his younger son leapt from the still moving vehicle to seek assistance from the hospital staff.

George ran into the hospital, demanding help, returning to the parked vehicle followed by a doctor and two nurses dragging a wheeled stretcher between them.

They stood back, allowing the medical staff to take over, lifting the unconscious man onto the gurney. The doctor shone a light into Sampi's eyes one at a time, but his pupils were fixed and unresponsive.

"Straight into the trauma unit, please, nurse," he barked. "He needs to be fully assessed, bloods, oxygen saturation and then a CT scan." The doctor turned to Whitaker, instructing him to register Sampi at the reception.

"Oh, is he allergic to anything, antibiotics, that sort of thing?" he quizzed, walking backwards as he waited for their answer.

All eyes focused on Angie.

"Um, err, no. No, he doesn't have any allergies." Angie touched the young physician's arm. "Is he going to be alright, doctor?" She mentally kicked herself, how often had she heard relatives of her own patients ask the same question before the doctors had a proper chance to evaluate.

"You are?"

"Angela Sampi, Joe's daughter."

The doctor shook his head, "It's too soon to say, Ms. Sampi. I'm sorry I can't give you more of a prognosis at this stage." He softened his tone. "Try not to worry, I've got a first rate team. He'll be in good hands."

"Please do your best," Whitaker said, "that's all we ask."

The doctor acknowledged him with a curt nod of his head.

"The reception staff will tell you where the relatives waiting area is. Someone will come and find you there later."

He turned and ran after his colleagues, pushing the gurney from behind as they disappeared into the glass building.

Three hours later the door to the relative's waiting room swung open. Everyone looked to see who had entered the room. A middle aged man, dressed in surgical greens walked in, grey hair protruded from under the surgical scrubs cap he still wore.

"Ms. Sampi?"

Angie and Connie jumped up.

"My name is Daniel Hodges. I'm the consultant trauma surgeon," he explained, extending his hand to each of them in turn. Addressing Angie, he smiled. "Your father is in the recovery room. I am afraid to say the CT scan showed extensive bleeding from a ruptured spleen."

Angie swivelled to look at Whitaker, his diagnosis of internal bleeding was correct. Connie started to cry as the doctor continued.

"I'm afraid the spleen couldn't be saved, it was too damaged so I have had to remove it, along with one of the nodes from the liver."

"Is he going to die? You need your liver don't you?" Connie sniffed.

Hugh gasped, this was worse than he had imagined.

Hodges glanced at the faces in the room. They were hanging on his every word.

"It has to be said it's better if you can keep all your organs, but it is possible to live a healthy life without a spleen. The liver is a little different. The damage isn't life threatening, in time it will repair itself."

Hugh exhaled, "Phew, thank goodness for that."

The doctor continued, "Your father is in remarkable physical condition for a man of his age. He isn't out of the woods yet, but I was astounded at his physique and good health. If it wasn't for that, he wouldn't have survived the journey, let alone the surgery. All we can do now is hope his recuperative powers are as good."

Doug Langdon, who had arrived about half an hour after the rest of the group, stood up and thanked the surgeon, a look of relief washing over his face.

"I know the question you are dying to ask is what are his chances." Mr. Hodges addressed the room as he spoke. "I'm not a betting man, so I won't give you any odds, but I am optimistic. Given time to rest, I think he will make a complete recovery."

"Can, can we see him? Hugh stuttered.

"Immediate family only tonight, young man."

Hugh felt his father's hand on his shoulder. He half twisted to look at him.

"We'll come tomorrow, Hugh. I promise."

Disappointed, Hugh nodded. There was little point in arguing. This was the rule of the hospital.

"I'll stay here and bring Angie and Connie home if you'd don't mind taking my boys with you?" Napoleon asked.

"It'll mean sitting in the back with the dog, we can't leave him here either, but if it's okay with Mikey and George, it's fine by me."

True to his word, Andrew Whitaker drove Hugh and Connie back to the hospital after school the following day. Angie had decided to stay overnight, she remained at her father's bedside in the high dependency unit leaving Connie in Napoleon's care.

Having located where Sampi was recovering, they tip-toed into the side room. Angie placed her finger to her lips indicating they should be quiet.

"He's sleeping," she whispered.

"Oh no I'm not," Sampi muttered, opening one eye to see who had entered the room. "Thank goodness it's you," he scowled. "I'm fed up with having my blood pressure taken, a thermometer shoved in my ear and drips connected and disconnected. I'm thinking of discharging myself."

"Oh no you don't!" His visitors exclaimed in unison.

A look of resignation clouded the old man's face, "We'll see about that," he mumbled to himself.

"You need some of your medicinal concoctions," Hugh laughed. "That'll soon get you on your feet. I can still remember the taste."

"That good, eh?" Sampi grinned as he patted the side of his bed, indicating it would be alright for Connie to perch beside him.

"Listening to what the surgeon said last night, you are very lucky, Joe."

"My body might not agree with you, Andrew, but you're right."

"Are you up to telling us what happened?"

Sampi nodded, "As much as I can remember. Can you pass me a drink, darl?" He smiled, sipping the luke warm water his granddaughter gave him. "Things are a little hazy but I remember walking down from Sullivan's Rise, I'd been watching what was going on at the site below."

Everyone nodded, that much they knew already.

"I noticed a couple of lads hanging around." Sampi grimaced, rubbing his forehead as if he were trying to remember. "Ah yes, I asked one of them to make sure they put their cigarette out properly when he'd finished with it, we didn't need a fire on top of everything else that's going on."

"We've found the cigarette stub, Joe," Hugh interjected. "We can use it for DNA."

Sampi smiled, "You've been reading too much Sherlock Holmes."

Hugh cocked his head, "DNA hadn't been discovered when those were written, Joe."

Joe Sampi wrinkled his nose, "I know!" He took another sip of water and licked his lips, which were cracked from the dry atmosphere of the air conditioned room. "Anyway, one thing led to another and all hell broke loose and I woke up here."

"It's a bit of a long shot but I don't suppose you recognised either of them?"

Sampi looked at the vet, "One of them was a kid called Lennie Watts. I didn't recognise the other one."

Angie twisted to look at her father.

"I thought he was in prison?"

Her father bobbed his head in agreement, "That's what I thought, but I was wrong."

"Is he related to Nigel Watts?" Hugh whispered to Connie.

"Dunno, hang on I'll ask. Grandfather is that Nigel Watts' brother?"

Sampi nodded.

"Yes, Lennie's a few years older than Nigel."

"I'm gonna have words with him at school tomorrow."

"Don't you dare, Hugh," Angie rebuked. "The Watts family have inflicted enough damage and pain without you getting into trouble. If one of them can do this to Joe, what do you think they'll do to you?"

Fuming, Hugh fell silent. They may not think he was capable of taking care of himself, but somehow he'd get Lennie and Nigel Watts back for what they'd done.

"I know I'll have to make a statement to the police, but I don't feel up to it at the moment. They'll ensure Lennie Watts gets what's coming to him," Sampi said, directing his comments to Hugh as if he were able to read his mind. "They'll arrest him and I'm sure, like most cowards, he'll roll over and give up his accomplice. I can't see him taking the heat for this on his own, he's not that stupid."

Connie kissed her grandfather's cheek.

"What was that for?" Her grandfather asked, blushing at the unexpected show of affection.

"I'm pleased you are okay," Connie smiled, "that's all."

Sampi laughed, his face creased in pain as the jolting movement aggravated his wound.

"I wouldn't go as far as to say I'm okay but I'm getting there, darl. I'm getting there."

Chapter Twenty-Four

With Joe Sampi's on-going recovery dominating their conversation on the way to school the following day, Hugh left Connie putting her track kit into her locker, excusing himself by telling her he needed to see his maths tutor before the start of lessons. Snatching a glance over his shoulder he could see her trying to push her bag into her crowded locker. He'd told her to take some of her stuff home on Friday, goodness knows what she had stashed in it, after all, the term was just a few days old, what on earth could she had accumulated in that short time?

He hurried along the corridor and made his way towards the boy's toilet block, he knew that's where some of the kids hung out for a smoke. Turning the corner, he stopped, hesitating, perhaps this wasn't such a good idea after all?

"Whitaker!"

It was too late now, he'd been spotted. Hugh clenched his fists, his eyes wide like a trapped animal.

Nigel Watts was surrounded by five other lads, all similar in age.

"Ha, it's that pommy shit who talks with a plum in his mouth – Hugh Whitaker!" Watts sneered, spitting his name as if it was a bad taste in his mouth.

"Is your brother called Lennie by chance?" Hugh heard himself ask.

"Is your brother called Lennie by chance?" Watts repeated, mimicking Hugh's accent.

Hugh gritted his teeth, readjusting his weight so he was more balanced, there was no way he'd be able to take them all on but he would give it a go if needs be.

"Yeah, he's my brother. What of it?"

Hugh's nostrils flared as he became angrier by the second.

"That bastard hurt a very good friend of mine."

"Do you mean that stinking black abo that's taking on all those airs and graces, pretending to be a park ranger?"

"There's no airs and graces about Joe Sampi," Hugh snapped. "You take that back!"

"Let's pulverise the fat bastard," said one of the lads Hugh didn't recognise.

Nigel Watts raised his hand.

"No one move, he's mine, all mine," he growled.

Without warning, Watts lunged towards Hugh. In spite of the extra weight he carried in comparison to Watts's willowy frame, the unexpected assault threw Hugh off balance. He took a step back to steady himself, raising his fists as they squared up.

"Oh look at little Lord Fauntleroy, he's following the Marquis of Queensbury's rules," the same voice taunted.

Watts smiled, his friend's goading seemed to be having an effect on Hugh.

"Come on big man, come on."

"Argh!" Hugh screamed, lunging at Nigel, with his full weight behind him.

Watts fell backwards, he shouted to his friends not to join in as they formed a circle around the two boys. He'd never live it down if he needed help to smash the face of a wimp like Whitaker, after all he was Lennie Watts' brother. Reaching up he grabbed Hugh's hair and yanked his head backwards.

Hugh yelled, his specs went flying as Nigel sank his teeth into his arm. With a yowl he landed a punch, splitting Nigel's lip.

Watts pushed Hugh off him, wiping his mouth on his hand. He stared at the smear of red on his skin. While Hugh scrambled to his feet, Watts lashed out, landing a punch on Hugh's nose.

"Break it up, boys, that's enough. I said break it up!"

Hugh felt someone yank his collar.

"Get off me," he yelled, his arms swinging in all directions.

"Whitaker, calm down."

Mr. Ford, the deputy head held both boys at arm's length as he frog marched them towards the head mistresses' office.

"Stand there, Whitaker. Don't you move," he instructed. "Right, Watts, you will see the head first," he said, guiding Nigel Watts towards the door of the head mistress's office.

Hugh wiped his nose with the back of his hand, it was bleeding. Pulling up his polo shirt, he dabbed his nostril to wipe the blood away, the stain growing as the grey fabric absorbed the bodily fluid.

He daren't think what his father was going to say. Removing his specs, he placed them on the chair beside him. *Bummer, they're bent.* No wonder he couldn't see properly; they must have been damaged when they went flying off his face. Gritting his teeth, he tried to straighten the arm, careful not to apply too much pressure, he couldn't afford to snap it off, he didn't have any spares.

The door opened, Hugh jumped up, pushing his specs back into place, but Mr. Ford indicated he should remain where he was.

"I'll escort you to pick up your belonging, Watts, and then see you off the premises. The school secretary will contact your mother. You are suspended for a week."

Watts leered at Hugh as he passed, whispering the word 'loser' as he walked by.

The school secretary put her head out of her office door.

"Mr. Whitaker will be here in a few minutes."

Hugh swallowed, the enormity of his actions was beginning to dawn on him.

"Thank you, Mrs Dean. Right, Whitaker, follow me," the deputy head clicked his fingers and led the way into the headmistress's office.

Hugh didn't move. He was still trying to absorb what was happening.

"Whitaker!"

"Sir, sorry sir," Hugh jumped up and followed Mr. Ford into the office and stood in front of the head's desk while she finished writing a note.

Marjorie Harris was gearing up for retirement, though with less than two years to go, she was still very progressive. She was well respected by her staff and pupils, relishing in their achievements.

Many head teachers may have regarded the headship of the Sullivan Academy as a side step on their career path, but not Marjorie Harris. In the ten years she had been at the school she had transformed it from a failing institution where pupils were disillusioned and often truanted, to an academy which achieved in the fields of science, maths as well as the arts in addition to having one of the best athletics teams in northern Tasmania.

Hugh looked around the small room. Two certificates jostled alongside a photograph of the entire school taken at the end of the previous term. On the top of a filing cabinet stood a geranium plant in full bud next to a photograph of a black and white cat.

Finishing her note, the headmistress looked up.

"Sit."

Hugh did as instructed, trying to ignore the butterflies flipping somersaults in the pit of his stomach. This was the first time he had ever been summoned to the head teacher's office, and it was not an experience he would be looking to repeat. He gripped the sides of his seat so tight the whites of his knuckles were showing, beads of clammy sweat dotted his forehead and upper lip as he waited.

A single knock on the door startled him.

Mrs Dean entered the room, announcing that Hugh's father had arrived.

"Please show him in."

Hugh swivelled in his chair. His father's face was devoid of emotion.

The headmistress stood up and extended her hand.

"Pleased to meet your, Mr. Whitaker. My name is Marjorie Harris, I'm sorry it's under such circumstances."

Hugh watched as his father shook hands before taking a seat on the empty chair next to him. They listened in silence as she recounted the events leading to his summons to the school.

"I'm afraid, under the circumstances, I have no alternative but to suspend Hugh for the rest of the week. He will be allowed to return to school on Monday."

Hugh studied his hands, his face burning as the two adults discussed him as if he wasn't there.

"All I can do is apologise for my son's behaviour, Miss Harris," said his father. "I can make one excuse in mitigation for his actions and that is to say he was very upset at the assault on a close friend of his, Joseph Sampi."

"Connie Sampi's Grandfather?"

Whitaker nodded, "He is in hospital, I'm afraid he suffered severe injuries following a brutal beating."

He waited while the head made a note to speak to Connie later.

"I hope you will believe me when I say this is not in keeping with Hugh's character."

The head nodded, "I agree, I have received a copy of his file from his previous school and they have commended his behaviour. Providing there isn't a repeat of this I don't think it will have an impact on your career in the school, Hugh," she said, directing her comments to her student, "but the suspension remains in place."

"What do you have to say for yourself, Hugh?"

Hugh looked at his father and then at the headmistress.

"I'm sorry, Miss Harris. Very sorry, it won't happen again."

Satisfied, Miss Harris smiled, the gesture softening the stern features of her thin face. She stood up and smoothed the crinkled fabric of her skirt before extending her hand.

"Once again it's a pleasure to meet you, Mr. Whitaker."

Outside the office, Whitaker pushed his son in front of him, "Get your things. I'll meet you in the Land Rover, I'm parked outside the gate."

"I'm afraid Hugh isn't allowed to wander around the school grounds while on suspension."

"Oh I see, may I accompany him to his locker to collect his belongings, I think we've taken up too much of everyone's time as it is."

Mrs Dean smiled.

"I'm sure that will be alright."

The journey home was completed in silence. Hugh tried to apologise but his father cut him off. They would discuss it when they got home.

Hugh followed his father into the bungalow. It was turning into a scorcher of a day but he felt sick and chilled to the bone. He turned to shut the door behind him before facing his father.

"What have you got to say for yourself?"

Hugh tried to fight the redness creeping over his skin. *Why am I blushing, I haven't done anything wrong?* he thought to himself

"Hugh, I'm waiting for an explanation."

"I'm sorry, Dad."

"Sorry. You're sorry," his father fumed. "Imagine how I felt when I got the call from the school. I had to leave a patient, thank goodness it was a puppy for vaccination, not something serious." He slapped his arms by his side, "I've got an operation waiting and some slides to fix before posting them to the Animal Health Laboratories in Launceston, how irresponsible can you get?"

"Dad, will you stop shouting and give me a chance to explain?"

"Don't be so damn cheeky," snapped his father, raising his hand as if to hit his son.

Hugh gasped, screwing his eyes shut in anticipation of the impact. That was enough to bring his father to his senses, he'd never struck his son before. Ashamed, his hand dropped to his side.

"I'm sorry, Hugh. You're right. Tell me what happened?"

Hugh shook his head.

"It's hard to explain how angry I was. When I got to school this morning, something inside me snapped. I had to find Nigel Watts."

"Who?"

"Nigel Watts, Lennie's younger brother."

Whitaker closed his eyes, the school hadn't revealed the name of the other boy.

"What on earth possessed you to do that?"

"I wanted, no, I had to find out if he was Lennie's brother, after all we know Lennie and his mate almost killed Joe."

"But that's a job for the police, Hugh. You can't keep doing this, taking events into your own hands."

"When have I done that?"

Whitaker rolled his eyes.

"Where do I start, let me see, ah yes, keeping the knowledge of the thylacine to yourself. Not telling me or Joe for that matter, that Spencer Tate was intimidating you, to name but two occasions. Hugh, you are a kid, stop trying to act like an adult."

Hugh stared at his father in disbelief. How could he stand there and belittle the things he and Connie had done over the past few weeks?

His son's shocked expression went unnoticed by his father who continued to berate his actions.

"You may be suspended for the rest of the week, but I'm grounding you for a fortnight."

"Dad, you have got to be joking. There's too much going on to be grounded."

His father shook his head.

"I'm sorry son, but actions have consequences. This is the consequence of your action today."

Hugh stormed into the kitchen.

"I need a drink," he muttered.

He lent over the sink and closed his eyes. How could his father do this? The thylacine was in danger and he was grounded. *Nah, this aint gonna happen*, he thought.

Without thinking of the fallout, Hugh stole a look over his shoulder, his father was out of sight. He opened the larder door and pulled the back panel away from the wall. It was ironic. Connie had shown him this tunnel on the day they met. It had been excavated by the previous inhabitant of the bungalow, a drug dealer who had used it to elude the police.

This was the second time he'd made use of the tunnel, once to evade Tate's clutches, and now to escape his father's wrath.

Sneaking another look behind him, he crawled into the tunnel. He had work to do.

"Hugh… Hugh." Whitaker walked into the kitchen, the door to the larder was open, but there was no sign of his son. "Oh, Hugh, what are you up to now?"

Chapter Twenty-Five

Without thinking his actions through, Hugh had left home without any provisions, he had no food or money, he might have escaped his father's grounding, at least for now, but he had the whole day to kill until Connie got back from school.

Emerging from the end of the secret tunnel, Hugh headed for Sullivan's Creek, at least Connie would have to come there to collect her bike from the shelter when she got off the bus. And, he hoped, this would be the last place his father would look for him, that's if he bothered to make any attempt to search whatsoever. After all, hadn't he said he had operations to complete, slides to fix, whatever that meant, and patients to see, and that was before he had a wayward son to add to the list? Yep, knowing his father as he did, work would come first.

He had to find somewhere to wait until Connie got off the school bus. He hurried along the footpath, keeping close to the buildings and shop fronts.

Checking to make sure he wasn't being followed, Hugh slipped down a side road which ran behind the saloon bar, 'Thirsty Work'.

The clatter of metal against metal startled him.

"Hey kid, are you okay?"

Hugh spun round, a short, red-haired woman was attempting to empty a bin into a dumpster. Vertically challenged, she was on tip-toes and having to lift it almost to head height in order to tip it over the edge.

"Err, yeah, I'm fine," he mumbled, conscious of his appearance, he must look awful, his blood stained polo shirt was now covered with mud and debris from the tunnel. A wry smile crept over his face as he remembered Connie pointing at his clothes the first time she'd shown him the passageway telling him was going to get dirty. Who'd have thought he would have needed to use the tunnel to 'escape' from his father.

"Here, let me help you."

Hugh took the bin and tipped it over the edge, emptying the contents into the filthy dumpster, wrinkling his nose at the stink from its rotting contents.

"Yeah, hums a bit, eh?" The woman said, nodding her thanks as he passed the bin back. "Look, tell me to mind my own business but you don't look fine to me."

Hugh wiped his hands down the front of his already stained shirt, not sure what to say.

"One good turn deserves another, how 'bout I get you a drink and something to clean yourself up with?"

Hugh hesitated, glancing at the open door.

"It's okay, I'm on my own. No one's going to see you like that."

"I don't have any money."

She looked at his face, smeared with blood from where Watts had landed a successful punch to the nose.

"Don't recall asking for any. If I can't spare a glass of water and a towel to clean a wound, then it's a sad day. I know a good kid in trouble when I see one."

His father's words ricocheted around his head, *don't talk to strangers*. How many times had he told him that when he was growing up, along with *don't get into cars* or *take sweets from people you don't know*!

"I'm Cath by the way. My old man owns this heap of shit."

"My name's Hugh, Hugh Whitaker."

"Come on in, I'll get you that drink."

Hugh didn't move. The woman could see he was wracked with indecision.

"It's fine, Hugh, I can remember my olds telling me not to talk to stranger's every time I want outside the front door."

"Gosh, I'm sorry, I didn't mean to imply..."

"Forget it kid. If you don't want to come inside, I understand." She pointed to a wooden crate. "Park your butt on that and I'll get you the drink I promised."

Hugh did as she suggested. Throwing the crate on its side, he sat down and leant against the rough brick wall.

"Here you go," Cath emerged through the open door carrying a tray, a towel draped over her arm. She'd brought him a tall glass of juice, a packet of chips and a bowel of water to clean himself up a little.

"Are you sure? This is very kind of you."

Cath smiled.

"Sure I'm sure. Most people would have watched me struggle with the bin. As I said, one good turn deserves another."

"Thanks, thank you very much." He grabbed the juice and downed it in one go, not realising how thirsty he was.

"Wow, I guess you needed that." She watched as he attempted to clean the blood and dirt from his face and hands, leaving a scummy mark on her towel.

"Sorry about that," he said with an embarrassed grin.

"Forget it, I've got more inside. Wanna talk? I've got a few minutes."

Hugh shrugged, "Nothing to tell, I got into a scrap at school."

"I sort of guessed it was something like that, it looks as if you and those specs came off worse than the other guy."

Hugh's eyes twinkled, "I got a couple of punches in though. It was worth getting suspended from school."

"Shouldn't you be at home then?"

Hugh stared along the narrow street.

"Yeah, maybe."

She placed a hand on his shoulder for a fleeting moment.

"Take a word of advice from an old woman?"

Hugh looked up at her, noticing for the first time a jagged scar running from her lower lip to her chin.

"Don't make a habit of fighting, Hugh. It'll get you into serious trouble one day." She placed the bowel of water back on the tray and went inside leaving him to his own thoughts.

He had no idea how long he sat there. He could hear the faint buzz from a television and the clatter of snooker balls coming from inside the bar. Grabbing the packet of chips he'd been given, he hurried to the bike shed. He could see their bikes still chained alongside one another. As far as he was concerned he had no choice but to wait for Connie.

The hours dragged, and with Sullivan's Creek, a town that couldn't be described as a hive of activity, there was little to watch.

At last the school bus pulled up. Hugh hung back. He could see it was the usual driver, his expression was one of annoyance at the noise his passengers were making and the inevitable mess they would leave for him to clear up.

Connie was the last to emerge. She had all but stepped off the platform before the driver closed the door and started to pull away.

"Hey!" She shouted, throwing him a withering look.

"Connie!"

She twisted on the ball of her foot, her agitation disappearing in an instant.

"Hugh, look at the state of you!"

He grinned.

"You should have seen the other guy," he joked.

Connie pulled a face, "I can imagine."

"Come on, let's get out of here," he suggested. "People keep looking at me."

"I wonder why."

They unlocked their bikes, at least he'd kept his key in his trouser pocket.

"Where do you want to go? My house, perhaps?" She suggested. "Mum's spending the day at the hospital before heading back to Hobart.

She's arranged to take a few days off when grandfather's discharged, she thinks that'll be more use."

"Wow, that's great for you."

Connie nodded, "Though with grandfather laid up, he won't have any money coming in, and he stresses about that. We'll be back to square one."

"That's a bummer."

Connie smiled.

"Forget it, we're used to it. My place then?"

Hugh shook his head.

"Nah, if it's okay with you I'd like to go to Sullivan's Rise. I know it's a long shot, with what Mikey and George said about seeing the thylacine a couple of miles away, but we haven't seen her in days, we could be lucky?"

"Fine by me. You can tell me what happened while we ride over. The whole year's buzzing with the news of your suspension. No one's been suspended so soon after starting at the school before."

"Wow, I'm famous at last, eh?"

Connie threw her head back and laughed.

"I don't want to ruin your fifteen minutes of fame, but the Head's sent some work for you to do while you are off."

"Gee, thanks for that," he said, the words thick with sarcasm.

"Hey don't shoot the messenger!"

Hugh started to pedal.

"Hugh."

He braked, waiting for her to catch up.

"You'll have to go home some time; you know that don't you?"

"Yeah, I know. Just not yet."

Warrugul National Park was proving to be the most troublesome development Laura Goodman had overseen since the formation of the Tasmanian Mining Corporation. She had endured an uncomfortable interview with a detective from Devonport that morning following the attempted murder of an Aboriginal Tasmanian, whose name she couldn't recall. Why they thought she'd had anything to do with it she didn't know. She'd denied all knowledge of the casual labour the site manager had employed. She shook her head as she glanced in the rear view mirror before accelerating past an old man driving at forty kilometres an hour.

"Bloody Sunday driver," she muttered under her breath as she flashed him a dazzling smile.

She was due to meet William Appleby at the Warrugul site. When she suggested local heavies who could look after themselves and bloody a few noses if necessary, she hadn't expected psychopaths who would half kill a bloke going about his business.

"Give a girl a break," she muttered under her breath, as her father would say, '*if you want a good job done, do it yourself.*'

She glanced down at her mobile and pushed the pre-set number. It went straight to voicemail.

"Where are you when I need you, Daddy?" She grumbled.

An hour later than planned, she arrived at the drill site. Appleby was already there, standing in the doorway of the portacabin. He watched as she swung her elegant legs out of the four by four, the patent leather of her designer shoes glinting in the sunlight. He smiled to himself, it didn't matter what she threw on, she always looked chic and elegant.

"Laura, sweetheart, you've made good time." He leant towards her to kiss her on the lips but she turned her head, causing him to miss her mouth and plant a kiss on her cheek. "It's nice to see you too," he muttered under his breath. It was obvious it was going to be a difficult meeting.

He followed her into the portacabin, watching as she peeled off her leather driving gloves and dropped them into her bag.

"Leave us!" She instructed.

The site manager didn't need to be told twice. He grabbed his cigarettes off the desk and hurried out of the office.

"This situation is getting out of control. I asked for an increased security presence and you employ monkeys."

Appleby held her gaze, he'd learnt at the beginning of their relationship not to let her see she intimidated you.

"Everything is going wrong, it started with that do-gooder vet trying to save the planet."

A slight smile crossed his lips as he listened to her, but it was gone in an instant.

"I assume you have looked into the incident with the abo?"

Appleby nodded.

"I've sent Pirlatapa over to Devonport to see him."

"Good, that's something I guess. What have you done about the men who attacked him? I'm assuming it was some of the casuals you employed, at least that's what the cops think?"

Appleby nodded, "Nothing yet. It will need careful consideration."

Goodman shot him a fierce look.

"If it needs *that* sort of consideration, make sure there are no bloody witnesses this time."

Appleby raised an eyebrow, "God, you are your father's daughter."

Goodman didn't respond to the compliment; this wasn't the time to acknowledge nepotism. She pulled the geological report from her bag and ran her finger down the figures.

"I'm in two minds as to whether I should pull the plug on this, we don't need the heat, but the numbers are so impressive." She tapped the page, "the bottom line indicates a potential multi-million-dollar profit margin. Our profile is so high at the moment, nothing else can go wrong."

Appleby kissed his teeth.

"I don't want to put a dampener on things, but I think you need to sit down."

He noticed her eyes fall on the black plastic chair covered in dust.

"I'm fine standing."

"One of the lads has made a discovery."

Goodman held his gaze.

"Go on."

"Perhaps it will be easier if you follow me," he said, reaching for a bunch of keys lying on the desk.

Goodman tutted.

"Can't you just tell me?"

Appleby shook his head.

"You won't believe me. You are going to need to see this yourself."

"Always a showman," she fumed, "an amateur showman!"

"Watch how you go," he advised, leading the way out of the portacabin. "Those heels are not the best footwear for traipsing around a site like this."

"Just get on with it, William."

She waited while he flicked through the bunch of keys on the ring before opening the door of the prefabricated building used to store additional equipment.

He flipped a switch, the strip lighting flickered on and off a couple of times before illuminating the long, narrow building. Appleby ushered her in, locking the door behind them

"What are you doing that for?"

"You'll see," he said in a conspiratorial way as he led her into the body of the building.

"Argh!"

Appleby twisted, "What's up?"

She slipped off one of her shoes and examined the heel.

"These stilettos are catching in the wooden flooring."

"I did warn you," he muttered to himself.

"What the hell's that smell?" She demanded.

"I'm about to show you. Follow me."

Holding her expensive shoes in her hand, she tip-toed after him, barefooted.

"Close your eyes."

"Get on with it. You know how much I dislike childish games. This flooring is killing my feet."

Appleby sidestepped to reveal a large cage containing three striped animals cowering in the corner.

"What the fuck!" Goodman shook her head as she took a step nearer for a closer look. "You've got to be kidding me?" It was more a statement of surprise than a question.

It wasn't often that Laura Goodman was lost for words, but this had to be seen to be believed.

"Is that, err, um, I'm not sure I believe what I'm looking at, but is that a thylacine, a Tasmanian tiger... wolf or whatever it's called?" She looked at the man standing next to her, "they're extinct!"

Appleby raised his eyebrows in surprise, "It seems not. The evidence is there in front of you, Laura. Not one thylacine, but three."

"That's amazing. Just amazing."

"And," he paused for a moment, "there has to be at least one more, a male, as the smaller ones are her pups."

"How many people know about this?"

"The two of us and the site manager."

"How much?"

Appleby looked confused.

"I don't understand what you mean?"

"How much to keep his mouth shut?"

Appleby ran his hand through his hair, "Why would he need to be paid to keep his mouth shut. This is an amazing discovery, Laura."

"Is it? You imbecile! I'm not even going to ask how they were captured. I don't want to know."

Appleby was astounded. They had re-discovered an animal that hadn't been seen since the nineteen thirties.

"Take that look off your face," she snapped. "It's obvious there was more to the alleged scandal about selling the thylacine than we thought, and I'm sure I read somewhere there's a massive bounty on them for proof of life." She clicked her fingers as she thought. "Yes, I'm sure of it. It'll be cheaper to pay him the equivalent, warn him to keep his mouth shut and tell him to get lost. Does he have any family?

"I've no idea, why?"

"Well it'll have to be a lottery win or something."

"Laura, sweetheart, this is an amazing discovery, we'll go down in history."

"Don't be so fucking stupid," she said, her tone thick with aggression. "If news of this gets out, the government will shut us down in an instant. You've seen the geological forecasts. I'm not going to walk away from a multimillion dollar contract for the sake of those creatures," she waved her hand in the vague direction of the cage. "They will have to go."

"You can't be serious, Laura. That's extreme, even for you. There in front of you are three specimens of one, if not the world's rarest animal."

"And under my feet is a vein of minerals that are going to make me a fortune," she said, walking back to the door. "Get rid of those stinking animals, I don't care how you do it. And make sure the site manager signs a water tight non-disclosure agreement. I don't want him taking the money and then blabbing to the press. Okay?"

Chapter Twenty-Six

Hugh and Connie lay on the grass, peering over the edge of Sullivan's Rise. They watched as Laura Goodman followed her lawyer into the building, which had been erected for use as a warehouse and equipment store.

"Wonder what she's doing here? Connie, what do you think?"

"Oh sorry, I was looking at what she was wearing. She always looks as if she is about to parade along a cat walk. Each one of her outfits must cost a fortune."

"I don't know why you worry so much, you and your mum always look nice, whatever you wear."

Connie twisted in order to see his face, his expression was neutral, he wasn't pulling her leg.

Satisfied, she rolled back onto her stomach.

"That's a nice thing to say, but you're a bloke, you wouldn't understand."

"Whoops, here they come." Hugh pushed himself up onto his elbows in order to get a better look. "She doesn't look happy, ha, look, she's turning to have a go at that lawyer chap!"

"Na, for such a pretty woman she's always got a face on her like a smacked bum," Connie joked.

Laura Goodman hopped on each foot in turn as she replaced her shoes.

"I'm not joking," she shouted at the top of her voice. "I want those creatures gone."

Connie gasped.

"Did you hear what I think I heard?"

Hugh's face was devoid of colour, "They've got the thylacine," he said, pulling himself to his feet.

Connie grabbed his arm but he yanked it out of her grasp.

"Don't be stupid, Hugh. We can't go charging about. Not until we are sure they've gone. Do you want to end up with a bullet in your back or something?"

Hugh stopped dead in his tracks.

"Why do you have to be so damn *sensible*?" He snapped. "If you've got a better idea, what do you suggest?"

Connie pouted.

"There's no need to be so rude all the time."

"I'm sorry. You know how I get when the thylacine is in danger."

She nodded.

"Yeah, but you forget I feel the same. Sometimes you are too much, Hugh." She shook her head before continuing, "she's as much my thylacine as yours, you know."

Hugh remained silent. As usual she was speaking the truth, not that he wanted to hear it.

"I feel so useless all the time. As soon as the thylacine is safe from one source of danger, something else pops up. We can't keep on like this."

Connie nodded.

"That's one of the most sensible things you've said. With the mine and such like, maybe," she glanced at Hugh, from his expression he seemed to know what she was going to say. "Maybe, the time is coming for the Government to be called, in. We keep saying it, but we always avoid making that decision. It's something we as a family, all of us, including Napoleon and the boys need to discuss, but at the moment we've got more important things to sort out. Look that Goodman woman's driving off."

"Good riddance," Hugh snapped.

"Let's see if we can get close to that building. There might be a window we can look in. I know it's a long shot but unless you can think of something it's that or we tell your Dad and Napoleon what we've seen."

Hugh shrugged, "Sounds as good a plan as any. Come on I'll race you."

He hurried to where they had left their bikes. He'd never beaten her in a race yet, but it was a laugh giving it a go, who'd have thought he'd become this competitive. It wasn't so long ago when the only competition he entertained was to choose between a Mars Bar and a Snickers! Laughing, he took his feet off the pedals and free-wheeled down the slope.

"Whooo!" He shouted, his feet splayed out in front of him.

They slowed their pace as they reached the bush which had become their new hiding place for their bikes. Keeping low, they skirted around the perimeter of the exploration site, Connie scuttled backwards, while Hugh kept an eye on the area in front of them.

"Hold up," he whispered.

They crouched low as he pointed to Appleby talking to the new site manager.

They couldn't hear what was being said, but it was clear from the expression on the site manager's face he was jubilant, it was obvious something had pleased him.

Appleby slapped him on the back in a good natured way as they walked into the portacabin.

"If we're quick we can make it to the toilet cubicles and then the back of the portacabin without being seen

Hugh agreed, "That'll leave five or six metres of open ground to the warehouse. I can't see anyone, can you?"

Connie shook her head, "Ready if you are?"

"As much as I'll ever be," Hugh grinned.

Shuffling forward on all fours, they paused behind the JCB and the van, which were now secured behind a portable fence.

Checking the coast was clear, they hurried past the toilet cubicles to the back of the portacabin. They could hear snatches of conversation but no distinct words, but they didn't hang around, they weren't there to eavesdrop, their target destination was the building Goodman had emerged from. They waited for a moment. They couldn't risk being seen.

"Shall I go first?"

Connie nodded, "Stay low and don't stop."

Hugh peered around the corner of the building. He filled his lungs before counting to three in his head. Making a dash for it, he ran towards the warehouse, sliding to a halt when he hit the shadows.

Turning, he gave Connie the thumbs up. She was just about to make her run when he held up his hand, his eyes wide in alarm. He put his finger to his lips and pointed to the front of the portacabin. She couldn't see it from where she hid, but a car had pulled up. Hugh held his breath as he watched the driver get out and hurry into the building.

They waited a couple of minutes, their hearts pounding with excitement before the driver emerged from the portacabin and drove away. Hugh gave Connie the all clear.

Keeping low, she hurried the short distance between the two buildings, smiling as she joined him.

"Thanks," she said, "that would have been too close for comfort, I couldn't see the front of the building from there."

"Forget it, my heart's still pounding ten to the dozen."

Keeping his back flat against the building, Hugh peeped around the corner. Nothing moved. With caution, they inched their way along the rear of the building, but they were out of luck, there was no window. Hugh wiped a trickle of sweat on his sleeve as Connie took the lead. She pointed to a window half way along the side of the wall.

"Bummer, it's quite high up."

"Maybe I can see in, that's if you give me a leg up?" She suggested.

"I've a better idea. Do you think you can reach if I kneel on all fours and you stand on my back, it'll be more stable?"

Connie looked up at the window, "Yeah, I think I can. Let's go for it."

They tip-toed along the side of the building. Hugh knelt on all fours, adjusting his position until he felt comfortable. Nodding, he braced himself as Connie climbed onto his back.

"This material is strange," she said, pushing the fabric of the building. "It's spongy, it feels like rubber."

Hugh tutted, "That's very interesting, Connie, but we don't have time to worry about that now," he hissed. "Can we get on with the plan?"

"Okay," she nodded."

Hugh inhaled through gritted teeth, this wasn't the time to tell her she was heavier than he expected.

Connie pulled herself up, moving her feet a little way apart to try and steady herself. Hanging onto the tiny window ledge with her fingertips, she stood on the tips of her toes.

"Damn, it's dark in there." She shuffled her feet, causing Hugh to wince as the fabric of his shirt rubbed his back. Stretching, she peered into the gloom of the building. "Hang on... um, I think I can see a cage!"

"Are you sure? Can you get a better look?" His face contorted as she wriggled about, the tips of her shoes digging into his back.

"No, it's wishful thinking, I can't be certain that's what it is."

"Oi! You there!"

The kids were startled by the unexpected shout. Standing at full stretch, Connie overbalanced, crashing to the ground, her head hitting the floor with a sickening thud.

"Connie!" Hugh screamed, the sound shrill, high pitched, and thick with fear as he crawled towards his friend.

"Don't move. Stay where you are."

Ignoring the instruction, Hugh cradled Connie's head and stroked her hair, smudging the trickle of blood oozing from a gash in her forehead.

"Connie," he whispered, "wake up, Connie."

"How touching," Appleby snarled. "Sykes, get your arse over here!"

Justin Sykes, the site manager, tore around the corner, a shotgun over his shoulder.

"Are these the kids I've heard about, the ones causing the damage?"

Appleby shook his head, "Dunno, but it seems a bit of a co-incidence."

"Yo, boy, what you doing, skulking around a site like this. It's dangerous," Sykes demanded, tapping Hugh's foot with his steel toe-capped boot.

Hugh didn't answer as he bent over Connie, stroking her face.

"She needs a doctor," he said, half twisting, he looked up at the two men. "Please, she needs help."

"Maybe you should have thought about that before you started to trespass and undertake little acts of vandalism."

"What do you expect," Hugh screeched, his face flushed with anger. "You've no right to destroy the environment like you're doing. We know where the funding for the company came from. We're going to expose you for the frauds and thieves you are."

Realising he'd said too much, Hugh fell silent.

Appleby narrowed his eyes, "Aha, so, you aren't just guilty of vandalism, you are guilty of computer hacking... I assume you know that's an offence too. Either that or you know who did it."

You've done it again, you bloody idiot, Hugh fumed in his head, *letting your mouth run away with you.*

"If you think you are going to get away with this, you've got another thing coming."

Sykes grabbed Hugh's arm and dragged him to his feet, causing him to yelp in pain. The site manager wasn't much taller than Hugh, but he prided himself on his physique, spending as many hours as he could in the gym, and when he was away from home, he had his weights and gym equipment in his lodgings.

"Can you manage the bitch?" He snarled at Appleby, taking control of the situation.

William Appleby leant over Connie, "I don't think she'd going anywhere at the moment. The kid may be right, perhaps we should get a doctor."

"What, and lose what we've got, nah, I'm taking my orders from the big boss now, Mr. Appleby. I want my money and then I'm gone."

Holding his shotgun in one hand, Sykes tightened his grip on the boy and dragged him round to the front of the warehouse.

"Don't move," he instructed, his gun trained on the boy while he fiddled with the keys before finding the correct one to unlock the door.

Appleby scooped Connie's limp body into his arms, and followed Sykes to the front of the building.

Shoving the door open, the site manager flicked on the light switch. He pushed Hugh in front of him, grabbing a coil of rope from one of the shelves as he passed.

"Oh my God. We were right, you have captured the thylacine."

Sykes looked surprised.

"So you are aware of the creatures, are you?"

Hugh started to struggle, trying to yank his arm free from the bigger man's grasp.

"You've got to let her go," he fumed through clenched teeth.

Sykes pointed the shotgun at Hugh, "Stop struggling, you little shit."

"Sykes! That's enough."

The site manager snarled, "Weak bastard," he muttered to himself. "Who else knows about the thylacine?" He demanded.

Hugh shook his head, more to clear his thoughts than anything else.

"Just... just us, Connie and me. We've been keeping it a secret."

Sykes yanked the boy up by his hair and stared into his eyes, "You sure about that, kid?"

Hugh nodded, grimacing as it accentuated the pain in his head.

"Yes, I'm sure. It's our secret."

"Prop her against the central support," Sykes instructed, dragging Hugh to the middle of the building. "Sit down," he commanded. "Sit down, I said. Sit! Don't you do anything at the first time of asking?"

Hugh felt the wooden pole against his back and slid down to the floor. Appleby lowered Connie to the ground. He lifted her head off her chest, "Looks like she's coming round."

"See, panic over!"

Ignoring the site manager's comments, Appleby tied the rope around the waists of the two kids, securing them to the wooden pole while Sykes tied their hands and feet with plastic ties, similar to those used by some police forces as disposable handcuffs.

Hugh tried to twist his body in order to see Connie.

"Is she alright?"

"Shut up."

"Please, tell me if Connie is alright?"

Sykes kicked Connie's foot causing her to groan.

"Yep, still alive." Sykes laughed, "I'm no doctor, but she's breathing. And if you get it into your head that you can scream and shout, well, the walls are thick. The rubberised material makes great insulation and sound proofing."

"If you don't let us go and release the thylacine, you're gonna be in big trouble."

"From where I'm standing, you're the ones in deep poo-poo."

Appleby glanced at his watch, "I've got to go."

Sykes nodded, following the lawyer out of the building he flicked the switch, plunging it into semi darkness as he pulled the door shut.

"Damn, damn, damn," Hugh cursed to himself. He tried to move, but the rope around his waist had been pulled tight, preventing him from shuffling more than a centimetre, and the plastic tie was cutting into his wrists. "Connie," he listened to see if she responded. "Connie, wake up, Connie."

Connie grimaced, pulling a face at the taste of blood, which had trickled down her face from the gash in her forehead.

"W, where are we?" She screwed her eyes up in an attempt to focus. "I, I can't see anything," she cried, her voice tinged with panic.

"Calm down, Connie, try not to panic, we're in the warehouse."

Connie blinked once or twice, "That's better, I can see a little clearer now, the double vision is settling down a bit."

"How do you feel?"

"Awful. Next daft question."

"They've captured the thylacine."

Connie nodded, closing her eyes as the diplopia made her feel sick, "I guessed that." She inhaled through clenched teeth, "these ties are killing my wrists."

"I know, mine too."

"Have they got the pups?"

"I saw one, maybe two."

"Bummer!"

"They asked how many people know about her. I said just us, our secret."

"Good move."

"I hope so," Hugh replied. "I think I said too much, I sort of hinted we knew where they got the money for the company from."

Connie groaned, but he was unable to detect if it was from pain or if she was annoyed with him.

"I can't help wondering if they are going to get rid of us as well as the thylacine."

"Na. It won't come to that. Either we'll escape or someone will find us. Napoleon or your dad will come looking."

"I hope you're right, Connie. I really hope you are right."

Chapter Twenty-Seven

Whitaker pulled up in front of the bungalow and leant against the steering wheel. What a mess. He knew he should have followed Hugh when he left the bungalow earlier that morning, but he had so much work on. He shook his head. When it came to his son there was always the pressure of work stopping him spending time with the boy. There was little doubt about it, he was a crap father.

He checked the time on his phone, eight pm. He knew he should go in but he couldn't face the inevitable confrontation.

"What's going on, Hugh?" He mused to himself. "I've never had to ground you before," he tutted, "then again, it's not that long ago that you never ventured out of your room."

Whitaker sighed. It was the typical catch twenty-two, for the first time in his life, his son had a friend and as a result he was doing the stuff that most kids of his age did, he was having fun. As his father, Whitaker knew he had to move with the times.

"Come on, Andrew, be the parent for once in your life!"

He grabbed his laptop off the seat beside him and went inside.

"Hugh, I'm home."

He dumped his bag into the nearest chair to the door and went into the kitchen. The larder door was still ajar and the back panel was propped against it.

"Hugh!" Whitaker cocked his head and listened. The bungalow was silent. He hurried into his son's room, it was empty, the bathroom door was open, it was clear his son wasn't home.

"If you're at Connie's you are in deep trouble!" He said to himself.

Retracing his steps, he jumped into the Land Rover and drove over to the small aboriginal community. He rapped on the door to Joe's cabin and waited, no one was home. Hearing the sound of the Land Rover, Napoleon hurried out of his cabin. The vet raised his hand in greeting.

"G'day, have you seen the kids?" Andrew Whitaker asked, glancing at his friend. "Napoleon, what's wrong?"

"I was just going to call you. Quick, come inside."

Whitaker waited a second, there was no movement in the cabin. The kids weren't here either.

"Andrew!"

The vet hurried after the Aboriginal Tasmanian. George and Mikey were standing around a large cardboard box.

"We've got big trouble."

Whitaker stared at Napoleon, "What do you mean?"

"The boys were repairing some fencing when they noticed a thylacine pup on its own."

Whitaker gasped, "You've got to be joking?"

Napoleon shook his head.

"Believe me, I wouldn't joke about something like this," he put his finger to his lips and pointed to the box.

The vet peeped over the edge, there, as Napoleon had said, was a thylacine pup, curled up asleep.

"We must have hung around for about an hour," Mikey explained, "waiting to see if the mother returned."

"But she had three pups."

Mikey nodded, "There was no sign of the mother or the other two. Looking at this one, they are on the verge of being weaned, but they'd stay with the mother for months yet."

Whitaker gripped the back of a chair.

"The kids are missing too."

"What?" Napoleon glanced at his sons, they shook their heads, they hadn't seen them all day.

Whitaker told them what had happened that morning.

"It's my fault, I should have checked he was alright earlier. I... I..." Whitaker bit his bottom lip in an attempt to stop it trembling. "I grounded him and he escaped through the secret tunnel."

George laughed, "Way to go, Hugh!" He was silenced by a stern look from his father, this wasn't the time to joke.

"We've got an interesting situation. Hugh and Connie have 'disappeared', and we have a missing thylacine and two of her pups," Napoleon observed. "I don't think it takes a genius to assume there's a connection."

Andrew Whitaker glanced out of the window, "It's getting dark, what are we going to do?"

"We'll start tracking at first light," Napoleon suggested. "In the meantime it's worth checking the mine site. It's a long shot but you know how much Hugh thinks of the thylacine, his thylacine as he calls her, they may have gone there. As we know, Sullivan's Rise is where they've seen her most often."

"What about the police?"

Napoleon pursed his lips, "You know how we feel about the heelers, Andrew, but Hugh is your son, it's your call."

The vet rubbed his chin between his first finger and thumb as he thought. Raising his eyes to the ceiling he muttered a prayer. He looked at the three men, "Okay, if we call the cops in I guess they will want to search these buildings, that's the last thing we want. We can't release the pup, we've got to reunite it with its mother and siblings. I just pray I'm making the right decision here."

George stole a quick look at his brother and smiled, Whitaker was on their side.

"Let's do as you suggest, we'll check the mine site now, and start to track them at dawn."

"What about Angie?" Mikey asked.

Whitaker looked at Mikey and pulled a face, "God help me if I'm wrong, but I think she's got enough to worry about. We'll call when we've got something to tell her."

"You boys stay here in case the kids turn up, and you can keep an eye on the pup," said Napoleon.

"No problem, Pop. How 'bout George stays here and I'll nip over to Andrew's place in case they head there?" Mikey looked at the vet for confirmation.

"Good idea," the vet replied, removing the front door key from his key ring and tossing it to the younger man. "There's plenty of food in the fridge."

"He'll be fine, Andrew," said his father. "He's not going to a party. Give him an invitation like that and he'll eat you out of house and home."

"Dad!" Mikey exclaimed, smiling as his father pulled a face. He knew his son too well.

The short drive to the exploration site was undertaken in silence. Whitaker parked alongside the portacabin which was being used as the site office and followed Napoleon to the door.

"G'day," Napoleon called, knocking once on the side of the building. The two security guards looked up from the game of cards they were playing. They had been drafted in at short notice and were under strict instructions to patrol the grounds every couple of hours, they had at least half an hour to kill before the next circuit.

One of the guards pushed his chair back and came to the door. Whitaker scrutinised the accreditation pinned to his shirt pocket while Napoleon engaged in conversation with him.

"We're looking for two kids, a boy and a girl, fourteen years old, have you seen them?"

The security guard shook his head, "Bruce, two kids are missing, have you seen them?"

His colleague shook his head as he shuffled the cards ready for another game.

"I can show you around the site, if you like, I'm due to walk round soon anyway, might as well bring it forward half an hour."

"That'll be great, thanks, mate."

Grabbing a torch, the security guard told his colleague he'd be back in a few minutes.

"Been here long?" Napoleon asked.

The security guard shook his head.

"That's the funny thing. We got the call late this afternoon, we were dragged off another job. The site manager came into a bit of good luck, well more than a bit. He's won the lottery, didn't check his numbers until today and resigned on the spot."

Whitaker turned to look at Napoleon, but he couldn't see his face in the darkness, things didn't add up.

"As you can see, this is where they park the vehicles, we've been told they've had a spot of trouble with vandalism, that's why the fencing has been brought in."

He swept the torch in a wide arc, over the portacabin and the prefabricated warehouse.

"What's in there?" Whitaker asked.

"To be honest, mate, I'm not sure. It's locked and we don't have the key. Having worked on sites like this, I'd guess its equipment, supplies, that sort of thing."

They walked to the end of the site and back again, but nothing seemed out of place.

"Sorry, mate, looks like the kids aren't here, do you want to leave a phone number, just in case they show up. As I said, we've got to make a sweep every couple of hours, a waste of time if you ask me, more like overkill, but I don't make the rules, I just follow them."

Back in the Land Rover, Whitaker hit the steering wheel with his hand.

"Something's not right."

"I agree, Andrew. There's too many coincidences. And now the site manager's won the lottery."

The vet nodded, "That bloke seemed genuine. I don't think either of them have seen the kids or the thylacine but there's more to this than meets the eye."

"I, for one, would like a better look inside the building they're using for storage. If no one's got anything to hide they'll let us have a good look round in daylight. I say we bring my boys back at daybreak and start by making a thorough sweep ourselves."

"Mmm, I'm not sure about that. Sneaking around, I mean."

Napoleon looked at his friend, it was obvious from his drawn expression he was wracked with guilt and worry.

"Come on, drive me home, we'll argue over it in the morning,"

Appleby waited for the waiter to leave. It was a considered risk but he'd decided to update Laura Goodman over dinner. At least she wouldn't be able to go ballistic in public – well, that was the theory anyway.

Reaching for his glass he watched her over the rim as he sipped the champagne, as usual her taste was impeccable.

She nuzzled into the corner of the booth, their booth, at the back of the restaurant, discreet and private, yet far enough from the kitchen not to be bothered by the comings and goings of the waiting staff. She had completed more than one business deal at this table.

"The problems of Warrugul are dealt with?" It was a statement, not a question.

Appleby ran his fingers up and down the stem of his glass.

"Things took a turn for the worse after you left."

Goodman focused her steel grey eyes on him, piercing, like two diamond tipped drills.

"Go on," the words were little more than a whisper yet they reverberated around his head as if they had been shouted by a town crier reciting a proclamation.

"I'll start with the good news. Sykes has gone. He lapped up the offer and is willing to hide behind the story of a lottery win."

"But?"

"But, the two kids who vandalised the vehicles came back."

"And the problem is?"

"And the problem is," he repeated, sounding like an echo. "The problem is they seemed to looking for the thylacine."

"That's ridiculous. I've done some research into that subject. The last footage to appear on the web is a grainy out of focus film of a dog, it's obvious that's what it is. The last verified specimen died in nineteen thirty-six, in Beaumaris Zoo. No one's seen one since, apart from us."

"Yes I know. But they claim to be aware of the animal."

"So why didn't they apply for the reward? I don't recall anyone in that god-forsaken-place being rich enough to ignore that amount of money."

"I've no idea. One of them, the girl is an abo. They regard the thylacine as some sort of spiritual creature, the heritage guy told me that."

You haven't told him, have you?"

Appleby shook his head.

"No, he told me something about it when we were talking about aboriginal culture, bored me rigid. Anyway, the boy claims no one else knows about it."

"What did the girl say?"

Appleby continued to play with his champagne flute, "She was unconscious."

Laura Goodman stared at him as he continued.

"She fell and hit her head. They were trying to look in the window of the warehouse when we surprised them."

"And you left her in that state. What the hell were you thinking?"

"Laura, you pay me to take care of things. The less you know about what's going on, the better it is for you and the Corporation. You said Warrugul will make you a prosperous woman. Leave me to deal with the problems we encounter in the process. Ah, that looks very appetising," he said, changing the subject as the waiter placed his first course in front of him.

With the sun peeping over the trees, Napoleon led the way to the perimeter of the exploration area. Whitaker had refused to remain behind, there was no way he was going to leave the search for his son to someone else. A sleepless night had left him exhausted, as he pondered on what a terrible father he'd been to Hugh over the past few years. Providing food and shelter wasn't enough. His son needed a parent who had time to spend with him. As his father, he would start to make time for him.

"So much for patrolling the boundary," Napoleon observed as they watched from the shadows thrown by two of the few tall celery topped pines the Corporation had left standing in the immediate vicinity.

They had been watching the portacabin for the last ten minutes. It was in darkness. Nothing moved.

"What do you suggest?"

Napoleon looked at the vet, "There's no point in asking you to wait here, just do what I say and we'll get through this. Together."

Whitaker nodded, his expression relaxing.

"I want you to go with Mikey and head over to that plant machinery, there's more cover to hide behind. George and I will go the other way. We'll circumvent the site from both sides, if they were here we'll find their tracks."

Whitaker turned to follow Mikey, but Napoleon grabbed his arm.

"Do everything Mikey tells you, Andrew, don't take any risks, we don't need a hero." He increased the pressure on Whitaker's arm. "I mean it, Andrew."

"Don't worry, Pop, I'll keep an eye on him." His son nudged the vet in a good humoured way, "stay close and stay low."

They waited while Napoleon and George skirted the edge of the clearing. George turned back and waved his hand from side to side, they hadn't found any tracks of note.

Mikey made an 'O' between his thumb and index finger, he'd got the message.

"Right, it's down to us, Andrew. Dad hasn't found anything over there. Don't forget, keep low and be extra careful near the portacabin. It looks as though the security guards are asleep but we can't be sure."

Andrew nodded, "Lead the way."

Unbeknown to Andrew and the others, the plant machinery had been moved closer to the portacabin the previous evening, as an additional security precaution, obliterating any tracks for Napoleon and George to find in that area.

Reaching the portable toilets, Mikey held up his hand as he scrutinised the ground. He pointed to a disturbance in the grass. The footprints they were looking at were too big for either Hugh or Connie.

Whitaker couldn't hide his disappointment.

"I hope we aren't on a hiding for nothing here, wasting more time."

Mikey smiled, he'd been tracking with his father since he was knee high to a grasshopper. It was as much about patience as it was about skill. His father had always said there was no point having a good eye if you were in too much of a hurry to read the signs.

"It's easy for me to say, but I wasn't expecting to see much here. Too many comings and goings," Mikey explained, "but we're heading for the portacabin, so we need to be silent."

Mikey hurried the short distance, stopping dead as he reached the side of the portable office, causing the vet to cannon into him.

The younger man put his fingers to his lips and then pointed to the ground. Whitaker shook his head; he couldn't see what Mikey was pointing at.

Speaking in a whisper, Mikey pointed to the tracks they had just made.

"See our feet are moving in one direction, facing east. These are facing south."

Whitaker scratched his head, "I don't understand."

Mikey stood with his back against the building, "They were standing like this, peering around the corner. I think they were looking to see if the coast was clear."

Whitaker whistled.

A look of alarm flashed across the face of the Aboriginal Tasmanian.

"Shush! Unusual sounds like that travel. You expect to hear bird song and insects buzzing around at this time of morning, not shrill whistles. This is why it may have been better for you to stay behind."

"Okay, I'm sorry," the vet hissed.

"No, I'm sorry, Andrew. I know you're worried." He waved to his father and brother, indicating they should meet them behind the storage building. "Right, let me go first and I'll call you over if the coast is clear."

With the vet following in his wake, Mikey led the way. Moments later they were joined by Napoleon and George.

"The kids were here, Pop. We saw tracks behind the portacabin. And look here," he pointed to the grass at their feet.

George moved a few paces, "And here, look, the whole area's been flattened. I think one of them was kneeling under the window, possibly on all fours, yep, look, I'm right."

Napoleon concurred.

"You're right, son. I think one of them was on the floor with the other one standing on their back, that explains why the grass is so flat. They were trying to see in the window. Way to go, son."

George grinned. He still had a lot to learn, but his father's praise meant a great deal.

"Whoa, there's blood here!" Mikey exclaimed.

Whitaker gasped, "Oh my God!"

"Let's not get ahead of ourselves, Andrew. We need to get a look in the window, George, you're the smallest. Climb onto your brother's shoulders and have a look."

Mikey lent against the building and cupped his hands ready to take his brother's weight.

"On three," he said, "one, two... three."

George bounced as his brother counted, leaping on three and scrambling onto his shoulders.

Mikey gritted his teeth as he took the strain.

"Thought you were on a diet," he grumbled.

"I heard that, bro!"

George clung onto the narrow ledge and peered in through the window.

"It's pretty dark in there," he said in a stage whisper. He squinted in an attempt to peer through the gloom. "Hang on, I can see a cage, yep, I'm sure it's a cage."

"Is it empty?" Napoleon called up.

"Can't see, Pop. It's too dark." He angled his hands over his eyes to cut out the light behind him, wobbling as he tried to balance on his brother's shoulders. "No wait. I, I can see a leg."

"What do you mean, a leg?" Whitaker demanded.

"Just what I said. I can see a leg. Someone's in there."

Chapter Twenty-Eight

"Help... Can anyone hear me? H-E-L-P!"

"Shhh, Hugh, stop shouting, my head hurts."

Hugh twisted as far as his restraints allowed.

"I'm sorry, I hate sitting here doing nothing."

Connie closed her eyes, as she tried to ignore the pounding in her head. Hugh raised his arms to his mouth and tried gnawing the plastic tie around his wrists, but it was pulled so tight it was cutting into this skin, preventing him getting his teeth close enough. He grimaced as he tried to separate his hands but it caused the plastic to cut deeper. It was obvious why so many police forces used this type of restraint, they were dirt cheap, light and easy to carry as well as very strong.

"Connie, Connie, answer me, Connie."

There was no response, she had slipped back into unconsciousness. Hugh realised the situation was becoming more serious by the minute, she needed medical attention, fast.

Behind him he could hear the thylacine moving in the cage, it was a scratching sound, as if they were trying to dig their way out. He had to save them as well as his friend.

Each movement caused the plastic to cut deeper into his flesh, for the first time he could imagine how a terrified animal felt, trapped in a snare. He was helpless, they were helpless.

Come on, Hugh, pull yourself together.

Napoleon tapped his son on the leg, signalling to him to climb down. George jumped to the ground, a look of excitement creased his face.

"We've found them, Pop, we've found them."

"Can you keep a look out, son?" Napoleon asked.

Mikey nodded, brushing the grass from his shorts as he walked to the corner of the building.

Napoleon pressed the spongy material of the building.

"I think this is rubber, galvanised rubber." He unclipped his hunting knife from his belt and pierced the material. The blade was razor sharp. To say it cut through the material like a hot knife through butter was an over simplification, but utilising a sawing action, Napoleon was able to carve his way through the back wall.

"Here, let me help, Pop," George offered, copying his father and cutting a horizontal incision.

"What's the time, Andrew?"

The vet snuck a look at his watch, "Almost seven."

Napoleon nodded, pausing to wipe the sweat from his forehead, "Time's knocking on, we need to hurry."

Mikey gave the all clear signal, at least there was no movement from the portacabin.

Tugging the rubber back to create a gap, George slipped through, leaving his father to enlarge the hole while Whitaker held the rubber flap.

"Pops, I've got the thylacine, there's three, mum and two pups in a cage. I'm going in a bit further. Oh no!" Spotting Connie, he hurried over to her slumped body.

"Dad – Dad, is that you?" Hugh whispered.

"It's me, George."

"Connie's hit her head, she keeps falling unconscious," Hugh replied, his throat hoarse from shouting for help.

"Right, she's still out cold," replied George, easing his knife between the support pole and Connie's body in order to cut the rope tethering them.

"Stay where you are, Hugh, I need to get Connie out, and then I'll come back for you." The Aboriginal Tasmanian scooped the young girl into his arms with ease and hurried to the hole at the back of the storage building where he passed her limp body out to his father.

Moments later Hugh was peering over his father's shoulder as the vet examined his friend. Connie groaned, screwing her eyes up as she started to come round.

"Andrew, is that you?"

"G'day," he smiled.

"How you feeling?" Hugh demanded.

"Stand back a little, Hugh. Give her some room, there's a good lad."

Behind them, Napoleon and George were trying to ease the cage out of the building.

"Hugh, if you're up to it, we could do with a hand."

Connie tried to sit up, gagging as the sudden movement made her feel dizzy.

Leaving his father tending to Connie, Hugh shuffled back to the building. He took the flap of rubber from Napoleon and pulled, trying to make the hole as wide as possible as the two men struggled to get the cage out.

Releasing the animals here was not an option, apart from the danger posed by the mining corporation they needed to reunite the third pup with its mother and siblings.

Leaning against the rubber with his full weight, Hugh laced his fingers through the metal of the cage as he helped pull the pen through the opening. They tried to keep their movements as smooth as possible, no one wanted to distress the thylacine any more than was necessary.

Mikey doubled back to help.

"Still no movement from the portacabin, Pop."

"I'm not worried about that now, son, with the evidence we have here, I don't think they'd be any trouble if they hear us. I can hazard a guess at the number of crimes the Corporation have committed, from kidnapping and illegal restraint to attempting to hide a protected species for some illicit purpose."

With the cage clear of the building, the three Aboriginal Tasmanians and Hugh took a corner each and headed to the Land Rover.

Ignoring her protests, Whitaker swept Connie into his arms, instructing her to hold onto his neck. She wasn't steady enough to walk.

Happy she was comfortable, he hurried to help the others. Minutes later they had loaded the cage into the back of the vehicle. Napoleon squeezed in alongside the terrified animals, the pups cowering behind their mother. Hugh and Connie sat alongside Whitaker in the front seat. With no more room, Mikey and George had arranged to meet back at their cabin.

George tapped the side window as he passed and gave the kids the thumbs up sign before trotting after his brother.

"Hey, Mikey, the speed Andrew drives, I bet we beat them home," he quipped.

"Oi, I heard that," laughed the vet, turning the key in the ignition.

As soon as they arrived back at Napoleon's cabin they carried the cage indoors. Having drawn the curtains of the boy's bedroom, they reintroduced the separated pup. They watched as the female sniffed her errant offspring while its siblings pounced on it, licking and snuffling its coat. Hugh smiled to himself, it looked as if the reunion was going well.

With a blanket covering two thirds of the cage, the thylacine were left devouring a chicken's carcase. They were starving, there was no evidence of food or water in the cage, a situation the Toba's had rectified as soon as they could.

Whitaker was bathing the gash to Connie's forehead with a mild antiseptic, it was bruised but not as deep as he had suspected.

"You look as if you've been in a Tom and Jerry cartoon," Hugh joked, "if I push the lump, it might disappear!"

"Don't you dare, it hurts too much," Connie laughed, groaning at the same time."

"I'm not taking closing arguments here; we are going to get you checked out at the hospital. Hugh says you lost consciousness more than once. Your mother will panic as soon as I tell her, if I can say you are okay she won't worry so much."

"Ah, Andrew, I'm fine."

"Don't 'ah, Andrew' me. We need to get you checked out and then you can visit your grandfather afterwards."

"Can we?" She gasped.

"Mmm, thought would make you change your tune!"

"Can I come?"

"Like we're gonna be able to leave without you," his father said, but there was no malice in his tone, and all mention of consequences forgotten. "Let me take a look at your wrists before we go."

He refreshed the bowl of antiseptic and bathed his son's wrists. Hugh inhaled through clenched teeth, he'd rubbed his skin so raw the dilute antiseptic solution stung the open wounds.

"Gee they are sore," his father observed, wiping the damaged areas with soaked cotton wool.

"I tried to bite through the plastic ties. I can understand how an animal chews off a limb when it's desperate to escape from a trap," Hugh closed his eyes at the thought, the image in his mind, terrifying.

It was an involuntary movement, but Hugh tensed his body as his father cleansed the area, wiping as much of the debris embedded in the flesh as he could without causing too much pain. Satisfied with his efforts, he smeared a liberal layer of antiseptic cream over the wounds before applying a light bandage.

With the kids and thylacine safe, Napoleon made his way to the ranger station while the boys promised to check the traps Whitaker had set the previous day; he was still looking for a healthy young male devil to place in quarantine.

There were mixed reports in the last update from the DFTD project. There had been a spike in the number of devils infected with the disease across the country. Work in developing a vaccine had stalled temporarily, while recent developments highlighting that the cancer tumours lack a critical molecule, which prevented the animal's immune system detecting the infected cells were investigated. On a more positive note, there was an indication that some devils were adapting to 'co-exist' with the disease, a bit like the rabbit population which was virtually eliminated when the man-made disease, myxomatosis, was introduced in the 1950's. Initially almost one hundred percent fatal, the rabbit population eventually produced a level of immunity which allowed them to co-exist with the disease.

After a cup of sweet, weak tea and a slice of toast, Connie seemed none the worse for her ordeal, apart from the physical bruises and gashed forehead, but she wasn't his daughter. And without Joe Sampi to consult, Whitaker had to get her checked by a doctor.

Two hours later, they were looking for somewhere to park, having made at least five circuits of the hospital car park. Hugh couldn't stop himself from commenting that Joe had completed the journey in less than ninety minutes when he was driving, and that he was also gasping for a drink and dying for a pee.

"Moan, moan, moan," muttered his father with a laugh. "Bugger!" he cursed under his breath as a nifty sports car nipped into the space he was heading for.

"There, Dad, that car's pulling out," Hugh said, pointing to a black Mercedes reversing out of a bay.

Minutes later they were heading towards the accident and emergency department.

Having been triaged, Connie was told to take a seat in the waiting area. With a head injury, the chances were the wait wouldn't be too long.

"Hey, is that young Master Whitaker?"

"Cindy, G'day. It's nice to see you," said Hugh, smiling as a nurse approached. "Hey, have you changed your name?" He asked, spotting her identity badge which now read Cindy Hawkins.

Cindy Hawkins, nee Houseman had been the nurse who treated him when he fell into a sink hole. He'd been following the thylacine when he fell through the overgrown vegetation, which had hidden the entrance to the underground cave, breaking his arm when he hit the ground.

"Yep, got hitched over the New Year hols," she said, raising her left hand to show him the thin yellow band.

"Congratulations. Was it a punk wedding?" He joked, referring to the short razor cut hair style she sported.

Cindy shook her head.

"I'll have you know it was a traditional do. Not my choice, but the white dress, bridesmaids, the whole shebang! I wore a hat so it hid my flowing locks," she laughed, rubbing her short, bleached platinum blond hair. "Anyway, young man, what are you here for, not falling out of a tree again I hope?" She asked, referring to the lie he told to explain his last visit.

Hugh shook his head, plunging his hands deeper into the pockets of his shorts to avoid unnecessary questions about his bandaged wrists.

"Connie had a fall, banged her head."

Cindy tutted, "You two should carry a health warning!" She joked.

"Constance Sampi."

Hugh sniggered as a look of annoyance clouded his friend's face, she hated her full name.

She glared at Hugh's father.

"Why'd you go and tell them that was my name?" She complained.

"I didn't. You were already on the system," Whitaker explained in his defence. "Go on, the doctor's waiting, I'll come with you, but you'll have to stay here, Hugh." He delved into his pocket for some change. "How 'bout you get us all a drink, please?"

Hugh watched as his father followed Connie into one of the consulting rooms. Memories flooded back from his experience, the moment he'd shared his secret with Connie, that he, Hugh Whitaker had seen a thylacine. A secret overheard by Spencer Tate. It was the moment he'd endangered the creature as Tate made it his business to follow him at every opportunity in an attempt to capture the animal and sell it on the black market.

Connie eased herself onto the examination couch while the vet sat on the chair alongside the table. He explained to the doctor her mother was working in Hobart and he was her temporary guardian while her grandfather recuperated in a ward here in the hospital. The doctor scribbled a note as the vet talked. Placing his pen on the table he swivelled his chair to face Connie.

"Right, Constance."

"It's Connie," she corrected, a hint on annoyance in her voice.

The doctor smiled, "Ah, I take it you aren't keen on your name, just like my sister. My parents saddled her with Andromeda."

Connie smiled.

"She won't answer to anything other than Andy. Our 'olds' were dye-in- the- wool hippies when we were born, you'd never believe it to look at them now," he explained, describing his parents.

"Dare I ask what they called you?" She asked.

"Ptolemy, I'm afraid. I changed it to Phillip, less pretentious. Saved me a hell of a lot of leg-pulling while I was studying at uni. though I may change it back if I gain a consultancy or professorship, I'm a snob at heart. Anyway, back to work."

Connie explained she'd fallen and hit her head, omitting she was balanced on Hugh's back on the time, or that she'd fallen unconscious more than the once she'd admitted to.

The doctor examined the gash in her head, it didn't need suturing and he doubted it would scar. He shone a light into her eyes, pleased at the way her pupils reacted. Adding another note to her records, he asked if she was experiencing any headaches.

Connie nodded, "Yeah, but they aren't as bad as last night."

"Nausea, black spots in your line of sight?"

She shook her head, regretting her action in an instant as the sudden movement made her feel queasy.

"Right, I don't think there's anything serious going on, but to make sure I'd like to take a couple of x-rays to rule out any skull fractures."

Whitaker thanked the doctor before collecting Hugh and traipsing to the x-ray department.

Two hours later, Connie had been given the all clear with strict instructions that she was to rest and return if she experienced any dizziness, black spots in her line of sight or nausea.

They waited in silence as they rode the elevator to the men's surgical ward. As visiting hours were not until later that afternoon, Whitaker asked for permission to visit Joe Sampi. The nurse pointed to a side ward consisting of four beds, they had moved him from the high dependency ward the previous day.

Connie led the way into the room. Sampi was sitting bolt upright, his brown skin was sallow and pale but he looked as if he were asleep or in a trance. If Hugh hadn't seen it before, he'd have been alarmed.

Connie touched her grandfather's arm.

"What's my favourite granddaughter doing here?" He smiled, "and why aren't you at school?"

Avoiding his eyes, Connie looked away.

"This isn't the best place to discuss it, Joe," said the vet, his eyes roaming the small room. All the beds were occupied; it was too public to tell him what had happened.

Sampi pushed the bedclothes back and swung his feet to the ground.

"Mr. Sampi," a nurse cried, hurrying towards him. "Where are you going?"

Sampi growled, Hugh studied the floor tiles, frightened he might laugh, the mighty Joe Sampi sounded like a grizzly bear.

"I feel fine, young woman. At my age I don't have time to laze around in bed."

The nurse took a step backwards. The Aboriginal Tasmanian was an imposing figure; he was not someone to be argued with.

"Please be careful. Would you like a wheelchair?"

One look from Sampi was enough to tell her he thought her suggestion was stupid. The nurse backed down, allowing her patient to go as far as the day room but no further.

Sampi raised an eyebrow. Hugh sniggered, he reminded him of Star Trek's Mr. Spock.

"Thank you, mam," Sampi replied with a curt salute.

The nurse watched as the old man shuffled towards the day room, his granddaughter and friends following behind him like a row of little ducklings waddling after their mother.

The room was empty. Sampi lowered himself into a chair and waited for Hugh to shut the door.

"So, who's going to fill me in?"

Hugh glanced at Connie and his father, but they were happy to let him start. He inhaled, for a second lost for words. *Come on, pull yourself together.* He realised Sampi was staring at him, unblinking. He had noticed the cut on his granddaughter's forehead and the bandages on the boy's wrists.

With precision, Hugh retold the story of how they had been watching the going's on at the site below Sullivan's Rise. He explained how Connie had fallen from his back when she tried to look through the window of the warehouse.

"Why weren't you at school?"

"Oh it was after school, but..."

"Ah, there's always a but. Do I want to hear this?" Joe Sampi asked, trying hard not to smile.

"Um, I'm suspended from school."

Sampi threw his head back and roared with laughter, his expression contorting as the jerky movements pulled his stitches.

"What are we going to do with you," he looked at Hugh and then at his granddaughter, "I've said it before, you two are a liability. A walking disaster zone."

"See, I told you he thinks I'm a bad influence on you," Hugh whispered to Connie.

"Don't be a dill," she whispered back through gritted teeth.

"So tell me why you were suspended."

"Fighting."

Sampi's expression was incredulous.

"It's true, I'm afraid, Joe," his father confirmed.

Hugh explained the events leading up to his suspension. Sampi listened without interruption, his jaw set as he concentrated. Whitaker continued the story, bringing Sampi up to date with how they discovered the kids and the thylacine held captive by the Tasmanian Mining Corporation.

Sampi stared at his granddaughter while the vet spoke, remaining silent for several minutes when he'd finished.

"I'm coming home with you."

"But Grandfather, you're..."

Sampi raised his hand, silencing his granddaughter.

"I'm feeling stronger by the minute. In the privacy of my own home I can brew," he glanced at Hugh who aimed two fingers at his mouth, pretending to induce vomiting at the thought of taking Joe Sampi's herbal medicine.

"I can brew one of my own 'concoctions'."

Hugh wrinkled his nose, he'd never forget the taste of the medicine the old man had prepared for him when he was suffering the effects of smoke inhalation having helped fight a forest fire.

"Are you sure that's wise, Joe?" The vet asked.

One look at the old man's face was enough to tell them his mind was set. It was not up for discussion.

"Once again someone has hurt my Connie. Hugh, not only tried to secure their escape, but he also got into trouble trying to help me." He smiled at the boy as he continued. "I'm grateful for that, but the Sampi's fight their own battles. I can't do that from in here. On a more important note," his eyes travelled to the door, checking it was still closed. "I will need to meet with the elders and commune with the spirits. I must seek guidance on finding a safe location for our thylacine." He turned to face the vet, "You will travel to Hobart, confront the mighty Tasmanian Mining Corporation and shut them down." It was an instruction, not a question.

Whitaker nodded.

"May I ask for one compromise?"

Sampi looked at the vet, waiting to hear his demands.

"Take Napoleon with you. Yes, I know you are fitter than most men half your age, but you almost died. For goodness sake man, you had your spleen and part of your liver removed."

Sampi remained silent for a moment, thoughtful.

"Agreed," he said, his voice little more than a whisper. "I have one suggestion to add to that. Your son," he acknowledged Hugh with a nod of his head, before looking at Connie, "and my granddaughter are no longer children."

A minute ago you said we were a liability, a walking disaster zone! Hugh thought.

"Oh I know we joke they are a danger to themselves," Sampi continued.

Hugh blushed, *How'd he know that's what I was thinking?*

"Sometimes their actions are hot headed and ill-thought out, but they are the actions of young adults. I suggest they accompany Napoleon and me to seek the advice of the aboriginal elders."

Shocked, Hugh dropped into the chair behind him.

"Are you joking?"

Sampi's face clouded for a moment.

"Hugh, you know me better than that. What I have suggested is sacred, it is not to be joked about."

Connie shook her head, "Do you know what an honour this is, Hugh? In particular, for someone who is not of aboriginal descent."

"If I didn't before, I'm sure getting the message. Joe, I don't know what to say."

"You keep telling me, she's your thylacine, here is an opportunity to observe part of the decision process, even if it's on the periphery of the decision making."

Hugh whistled, "I'm gobsmacked."

"The first plan of action is to get me out of here," Sampi whispered in a conspiratorial way, "anyone thought of an escape plan?"

Chapter Twenty-Nine

Having been prodded and poked by his surgeon, Joe Sampi ignored medical advice and discharged himself from the hospital, promising to rest and pledging not to consider returning to his temporary job with the Parks and Wildlife Service until he was re-examined in ten days' time.

Hugh and Connie led the way to where the Land Rover had been parked. Without argument they climbed into the back of the vehicle while Whitaker helped his friend into the front seat. A look of pain flashed across Joe Sampi's face as he eased himself into the vehicle, the effort straining his tender abdomen. Not that he would ever admit that leaving hospital so soon after surgery was not one of his brightest ideas!

As soon as they pulled up outside the cabins, Hugh and Connie hurried into Napoleon's bungalow and crept into the boys bedroom, which had become the temporary home of the thylacine. The three pups were nestled close to their mother, too big to fit in her pouch. George had prepared some fresh meat, which Connie placed in the cage.

They watched as the female thylacine sniffed the offering before dragging it over to the pups.

"At least they are eating," Hugh observed, "I guess that's something."

Connie nodded.

"And she's accepted the pup who was separated from her."

They stood watching the animals for a few minutes. This was the first time they had studied these magnificent creatures in such close proximity. It was an overwhelming experience. It was a joy to see the full beauty of the markings along their flanks which provided the perfect camouflage. It was little wonder that they blended so well with the shadows.

Using Whitaker's mobile, Joe Sampi had called the school to inform them of Connie's accident. In light of the fact she'd been knocked unconscious, he explained the hospital had advised her to rest for a few days.

The call to his daughter was altogether more arduous. She didn't take the news he had discharged himself well. He thought it better not to divulge what had happened to Connie at this stage. His granddaughter hadn't received any life threatening injuries, or required hospitalisation, it was better to tell her mother during her next visit home.

It was decided they would leave for their respective expeditions after breakfast the following morning. Mikey would accompany Whitaker to Hobart to confront the Tasmanian Mining Corporation, leaving George to keep an eye on the ranger's station, feed Boy-Boy and protect the thylacine.

Neither of them complained, both George and Mikey had received confirmation they had been accepted on the trainee ranger's scheme, subject to an interview with Doug Langdon, a virtual done deal. This was the opportunity of a lifetime. At last things were beginning to look up for them.

Later that afternoon, Andrew Whitaker and Mikey stood in the reception area of the Tasmanian Mining Corporation's head office building. In spite of the valiant efforts of the receptionist to send them away, their persistence had resulted in a hastily arranged appointment with Laura Goodman on threat of a phone call to the national press to divulge information they were sure she wouldn't want made public.

"Mr. Whitaker," Goodman's personal assistant walked towards the two men. "It's a pleasure to see you again." She looked at Mikey, waiting to be introduced.

"This is Mikey, I mean Michael Toba, friend and colleague," Whitaker said.

The PA nodded to the younger man and asked them to follow her, leading the way to the elevator and up to Goodman's office.

Laura Goodman pushed a stray hair back into place as she stepped from behind her desk. As usual she looked elegant, dressed in a geometric black and white patterned shift dress, she wouldn't have looked out of place on the pages of a glossy fashion magazine, not spending the day in her office surrounded by paperwork.

"Andrew, may I call you Andrew?"

Whitaker nodded.

Goodman smiled, "Andrew, please take a seat," she pointed to the Chesterfield couch on the opposite side of the coffee table. "May I offer you tea, some coffee perhaps?"

Whitaker shook his head, "No thank you, this isn't a social event."

Goodman's expression clouded for a fleeting second but she managed to mask her surprise as she moistened her lips with the tip of her tongue.

"In which case, how may I help?"

Whitaker glanced at Mikey as if seeking reassurance before starting to speak.

"I am sure the reputation of your corporation is of utmost importance to you."

"Paramount," she interjected.

Whitaker nodded in deferment, "Then I must advise you to listen and concentrate on what I am about to say."

Goodman raised her eyebrows, the false smile on her lips failing to reach her eyes, she wasn't used to being spoken to in such a brusque manner.

"It has been brought to my attention that the Tasmanian Mining Corporation was founded on proceeds from your father's company, Townsend Mines. Your father is Craig Townsend, is he not?"

As if playing for time while she cleared her thoughts, Laura Goodman crossed her elegant legs, the action slow and deliberate.

"I'm not sure what you think you know, Mr. Whitaker," she said, becoming more formal, "but you should be careful what you are implying. It could be construed as slander."

Whitaker smiled, "It's only slander if it's untrue."

Goodman stared at him, unblinking.

"What is it you want?"

"A woman, like you, with her finger on the pulse knows every movement her company makes."

Goodman didn't respond.

"I'd be very surprised if you were not aware that two children – my son and the granddaughter of my close friend, Joe Sampi, ah, I see you are aware of his name," he said, noticing a flicker of recognition in her expression. "Yes, Joe Sampi, the man who suffered a severe bearing at the hands of Lennie Watts and an unknown associate, but I digress. Our children were held against their will, injured and restrained overnight at one of your locations in a building owned by your company."

"I don't know what to say, Mr. Whitaker. This is the first I have heard of your accusation. Do you have any proof to substantiate your claims?"

"Let me see, well there's the medical records for Miss Sampi at Devonport Community Hospital and the bloody big hole we cut in the back of your building to rescue them. Will that do for starters?"

"Are you admitting to criminal damage?"

"Don't get smart with me, madam. My son and his friend were kidnapped and restrained. Stop being crass. You are in real trouble here."

Laura Goodman uncrossed her legs and leant forward.

"What I am about to say, I say without prejudice."

Whitaker ignored Mikey's confused expression.

"Go on."

"What will it take to make this unfortunate situation go away?"

Whitaker leant towards her. Their faces centimetres apart. Keeping his voice devoid of emotion, he started to speak.

"I want the Tasmanian Mining Corporation to pack up and leave Warrugul National Park. I don't care what excuse you make to explain why you are leaving, just leave the area."

"Do you know how much it will cost my company if I close the operation down?"

"I don't know, and I don't care. I thought these were exploratory bore holes. Once drilled and the information extrapolated, a consultative process was to begin. If that was the plan I can't imagine the cost to the company will be too great so far as drilling hasn't started," he said, holding Goodman's gaze as he spoke.

Playing for time, Laura Goodman studied her nails for a moment.

"I will need to consult with my lawyer, legal team and board of directors."

"Ms. Goodman, this isn't up for negotiation."

Goodman gave a curt nod of her head.

"I understand what you are saying, Mr. Whitaker. Now if there is nothing else I can help you with?" She stood, indicating the meeting was at an end, and extended her hand. "It's been a *pleasure*. I'll be in touch in a day or two. May I assume you will refrain from contacting the press in the mean time?"

Without waiting for an answer she walked the two men to the door and showed them out of her office. As they walked towards the elevator she closed the door and leant against it.

"Shit, shit, shit," she muttered, hitting her head against the opaque glass panel as she spoke. "If he thinks I'm going to capitulate to his petty threats he has another thing coming."

As the door to the elevator closed, Mikey turned to face the vet.

"Do you think she knows about the thylacine?"

Whitaker rolled his eyes, "I doubt she misses a trick."

Mikey nodded.

"That's what I thought. Do you think she knows we know about the thylacine?"

Whitaker's expression answered his question for him.

"Yeah, I suppose the hole we left in the wall is a bit of a giveaway, Hugh and Connie's escape and the disappearance of the cage says it all, huh? I wonder why she didn't mention it."

"I think I know the answer to that, Mikey. If anyone discovered the thylacine, she'd be shut down in an instant, at least until the potential impact mining would have on one of the world's rarest creatures is assessed. Then with the additional restrictions it would bring, it would be impossible to mine in Warrugul."

"What do you think they'd have done with them if we hadn't rescued them?"

"The thylacine?" The vet shook his head. "I don't want to think about it."

They stepped out of the elevator and headed towards the revolving door.

"Are you going to see Angie? I can wander around for an hour or so. There's plenty to keep me occupied?

The vet sighed, "I'd love to, but she's working a double shift, she's got some time to make up. She doesn't get off duty until seven tonight."

Meanwhile, with Joe Sampi acting as navigator, Napoleon drove the truck in the opposite direction to that taken by Andrew Whitaker. No one voiced their hope the vehicle would make the journey, but with the Land Rover un-drivable, they had no choice but to use Joe's battered truck.

The damage to the Land Rover was waiting to be assessed by the insurance company, it was probable it would be written off as the front of the vehicle had been caved in, the front axle was damaged and the exhaust was hanging on by a prayer. Sampi's assailants, as front seat occupants at the time of the impact, were lucky not to have suffered serious injury themselves.

Hugh and Connie spent much of the journey engrossed in conspiratorial whispers. They couldn't get over the fact they'd been allowed to accompany the older men to discuss the future of the thylacine with tribal elders from across the territory.

Arriving at their destination, Sampi pointed to where Napoleon should park, alongside an old white van. To a casual observer it would be difficult to decide which set of wheels was in most need of a paint job!

Joe Sampi tapped on the back window of the cab, indicating the kids could disembark. They hurried round to the door of the cab.

"I want you to listen to what I have to say," Sampi said, his tone grave. "I know I don't have to emphasise the seriousness of this occasion. You are to be on your best behaviour. I'm not going to tell you to wait until you are spoken to, or to be seen and not heard, you are old enough to know how to act. Be sensible and don't let yourselves down. Passion is acceptable," he directed his comment to Hugh as he continued, "stupidity and rudeness isn't."

Hugh nodded as he listened to the old man.

"What you are about to see is not to be discussed with friends at school, appear on that face thingy or whatever you kids call it. You may see or hear things you find strange; I don't care; you must remember this is an honour."

Connie nodded, "Yes grandfather."

"Hugh?"

"What... oh sorry, Joe, I wasn't being rude, I was trying to take it all in. It's so, so fantastic!"

A slight smile threatened to erupt across the old man's face but he turned away as he hauled himself out of the cab.

"Can you grab my rucksack for me, Hugh?"

Napoleon closed his eyes and turned to face the sun, relishing the heat on his skin. He filled his lungs and sighed.

"It's been so long since I was here," he said to his friend. "It feels good to be back; it's as if I've come home."

Sampi slapped his friend on the back.

"I know how you feel; it gets me like that too." He gave the parked vehicles a cursory glance. "It looks like we're the last to arrive."

Following the two older men, Hugh and Connie pointed out things of interest to one another. Joe Sampi headed towards a narrow gorge between two huge stone monoliths.

"This is what I expect Ayres rock to look like, only much, much bigger."

"Do you mean Uluru?"

Hugh looked confused, it was a word he hadn't heard before.

"I didn't know the rock had been renamed."

Napoleon smiled, "Not renamed, Hugh, the monument has reverted back to its aboriginal name."

Hugh nodded his understanding.

"I hate to disappoint you, but this is nothing like Uluru, that has a circumference of over nine kilometres, this is tiny in comparison."

Hugh placed his hands on the rock on either side of the gorge to steady himself as they walked along the narrow slope, the going made harder by debris from a recent landslide littering the floor.

Sampi steadied himself with his left hand, while his right lay across his stomach as if protecting the area where he'd had his recent operation.

"Are you ok?" Napoleon asked, his words almost inaudible in an attempt not to alarm the kids walking behind them, their excited chatter hanging in the air. He looked at his friend, concern evident on his face.

Sampi smiled, "I'm fine, a little tired, but otherwise, okay. This is something I have to do, you know that."

Napoleon nodded.

"It's something we both have to do."

The two men continued in amiable silence, enjoying the youthful exuberance exuded by the kids.

The narrow gorge opened into a wide expanse. The cliffs encompassing the basin towered overhead like leviathans made of rock. Their stony silence had borne witness to secret ceremonies for thousands of years. Aboriginal Tasmanians had met on this sacred site for as long as man had inhabited the island, with a single break at the end of the nineteenth century following the decimation of the indigenous population which had no resistance to disease brought by white settlers. Ceremonies resumed in the nineteen twenties when families like the Sampi's and Toba's emigrated from the mainland to protect the thylacine when it became apparent that the white settlers were hunting and trapping the magnificent creature to extinction.

Chapter Thirty

Hugh stopped dead, a group of men ranging in age from that of George and Mikey to Joe Sampi, stood in a circle as if waiting for their arrival. No one seemed surprised to see they had accompanied the two older men, but he couldn't help feeling a little intimidated by their welcoming committee.

An old man, his tight curly hair, white with age, stepped forward. Beaming, he shook hands with both Joe Sampi and Napoleon, the greeting warm and affectionate.

"When news of your unfortunate," the old man paused for a second as if choosing his words with care, "err, '*accident*' reached us, we were concerned to say the least. It is good to see you, Joe. It pains me when one of our number suffers an unprovoked attack."

Sampi looked away. Hugh couldn't remember seeing him blush with embarrassment before.

"I challenged two lads, asking them to extinguish their cigarettes with care. Perhaps, for someone with such apparent low intelligence, I seemed provocative, I don't know."

Hugh tried to smother a snigger, it was true, Lennie Watts couldn't be described as a brain of Britain, or in Watts' case it was more appropriate to say brain of Tasmania!

"Oi!" He exclaimed as Connie poked him in the back, reminding him of her grandfather's warning.

The old man looked straight at Hugh.

"Are these the young people you have told us so much about?"

Hugh felt his face redden, *Joe has been taking about us? Wow!*

Sampi looked at his granddaughter and then at Hugh and smiled, "Let me introduce you," he said stepping backwards. "This is my granddaughter, Connie Sampi, and this young man is Hugh Whitaker. Hugh, Connie, this is Jacob Rookh, known with affection as Uncle Jac."

Connie shook Uncle Jac's hand, "It's nice to meet you, Mr. Rookh."

The old man grinned, "It's Uncle Jac to my family and friends, this old bird is part of my family, so that extends to you, little lady," he said, nodding at her grandfather as he spoke. "That goes for you too, young man."

Hugh shook the hand offered by the old man, "Thanks, Mr. Um, I mean, Uncle Jac."

Each man in turn was introduced to the kids, names were announced but there was little hope of remembering them all. Hugh felt as if he was buzzing, a mixture of euphoria and anticipation coursing through his veins. It was as much as he could do to prevent himself from pinching his arm to make sure he was awake. But if he did that he might discover this is a dream and he was still in Warrugul - that would be untenable.

Joe Sampi explained he and Napoleon were going to accompany the elders to commune with the spirits. It was a ceremony seeped in mysticism and secrecy which could not be observed or participated in by outsiders. He squeezed Hugh's shoulder and brushed the top of Connie's head with his lips as he noticed their downcast expressions.

"I can imagine how you feel. I know its poor consolation but it's a great honour to be permitted to meet the elders here.

"I know, it's just..."

"It's just every time you get so far it's as if the thylacine is snatched from your care," Sampi said, finishing off the boy's sentence for him as if reading his mind. "I am going to leave you in the capable hands of Eddie Kwatkwat."

Sampi waved a young Aboriginal Tasmanian over. Hugh guessed he was a couple of years older than Mikey. He couldn't help feeling a little jealous at the glance Connie gave him. There was no doubt he was a good looking lad, his muscular torso evident through his tight fitting tee shirt.

Hugh sucked in his stomach, pulling himself up to his full height as Eddie walked over, he raised his hand in greeting, flashing them an easy smile.

"Wow, I love your ink," Connie enthused, pointing to the cuff of blue-black artwork circling the young man's wrist.

"Thanks," Eddie raised his arm so she could get a better look. The intricate design was a mixture of tribal symbols intertwined with some mythical creatures neither of them recognised.

"What's that?" She asked.

Eddie pointed to each of the three creatures on his wrist, "That's a bunyip, said to lurk in creeks and billabongs, this is Akurra a great snake deity often associated with the Rainbow Serpent, and here, of course, is the Tassie tiger."

Hugh pretended not to be interested, but snuck a surreptitious look, he had to admit the art work was impressive. He doubted his father would let him get a tattoo until he was at least forty- boring fart.

"Can I look at the cave paintings?" He heard himself ask.

Eddie turned to look at the rock face, "The Petroglyphs? Sure."

"Petroglyphs," Hugh repeated.

Eddie nodded.

"Come on, I'll show you."

Hugh was absorbed by the aboriginal art. Eddie explained the oldest examples dated back thousands of years, they had been etched into the rock using stone tools.

Hugh nodded.

"Joe told me the aboriginal people died out after the white settlers arrived".

Eddie bowed his head as he started to speak, "It's a tragedy suffered by many indigenous people such as the Aztec, Inca's etc. Living in isolation as they did, they had no resistance to diseases conquerors and settlers brought with them. Some of these civilisations were decimated not only by killers such as smallpox and tuberculosis but sometimes, something as simple as the common cold. But then the new countries bit back. Settlers died from eating poisonous plants, fruits and berries or were killed by predators, but these numbers were small in comparison to the countless indigenous people killed."

Hugh took a step closer to examine the faint scratches carved into the rock face. They were a little hard to see in the harsh sunlight. Eddie called them over to a slight overhang.

"Here, it'll be easier to see the drawings in the shadows. See here, that's a kangaroo, and here, a wombat."

"Hugh, look, a thylacine!" Connie exclaimed with excitement. She glanced at Eddie for confirmation.

Hugh went to trace the creature with the tip of his finger but Eddie slapped his hand away.

"Ouch, what did you do that for?"

"Sorry, Hugh. I didn't mean to use as much force as that, it was a bit of an automatic reaction. The carvings are too precious to touch."

Hugh couldn't hide his embarrassment.

"Nah, I should have realised. I'm sorry, Eddie."

"Here, look at these," Connie called from the other side of the basin.

"This artwork is much more recent," Eddie explained, walking across to where Connie was standing. "These date back to the nineteen thirties."

"Ah that's not long after families like the Sampi's and Toba's started to return to Tasmania?"

Eddie nodded, "You know a lot about our history, young man."

"What sort of paint did they use, that's if it's paint as we know it?" Connie asked.

"It's ochre, charcoal and clay." Eddie glanced at Hugh, he was absorbed with what he was telling him. "The pigments are ground with a grindstone and mixed with a binding agent such as water, saliva, egg white, animal fat, even blood to form a paste. It's also applied to the body as decoration for ceremonies or nowadays for tourist displays." He side-stepped a couple of paces. "Look here. This is a series of paintings which tells the dreaming or mythical story of how the thylacine got its stripes."

Fascinated, Hugh crouched on his haunches and asked Eddie to tell them the tale.

Eddie pointed to the paintings, "It goes something like this... the Tiger loved to sing. One day he was singing at the top of his voice but it was too loud for his friends. Each in turn told him to be quiet as he passed by, Platypus, Bunyip, Kanga and Great Bird. Walking towards the river, Tiger noticed a fire burning in the forest, he called to his friends but, fed up with his singing, they had left the area. It was down to Tiger to save the forest."

Eddie's hands hovered over the paintings as he interpreted the art work.

"Tiger ran backwards and forwards to the river carrying water to extinguish the fire, each time, the flames burnt a strip of fur along his back. At last the fire was out, but poor Tiger had lost his voice, he would never sing again and his fur was burnt and singed with stripes of soot which, as you know, can still be seen today."

Grinning, Hugh turned round and looked at Connie. The story was perfect.

"How do you stop tourists coming here?" He asked.

Eddie shrugged, "It's not easy. At least this is way off the usual tourist trails."

Hugh nodded, they had driven along a rough track for a couple of kilometres, he doubted he'd be able to find it again.

"There's a small sign at the top of the gorge asking that visitors respect our culture and heritage. This is a very spiritual place especially as Aboriginal people believe in animism."

"Animism?" Hugh repeated, getting more and more confused.

Connie nodded, "It means we embrace the belief that the spiritual and physical worlds are one. We believe that animals have souls and spirits, but also plants, trees and geological features such as stone monoliths and rivers."

Hugh was transfixed.

"Bet you think that's stupid."

Hugh was vehement, he shook his head, "Not at all. I love the thought of animals having souls, it's, it's kinda comforting and I know a lot of the owners of Dad's patients would be consoled by that too."

Eddie continued, "These mountains have a special spiritual significance for us because of the gorge and basin formation, the way the gorge opens is representative of a womb, the stone monoliths protecting the unborn. Here spirits are safe and protected."

"It's funny, that's how I feel, safe and protected too. I felt it as soon as we arrived. I feel as though my mother is nearby."

Connie touched his arm, "That's a wonderful thought, Hugh."

Hugh nodded as he explained to Eddie that she had died when he was little, she'd committed suicide when she could no longer take the pain from a brain tumour.

Eddie was quiet for a moment before whispering, "She is very proud of you, Hugh."

His words hung in the air as Hugh spun on his heel and walked away, too choked with emotion to respond.

"Um, I don't know about you, but I'm starving," said Connie, looking to deflate the charged atmosphere.

"They could be gone ages yet," said Eddie. "I've got some dried moon bird in my bag if you want to share?"

"Moon bird?" Said Hugh, "I've never heard of that."

"Yolla, or moon bird, as it's more commonly called, is an aboriginal delicacy," Connie explained. "They are now harvested on a commercial basis, or at least the chicks are. The meat is eaten and the oil from their stomachs used to make health products such as vitamins as it is high in omega compounds."

Eddie removed a plastic food container from his bag and prised the lid off. He offered it to Connie and then to Hugh.

Hugh sniffed the meat and then nibbled the edge, "Guess there's a first time for everything," he joked.

"Don't be offended by him smelling it," Connie laughed, "he always does that when he's trying something new."

"It doesn't taste too bad, but I don't think I'd rush to have it again. I've never heard of moon bird or whatever its traditional name is."

"Yolla," Connie repeated.

"You might know it as short tailed shearwater," Eddie explained.

"Oh yuk, that's disgusting!"

Eddie looked at Connie and raised his eyebrows.

"Don't worry about him," she said, "he's just a mad pom, I think it's delish!"

Joe Sampi emerged from the cave, his torso above his bandaged midriff was daubed with symbols in red and yellow ochre. He looked exhausted.

Connie gasped as her grandfather lent on the rock for a moment, steadying himself before walking over to join them. In spite of the red ochre on his face, his complexion was pale, almost ashen, these ceremonies were arduous and on top of his recent surgery, she could see he was shattered. Napoleon followed two or three paces behind his friend, a look of concern on his face.

Hugh wanted to hear what had taken place, but it was clear Sampi was in no state to be cross examined with him firing questions at him.

"Are we going home?"

Napoleon nodded, "Yes Hugh. We'll tell you everything when we get home, that way Joe can rest on the journey and we don't have to repeat ourselves for your dad and my lads."

Disappointment washed over him, but Hugh nodded. He felt as though he was about to burst with unasked questions but even he could see Sampi wasn't up to it at that moment.

Connie thanked Eddie for his time, shaking her head when he asked for her number, explaining they didn't have a phone, but jotted her address onto a scrap of paper for him.

"It's been great, Eddie, well except for the moon bird," Hugh said, with a wry grin.

Connie hung back as her grandfather and Napoleon made their way back along the narrow gorge.

"Hugh."

He stopped, waiting for her to catch up.

"I'm worried about my grandpappy."

"Me too, it looks as though it's been a bit much for him. I feel I'm gonna burst with the questions I have but as Napoleon says, the ride home is an opportunity for Joe to rest, perhaps get some sleep."

Connie forced a smile but it was clear from her expression she was worried sick. Hugh reached over and pushed a stray hair out of her eyes.

"He's gonna be fine, Connie," he said with more conviction than he felt. "He is as strong as an ox; we both know that. Most people would still be flat on their back, but not Joe. I think we forget how old he is, but I am sure he'll be fine. He's strong, real strong."

The journey home was subdued. Sampi slept for much of the way, but once they had reached the motorway it was plain sailing, and Napoleon no longer needed a navigator.

Hugh was wrapped up in his own thoughts, he'd pondered every scenario he could think of. Not knowing what the elders had decided was eating him up. The fate of the thylacine, his thylacine had been decided by a group of strangers, and although he and Connie had been on the periphery, they weren't a part of the decision making process. Was Joe well enough to fight on their behalf? He knew they couldn't participate or witness the spiritual ceremony, but no one had asked their opinion.

Pull yourself together, Hugh. You're thinking like a spoilt brat, you know Joe better than this and you haven't given him any credit. What was it he said... Hugh wracked his brains as he tried to remember... *Ah yes, Joe, Napoleon and the boys stayed, in spite of the lack of work and prospects, they stayed to protect the thylacine.* Hugh nodded his head as he thought, *Joe would fight for the thylacine until his dying breath.*

Connie gave Hugh a funny look.

"What are you doing?" She asked, "you look like a nodding donkey."

Hugh laughed, "Well you called me a crazy pom, I was just thinking, that's all, just thinking to myself.

It was nine pm before they pulled up outside the cabins. Boy-Boy came charging out of Joe Sampi's cabin, as usual barking like a banshee, his tail a blur as it wagged from side to side. With the thylacine in the boy's bedroom, it was decided the scruffy mongrel should stay with the Sampi's so he didn't add to the thylacine's distress.

Hugh leapt from the side of the truck and hurried to open the cab door for Joe. The Aboriginal Tasmanian smiled, he looked better after his rest.

"I'm not ready for my wooden box yet, young man," he joked.

"Ha, I'd like to see you drink one of your medicinal concoctions yourself if you were about to be pushing up daisies," Hugh replied with a laugh.

Sampi aimed a playful punch at the boy's arm.

"You're too cheeky for your own good, young Whitaker!"

Hugh's father, Mikey and George waited to greet them, both parties had a lot to tell.

"How's the thylacine and her pups?"

Mikey and George exchanged glances. Mikey had won the bet; Hugh hadn't even crossed the threshold before asking after the animals.

"Fine, Hugh, they're all fine. George says they're eating well and drinking, so they seem none the worse after their ordeal."

"We thought you'd be hungry so George and Mikey have been practising their culinary skills, they've made some sandwiches, there's the choice of cheese, egg or tuna," Whitaker explained, reaching over the table and removing the silver foil from the plates. There's coke in the fridge. Joe, Napoleon do you want a stubby or a hot drink?"

Joe Sampi put his finger to his lips in a conspiratorial way, "Don't tell my surgeon, but I could murder a cold stubby, please."

Tucking into the plate of sandwiches, Hugh was amazed his father had the forethought to provide food for their arrival, with his stomach beginning to think his throat had been cut he'd assumed he'd be left to make himself a snack when he got home.

Sampi closed his eyes for a moment and relaxed in the chair.

"Joe, oh sorry," Hugh grimaced as Sampi opened his eyes. "I didn't mean to wake you."

"Just resting my eyes, boy, just resting my eyes." Sampi shuffled in his chair. "How did you get on with the elusive Ms. Goodman, Andrew?"

Whitaker shrugged, "How would you say it went, Mikey?"

The. young Tasmanian swallowed the food he'd been chewing, "She's a tough old bird."

I bet she wouldn't be pleased to be referred to as old, Hugh thought to himself.

"She's hard to read."

Whitaker agreed, "She said all the right things to begin with. She seemed surprised to learn Connie was your granddaughter, but she knew who you were, at least she recognised your name so she's been briefed on your attack."

Sampi's expression remained unchanged as the vet continued speaking.

"The old adage 'a leopard doesn't change its spots' rang true with her. It was obvious she takes after her father when she asked what it would take for this unfortunate incident of kidnapping to go away."

Hugh reached for his glass of coke, "Do you think she's knows about the thylacine, Dad?

Whitaker clicked his tongue against the back of his teeth.

"That's a question we asked ourselves, Hugh," he said, nodding in Mikey's direction to include him in the statement. "It was the elephant in the room, so to speak, neither of us mentioned it, but I got the distinct impression she knew all about it."

"That's good then, isn't it?" Hugh asked, his face a picture of innocence.

"I'm not so sure."

Confused, Hugh looked at Sampi, "No one would kill the thylacine, would they?"

Sampi cocked his head to the left a little as he spoke, "I think she is a chip off the old block. She'd do anything to get what she wants."

Hugh looked at Connie, who shook her head, her expression one of desperation, everything was falling apart.

"Your turn," said the vet, "how did you get on, Joe?"

Sampi addressed Hugh, "Do you want to tell your father what you got up to?"

Whitaker, groaned, "Got up to?"

A look of annoyance flashed across his son's face, as usual his old man had jumped to the wrong conclusion.

Sampi held up his hand, "Whoa, that was the wrong choice of words. Better to say do you want to tell your dad what you saw?"

Hugh threw Andrew Whitaker a look that could have turned him to stone. As far as his father was concerned, he'd made his mind up before he knew all the facts.

"Go on, Hugh," Connie urged.

Still annoyed with his father, Hugh started to speak, but it wasn't long before his eyes started to twinkle and he became more animated.

"Joe and Napoleon drove us to a holy site."

"I think spiritual is a better description, Hugh."

Hugh smiled at the old man, "Spiritual," he said in correction. "It was at the end of a narrow gorge, which opened into a basin. The rocks that made up the walls were covered with p, petroglyphs." He looked at the old man to check he'd got that right. "Dad, it was fantastic. We learnt how the thylacine got its stripes, and we tried moon bird, it wasn't great," he said, sticking out his tongue to emphasis the fact.

"He means it was delish," Connie rebuked.

His father smiled, wrinkling his nose.

"Hugh's like me, not always the first to try new foods."

An expectant silence fell over the room as they waited to hear what the elders had decided following the commune with the spirit world.

Sampi drained the rest of his bottle, aware everyone was watching him.

"Elders from communities across Tasmania, as well as three brothers from the mainland met with us at Tjuta. It was an honour and a privilege to commune with so many brothers, but as we know, the issue was of great importance."

A general murmur of agreement rippled around the room as he continued speaking.

"We conversed with the spirits of our ancestors as well as the spirits of animals."

Whitaker raised a sceptical eyebrow, a movement which didn't go un-noticed by the Aboriginal Tasmanians.

"Our rituals and beliefs are based on animism," the old man explained. "We believe that animals, plants and what you class as inanimate objects such as mountains, have spirits, along with rivers and trees."

The vet nodded, "I apologise, I didn't mean to offend."

Sampi continued.

"You are aware that we have tried to protect the thylacine from the moment we realised it was endangered, and have continued to do so long after the rest of the world thought it extinct. We have been able to discredit sightings, destroy evidence, anything to keep our creatures safe. The capture of the thylacine and her pups was our first failure."

"It's not a failure, Joe."

Sampi silenced Hugh with a look. This wasn't the time for interruptions, no matter how well meaning.

"The influx of people the mine will bring if you're warning goes unheeded, will make it almost impossible to protect the thylacine within the park. With the arrival of this season's pups we have twenty-five thylacine living within Wurragul's boundaries."

Connie gasped, "Wow, twenty-five."

Sampi smiled at his granddaughter, "It's been a good year, and before you ask, this isn't the time to show you the others!"

Amused, Hugh smiled, once again Joe Sampi seemed to read their minds.

The Aboriginal Tasmanian paused, his eyes travelled around the room, resting on each of the occupants in turn, they were engrossed in what he was saying.

"Guided by the spirits, it is the decision of the elders that the existence of the thylacine must be made public."

Hugh felt as though he was going to throw up. It was the worst news he could have imagined. If he was rational when it came to the thylacine he'd realise this was the only sensible course of action. It was the only way to protect them.

Aware everyone was watching him, Hugh jumped to his feet.

"That can't happen, Joe, it's not safe."

Sampi nodded, "I understand why you feel like that, Hugh, but let me finish."

"I've gotta get some air."

Chapter Thirty-One

Whitaker got up to follow his son.

"Wait, Andrew, give him five minutes, he'll be back, rest assured."

Whitaker nodded his understanding and took the opportunity to open another bottle of beer, he offered the beverage to Joe Sampi who shook his head.

"I'm fine, thanks. I don't want to push it with the medication I'm on."

"Ha, overdo it and Napoleon will be forced to brew one of your concoctions," Hugh laughed, returning to the room and retaking his place next to Connie.

"Better?"

Hugh nodded, "Guess so."

"Look, you know my grandfather would never put the thylacine in danger. None of us would. Let's hear what he's got to say," she said.

Hugh didn't want to acknowledge his friend was being sensible, as usual, but deep down he knew he was running out of ideas to protect the thylacine.

Sampi gave Hugh a conspiratorial wink, perhaps everything was going to be alright?

"As I was saying, the elders have decided that we make the existence of the thylacine public here in Warrugul."

"What did they suggest?" George asked.

"At no time do we produce an animal for inspection or disclose where they can be found. In the first instance we will take a photo of our female and pups in a non-descript place the authorities can't identify. We'll require reassurance that the thylacine still has the full protection of the Government. We shouldn't forget the one thylacine to obtain that safeguard, if it can be called that, was Benjamin, the last *known* specimen, back in nineteen thirty-six. Once we have those assurances we can disclose the location and ensure Warrugul will be upgraded to a sanctuary. The Tasmanian Mining Corporation will be shut down hook, line and sinker."

The room remained silent while the occupants absorbed Sampi's words. Mikey crammed a handful of chips into his mouth and crunched, the sound shattering the silence, much to the amusement of Hugh and Connie who started to giggle as their friend tried to brush the shower of crumbs he'd produced from his shirt.

"Okay, for the plan to work," Hugh sniggered, "Who do we tell?"

Sampi smiled, their amusement was infectious.

"That's the problem. It has to be someone we trust at a high enough level, who will take our evidence seriously."

"The newspaper, err, what's that awful woman's name?" Mikey clicked his fingers as he tried to remember.

"Patricia Collins?"

Mikey pointed at his father, "That's her, Dad, Patricia Collins."

Sampi and Napoleon shook their heads in unison.

"Good idea, Mikey, but that sort of publicity will cause too much of a furore too soon, people, sightseers, scientists, they'll all come hoping for a sighting. But certain things need to be in place before the hordes arrive," Napoleon explained.

Sampi nodded, "I agree, the marauding hordes, as Napoleon described them, have to be controlled, even if it means new legislation has to be written, but that will take time, and at the moment, time is something we don't have."

As much as he hated what he was hearing, Hugh was forced to admit to himself it was the best plan under the circumstances. Things were beginning to spiral out of their control, and that put the thylacine at risk.

"What about Doug Langdon?" He heard himself suggest.

"Yes, Doug Langdon. He's a good bloke."

Hugh smiled at his father, pleased he supported his suggestion.

"Yes, I agree, Langdon is a reliable, honest man. At least that's how I've always found him, but I think this is something bigger than Langdon can control," mused Sampi, as if thinking aloud.

"But he could be the best person to ask for advice," George suggested.

Sampi looked at Napoleon who nodded, it was a fair idea.

"What are we going to do with the thylacine in the mean time?" Hugh asked.

"They can't be kept here, Hugh. I seem to remember you saying you didn't want them to be gawped at in a zoo."

Hugh grimaced, that was true.

"If Napoleon is up for it, perhaps he can drive me to the far side of the park, we know there are no thylacine there. We'll release them and with a great deal of luck they will stay there and not make their way back. There's a good source of food, so in theory they have no reason to wander far, at least in the short term."

"When will you do it?"

"No time like the present. That's if you are up for it, Napoleon, you've done a lot of driving today?"

"But?"

Sampi ignored Hugh's interruption.

"By the time we get there it'll be about dawn, that'll give them the day to hole up before they start investigating the new territory, with the pups almost weaned, it's ideal."

Not for me, Hugh fumed.

"Grandfather, I'm gonna be off school for a few days, Hugh's suspended, is there any chance we could come with you, *please?*"

Sampi looked over their heads at Hugh's father, the vet nodded his head once.

"It's fine by me," he said.

Hugh threw his father a look of thanks, surprised he had agreed without cajoling and begging.

"Can you call Langdon over, say, for late morning?"

Whitaker nodded, "On what pretext?"

"I'll leave that to you. I'm sure you'll think of something," Sampi said. The old man stood, wavering as if trying to regain his balance.

"Are you sure you are well enough for this, Joe, after everything you've been through today?"

Sampi smiled, "This is something I have to do. It's as important as communing with the spirits."

As the kids were insistent on accompanying them, it was decided they would take Sampi's truck, there was no way they would all fit in the Land Rover along with the cage containing the thylacine.

The cage was hoisted onto the back of the battered vehicle, a blanket draped over it in case they passed other vehicles en-route.

Sampi sorted out some warm clothing for Hugh to borrow. In spite of protesting he was fine, the old man was insistent. The night would be at its coldest just before dawn.

Having administered a sedative to each of the animals to minimise their distress during the journey, the vet watched until the tail lights of the truck disappeared into the blackness.

Napoleon drove towards the agreed destination. They had won the argument with the elders to keep the thylacine in Warrugul, but the male pup and one of the females would be exchanged with animals from other territories when they were older. With such a small population they had to ensure they maintained the genetic diversity of the species. It was an exercise the Aboriginal Tasmanian's undertook every couple of years, made all the more important this year as the thylacine killed in the forest fire before Christmas was a male.

As the sky began to lighten, Napoleon parked the vehicle.

Hugh looked at Connie, "I guess this is it."

"Are you okay?" She asked.

Hugh smiled, but his eyes were full of sadness.

"I'm fine," he lied.

He jumped down and offered Connie a hand to help her down, which she smacked away with a laugh.

"Anyone would think I'd been knocked unconscious," she joked.

In spite of his protests, Joe Sampi was not allowed to help lift the cage to the ground, it was too great a risk following his recent surgery and exertions over the last twenty-four hours.

Between them, Hugh and Connie pulled the cage towards the tail gate while Napoleon pushed from behind.

"Can I touch her?" Hugh asked, turning to face Joe Sampi.

The old man could see the boy was choked with emotion, he nodded, "Be careful, she could bite."

Hugh shook his head, "No, she'd never do that."

He reached through the bar and stroked her elegant head, surprised at how course and gritty her coat felt to the touch. Connie ran her finger down the female's back.

"Beautiful," she whispered, "just beautiful."

Napoleon opened the cage as they stood back. With the effects of the sedative having worn off, the female led the way to freedom, her head held high as she sniffed the air. She stopped and looked back, her eyes locking with Hugh's for a split second before trotting into the undergrowth, her pups following, one of whom stopped by a tree and squatted for a pee.

Connie held up the camera and showed Hugh the photo's she'd taken. She'd borrowed a small digital camera from their neighbour, Aggi's niece.

They stood in silence for several minutes, a silence broken by a series of short sharp yaps.

"What's that?" Hugh demanded.

"That's the sound of the thylacine."

"Is it a distress call?"

Sampi shook his head.

"It can be a call of alarm, but that's our girl establishing her territory. I promise she'll settle, Hugh and we'll keep an eye on them." The old man looked at the boy, "have I ever let you down?"

"No," he replied, his voice little more than a whisper, but in his mind he shouted, *there's always a first time, please don't let it be this.* He felt his body stiffen as Sampi draped his arms around his and Connie's shoulders.

"Come on, it's late. You may be wide awake, but I feel awful."

Connie kissed her grandfather on the cheek.

"You sleep on the way home. Hugh and I have the blanket; we can snuggle into that if we get cold."

Hugh slipped out of Sampi's embrace.

"I'll help you lift the cage back on the truck, Napoleon."

"Good lad."

Chapter Thirty-Two

Hugh looked up from the crossword puzzle he was attempting to complete with Connie.

"Three score and ten, eight letters, starting with L, blank, F."

"G'day to you too, Hugh," Langdon laughed, placing his briefcase on the desk as he squinted at the half-finished puzzle. "L, blank, F." He drummed his fingers on the table as he thought. "Ah, got it, it's 'lifetime'."

"Wow, thanks, Doug. I don't think we'd have ever got that," Connie grinned.

"Why aren't you kids at school?" He asked as the vet and Joe Sampi came out of the lab at the sound of his voice.

Hugh didn't look at his father, there was no point in lying.

"Err, I'm suspended."

"Suspended!" Langdon exclaimed, his tone thick with incredulity. He shook his head. "Dare I ask what for?"

Hugh bowed his head, he felt sheepish to say the least, "Fighting, I'm afraid."

"Way to go, Hugh," Langdon raised his hand for a high five. "I was always scrapping when I was a lad."

Whitaker cleared his throat.

"I hope it's a one-off, I don't condone violence."

Serious, Langdon agreed.

"But kids will be kids," he added, making a thumbs up gesture to Hugh behind his father's back. "And you, miss, you weren't his boxing second were you?" He asked, directing his question to Connie.

"Second what?"

Her grandfather laughed, "That's the person who aids the boxer in between rounds, rubs them down, gives them a drink, that sort of thing, they are sometimes called a corner man, darl."

"Ah, I see. No, I wasn't his second," she laughed, "I'm off school because I had an accident."

Langdon's face clouded.

"I don't think I've ever met such calamity prone children."

Whitaker concurred, "Tell me about it."

Langdon perched on the corner of the desk and looked at Sampi for a moment before speaking. Hugh could see from the ranger's expression, he was concerned.

"Is this the best place for you, Joe, being so soon after your surgery? You were injured working for me, I'm happy to pay you a retainer while you recuperate?"

Sampi's face clouded at the mention of money, but he masked his expression before responding, "I wouldn't be anywhere else, Doug."

"He's fair dinkum, Doug, as strong as an ox!" Hugh quipped.

Connie stared at her friend, laughing, "You sound so funny when you try and talk like an Aussie," she giggled, "it sounds wrong with your accent."

"Where's Napoleon's lads?"

"Outside," said the vet, "shall I give them a shout?"

Langdon twisted off the cap from a bottle of water while he waited.

"G'day," said Mikey in greeting as he led the way into the office, followed by his brother and father.

"I've got good news for you both."

The boys exchanged glances.

"You are both accepted on the training programme."

"No way," George yelled, punching the air.

"That's fantastic, Doug," said Mikey. "What about the interviews we were supposed to have?"

Langdon waved his question away.

"I've got your offer letters with me. There'll be an induction programme in Hobart, which is why I need Joe at his best and then, well, that's a way off down the line." He handed a letter to each of them as Hugh slapped them on the back. It had been the news they had been waiting for.

"I'm sorry I've stolen your thunder, Joe. Andrew said you had something important to tell me, but I wanted to tell the lads as soon as I arrived."

Napoleon was reading the letter over his son's shoulder.

"It's fine, Doug. You've made their day."

"They got the offers on merit, Joe. I've been impressed with the work they've done over the last weeks."

"We heard the Tasmanian Mining Corporation was pulling out," Whitaker said.

Langdon looked puzzled.

"Oh, that's news to me."

Whitaker turned to look at his colleague.

"What makes you think that, Andrew?"

"I had a conversation with Laura Goodman yesterday and that's the distinct impression I got."

Langdon sipped his water, "Strange, I got a call first thing this morning to say they'd be in a position to start drilling the bore holes by the end of the week."

Hugh gasped but was silenced by a frown from his father.

"Is there a problem I should know about?"

George closed the door to the office. They didn't want to risk being overheard.

Langdon glanced around the room, a worried look creased his face.

"Wow, I'm feeling a little nervous."

The strained silence was broken by the sound of Langdon's mobile. He tapped his pockets to locate it before switching it off.

"They can leave a message," he said. "Is someone going to tell me what the problem is?"

Hugh was about to speak but his father stopped him, "It'll be better coming from Joe."

Hugh nodded, his father was talking sense.

"You'd better sit down again, Doug. What we've got to say is going to take an open mind."

"Don't tell me, you've seen a flying saucer," the ranger joked in an attempt to make light of the situation. He'd known the Aboriginal Tasmanians for many years and never seen them so serious.

"It's not a joking matter, Doug. Little green men could be easier to explain." Sampi said, opening a drawer in the desk and removing a large envelope, which he handed to the ranger.

Langdon slipped his finger under the flap and eased it open, pulling out the printed page face down, adding to the atmosphere of suspense. He licked his lips, "I'm almost frightened to look."

"Go on," Hugh urged. "Look at the picture."

With deliberation, Langdon turned the page over. Stunned, he studied each of the four images in turn.

"Oh my goodness!"

He stared deep into Sampi's eyes. The old man returned his stare.

"The photos are genuine. The originals are on this stick," Sampi passed the ranger a USB stick explaining that Connie had downloaded the photographs for him.

It was clear from Langdon's face he was gobsmacked. Hugh smiled to himself, remembering his reaction when he'd seen the thylacine for the first time, it was the most amazing experience of his life.

Langdon looked at each of the photographs again, lingering over the last image of the female thylacine looking back before leading her pups away. He shook his head.

"It's a thylacine. I don't know what to say, it's a friggin' thylacine." He glanced around the room. "I can't believe what I'm looking at." He stared at the page, shaking his head in disbelief. "How long," the words caught in his throat as his mouth went dry. "How long have you known or was this a chance encounter?"

"I saw her for the first time before Christmas," Hugh smiled.

"I suppose it co-incided with your accident when you broke your arm. No, don't tell me, I don't think I want to know." Langdon closed his eyes and held his head in his hands. "I'm guessing you and Napoleon have known for longer?" He asked, directing his question at the Aboriginal Tasmanian's.

Joe Sampi remained silent for a moment, as if thinking about his answer.

"Now the secret is out, there is no point in lying. I'm going to say the same as I said to Hugh and his father, the aboriginal community have kept the secret of the thylacine since before the death of Benjamin."

"The last known specimen?" Langdon interrupted.

Sampi nodded as he continued.

"Unlike the Tasmanian Government, we recognised the danger signs at the beginning of the twentieth century. The thylacine was becoming rarer, the numbers the settlers were trapping were getting lower and lower. Our families moved from the mainland, along with other indigenous native families to protect the thylacine. We couldn't allow a spiritual creature to disappear while we had breath in our bodies."

Langdon nodded.

"I have no idea how you managed to keep this a secret."

Napoleon smiled, "It hasn't been easy, it's gotten harder as the island population grew."

"Imagine how we felt when we heard about the discovery of Scandium," Hugh interrupted, he couldn't keep quiet any longer.

Langdon swore before apologising to the kids for his bad language.

Hugh and Connie laughed, they'd heard and used a lot worse.

"The Mining Corporation know about the thylacine," said the vet.

Langdon's jaw fell open.

"I don't understand."

Whitaker explained about the events leading to Hugh and Connie's capture for 'snooping' around the mine site, and their subsequent rescue.

Langdon held his hands up, "This is so much to take in. Are you telling me the Tasmanian Mining Corporation captured a thylacine and didn't inform me?"

"Three," Connie corrected, "they captured the female and two of her pups."

"W...w... What happened to the third pup?" Langdon asked, looking at the photo again.

"Mikey and I found it, wandering alone, that's when we realised we had a problem."

"I understand. I think. And it seems there is still a problem. Laura Goodman's company captured three protected animals and didn't inform the Parks and Wildlife service. I may be wrong but the evidence suggests the corporation was prepared to put profit ahead of the law and the conservation of one of the world's rarest animals. That's before we factor in the illegal restraint of two children."

Hugh was finding it difficult to contain his excitement. *Yea!* He yelled in his head, *this was fantastic*, Langdon's responses were more than he could have hoped for. He turned to face Connie, her eyes shone with happiness, it was obvious she was as thrilled as he was.

"What happens now?" He heard himself ask.

Langdon took another swig from his bottle of water.

"I know you've produced these photos and they're brilliant," he added with haste. "But there will have to be a formal investigation."

Aghast, Hugh stared at the ranger.

"What, what's wrong with just showing the photos?"

"He's right, Hugh," said Joe Sampi. "Photos can be faked or doctored. Look at what film makers can do - they produce environments from other planets, extra-terrestrials, ghosts, etc. It wouldn't be difficult to produce a credible photo of a thylacine. I'm not saying we are going to renege on what I said earlier, the conditions laid down by the elders, but we may need to adapt."

Hugh nodded, in his head he was shouting *I give up. What the hell do I have to do to keep the thylacine safe and secret!*

Langdon was observant, "I can see you're troubled, Hugh."

Hugh couldn't help thinking he should let rip and tell the ranger what he was thinking. He was aware everyone was staring at him so perhaps this wasn't the right time to bare his soul.

Langdon took control of the situation, "I understand you are worried. Even in the time I've known about the thylacine, what, all of ten minutes, it's apparent how you feel, Hugh, and you too, Connie," he added. "As for the safe welfare of the thylacine, I don't know what assurances I can give you to allay your fears. The investigation into your discovery has to take place to give it credibility and assure the world that the thylacine is still alive." He paused for a moment to wipe his forehead. "Look, I'm dripping in sweat, I'm so excited. I think this is the biggest thing since the discovery of the okapi! Bigger, actually. Once the investigation endorses your evidence, the thylacine will have the full protection of the Tasmanian Government behind it."

"Will an ark population be created?"

Langdon smiled at the lad.

"I think you're jumping the gun a bit, Hugh. The aboriginal community has done a fantastic job by all accounts. With their help, various assessments will need to take place to establish the population level and the genetic diversity, but that's a way off yet, I could go on and on.

"Hang on a minute, Doug."

The ranger looked at the vet.

"There's one thing Hugh is very worried about, he's frightened the thylacine will end up in the zoo or being gawped at and poked by scientists."

Langdon shook his head.

"Don't worry, Hugh. We'll be taking the advice of the experts," he nodded towards Sampi and Napoleon as he spoke. "These guys have done a fantastic job. I'm sure any decisions we make will be in full consultation with the aboriginal community."

Following a phone conversation with one of his most trusted colleagues, Doug Langdon returned to Warrugul with Kennedy Smith the next day.

Hugh and Connie hurried to the ranger's station as soon as they were aware of the news. They burst through the door in time to hear Langdon insisting they were taken to where the thylacine had been spotted.

"No. That's not what we agreed. I don't understand why the photographic evidence isn't enough?" Hugh exclaimed, his fists clenching into tight balls at his sides.

"Ah, you must be Hugh," Smith observed, "and Connie?" He added, looking over the boy's head. In spite of his recent growth spurt, Connie was still a couple of centimetres taller than him.

Not expecting the stranger to know their names, Hugh became flustered.

"Err, yes, um pleased to meet you," he stuttered, looking at the short man standing in front of him.

Kennedy Smith was immaculate, his ranger's uniform looked as though it was a bespoke made to measure outfit. He would have seemed more in place in a trading room than out in the field protecting the environment.

Langdon's colleague extended his manicured hand to each of them in turn.

"I've heard a lot about you."

Hugh raised an eyebrow.

Smith raised a hand, "Don't worry it's all good, and without you taking it the wrong way, for two youngsters, you've behaved in a remarkable way. I'm trying to impress on Mr. Sampi the importance of letting us see the thylacine. We need to substantiate these stunning photos. And before you voice the arguments I can see in your eyes, I believe the evidence you've produced. It is the best I have ever seen, but we need more."

Hugh was bewildered, he didn't know what to think.

Sampi sat behind the desk, his hands pressed together, deep in thought. After several minutes he started to speak.

"I'm a good judge of character. I think you are honest. Doug Langdon appears to vouch for you and that's good enough for me. I am going against what we decided with the elders of the community, but if Napoleon is in agreement we will take you to where we sighted the thylacine."

Hugh tried to mask his expression, but not before Connie caught a glimpse of the surprise evident in his eyes.

"However," Sampi continued, the word hanging in the air as he looked from one ranger to the other. "There is one condition, and this is non- negotiable!"

"Name it," Smith demanded. It was clear he was finding it hard to contain his excitement.

"You will be blindfolded."

Smith stamped his foot like a petulant child, "Don't be absurd."

Sampi angled his head as he spoke.

"That is the condition I make, and I repeat it is non-negotiable!"

Smith looked at his colleague.

"We agree," said Langdon, responding for both of them.

Sampi directed his attention to Hugh and Connie, "Before you ask, the answer is yes. You can both come too."

"Yippee!" Hugh muttered under his breath.

The day dragged. Hugh couldn't stop himself checking the clock every few minutes. Langdon and Smith took the opportunity to accompany Napoleon to the mine site, returning with the news that Laura Goodman had moved heavy machinery on site during the course of the day. A recruitment company had been engaged to employ more casual labour. It was imperative the rangers started their investigation into the sighting as soon as possible.

For Hugh, the afternoon couldn't pass soon enough. In spite of joining Connie on a ride into town to complete a few errands for her grandfather, he was agitated. They would both be returning to school on Monday, there was no way he could settle into his regular routine knowing he hadn't done as much as possible to ensure the safety of the thylacine.

With the vet driving, Joe Sampi sitting alongside him and Langdon and Smith blindfolded in the back of the Land Rover, Napoleon followed in Langdon's vehicle with Hugh and Connie as they made their way to the release site.

On Sampi's instruction the ranger's removed their blindfolds, blinking in an attempt to focus in the evening sunlight.

"I don't know about you but I feel like I've stepped into a 007 movie," Smith whispered to his colleague as he smoothed down his hair, "everything's so cloak and dagger!"

"Are you okay?" Joe Sampi asked as the two men tried to acclimatise to the light, "I don't want you falling and breaking your necks."

Smith grinned, "Apart from the blindfold giving everything the aura of a James Bond adventure I feel like a kid in a candy shop, I'm so excited."

As Napoleon started to lead the way to the release site, Joe Sampi whispered to Whitaker.

"I can't help feeling the insistence on seeing this place is to satisfy Smith's personal needs rather than substantiate the sighting!"

Whitaker nodded, "The blindfolds were a good idea, Joe. At least they won't have a clue where they are."

Catching the group's attention, Sampi explained there was no guarantee the thylacine would have remained in the immediate vicinity. They could have moved on while establishing their new territory.

Kennedy Smith scanned the area trying to memorise trees and landmarks, but with little success, one group of trees looked very much like the next.

"Don't waste your time," Napoleon said, "the blindfolds will disorientate you when you put them back on again. You won't remember."

Smith grinned, "You can't blame a guy for trying. I don't mind admitting I will be so disappointed if we don't see them."

"Don't even go there," his colleague warned. "I don't want to tempt fate."

"I didn't peg you as superstitious, Doug," Whitaker replied.

Langdon threw him a withering look.

"Andrew, as a rule I'm not, but if there's a chance to see an animal the world thinks are extinct I don't want to put the kybosh on it in any way."

"Hark at them," whispered Connie.

Hugh swivelled to face them, "They sound like a couple of kids."

Connie giggled, "What, like us you mean?"

"This is where we let them go," Napoleon announced.

Langdon shivered.

"Cold?" The vet asked

Langdon dismissed the idea, "Na, just excited."

The vet smirked, "Yeah, the thylacine gets you like that."

"Make yourself comfortable," Sampi instructed. "You could be in for a long wait."

Langdon and his colleague talked in excited whispers for about an hour until the novelty of waiting wore off.

Smith shivered, "It's getting cold. If they don't turn up soon it'll be too dark to see anything," he said, his voice tinged with frustration.

"I don't think you'll be disappointed. Look." Napoleon pointed to a thicket of trees towering over an expanse of dense undergrowth. "Left of those," he added.

Two of the pups fell out of the bushes as they wrestled with one another.

"Where!" Smith exclaimed, a little on the loud side.

The animals froze.

Hugh shook his head, *call yourself a ranger,* he thought to himself.

Smith stared, transfixed, as the female crept out to join her pups, her nostrils flaring as she sniffed the air.

"Oh my God, oh my God," Smith repeated over and over.

Langdon poked him in the ribs, "Shut up," he hissed through clenched teeth. "You're gonna frightened them off. I thought you were experienced at this?"

Mesmerised, Hugh watched in silence. The sight of 'his' thylacine never failed to amaze him. He was as awestruck as the two men beside him, witnessing the spectacle for the first time.

"Stunning, aren't they?" Said Hugh.

They watched in silence until the female led her pups back into the undergrowth, pausing as she rubbed her body against one of the trees. Smith and Langdon strained to get a last glimpse of them, but to no avail, they had disappeared.

Joe Sampi was the first to break the silence.

"We've kept our end of the bargain. What happens now?"

"First thing in the morning, Kennedy and I will file a report."

"It won't get lost in the system, will it?"

Langdon smiled.

"Hugh, it never fails to amaze me, what lack of faith you have in the establishment for one so young."

He shrugged.

"I guess Connie and I have learnt the hard way. We know how much the thylacine is worth."

"But *once* the sightings are made public, as soon as the appropriate *protection* is put in place," Sampi said, emphasising the points as he spoke, "the thylacine will be safe from exploitation."

"Don't take this the wrong way, but as much as I hate to admit it, they might be safer than when we were responsible for them, Joe."

A sadness clouded Joe Sampi's eyes.

"I never thought I'd hear you admit that, Hugh, but I agree, things are different now. The arrival of Ms. Goodman has seen to that."

Hugh was thoughtful for a moment.

"How do you gather evidence to substantiate their existence?"

Landon deferred to his colleague to explain, he had the experience of investigating reported sightings.

"The photos are fantastic, and their resolution is so high they will be verified as authentic, but if we didn't have them we'd be looking for physical evidence, foot prints, faecal samples, hair, anything."

Connie gasped, "You look like you've been hit by a bolt of lightning, Hugh."

"That's 'cause I feel as if I have. Joe, the rangers need physical evidence, the female just rubbed against that tree, there could be hair snagged on the bark, and one of the pup's pee'd when we released them."

Sampi hit his forehead with the palm of his hand, "How stupid of me, my father often said you're never too old to stop learning."

"That's right, where's the tree?" Smith asked, almost unable to contain his excitement.

"Lead the way, kids, but don't touch anything, you don't want to contaminate the evidence," Sampi instructed.

Connie and Hugh stepped forward, walking with caution.

"Hugh!"

Hugh swivelled on the ball of his foot, his gaze following in the direction she pointed.

"There."

He bent forward, twisting to smile up at her, she was right, there, caught in the rough surface of the bark were several strands of hair. He went to take a step closer, but Connie grabbed his arm and pulled him back.

"Hold up, they might not be able to get anything, but that's where the pup pee'd."

Hugh rolled his eyes at his rashness.

"Yeah, you're right."

He took a step backwards as Connie waved the rangers over. She pointed to the ground in front of them.

"Here's where one of the pup's pee'd, and there, on the tree is some hair."

Crouching, Smith pulled out some sealable bags from his pocket.

"I'll take a sample of earth but I doubt we'll get much. Urine is hard to get a DNA sample from, most of it is water with a dash of urea and uric acid, I'm afraid. Unless the urine contains some cells from the skin or suchlike there's no chance of getting a DNA profile," he explained.

Langdon asked them to step back as he removed his mobile from his pocket and started to take photos, documenting the evidence in situ before Smith collected it and sealed it in the bags.

"How long before you get the DNA results?" Sampi called from where he watched with the other two men.

"Longer than you expect, I bet, Joe. It's nowhere near as quick as they get it on the telly I'm afraid. This will be given our top priority."

"Do you get many reported sightings?" Whitaker asked.

Standing to ease the strain on his back, Smith nodded.

"Yes, several every year, more if there's been something in the press, though prior to this I've only had one 'sighting' to investigate in the last six months. I'm sure this will bring out a feeding frenzy as soon as this hits the news."

"Hang on a minute, Kennedy. This won't be published until the appropriate safeguards are in place, will it?"

Smith held the gaze of the Aboriginal Tasmanian, staring him square in the eye.

"I can't stress enough, Joe there is no need to panic. Written in the Threatened Species Strategy are legal obligations laid down by the Government that will be followed. The safeguards are already in place. They are proving successful for the devil; they will work for the thylacine."

"And the mining?" Hugh asked.

"Substantiated proof such as we have here will stop the mining operation dead. Depending on the geographical extent of the population, it may have repercussions for the exploratory bore holes at the other sites. It will have the knock-on effect of aiding your work too, Andrew."

"Yes, I was thinking that. I was worried what impact the damage to the environment would have on the devil population. For me this is a win-win situation. I'm well pleased."

When the collection of evidential samples was complete they walked back to the vehicles.

"I'm sure you know what's coming next," Napoleon said, reaching for the blindfolds off the front seat.

Smith gasped, "Do we have to? It's bloody nauseating riding in a vehicle with your eyes covered."

"That was the condition you agreed to," Whitaker reminded them.

"Yeah I know," he said, taking the scarf Napoleon held out, "as I said before, you can't blame a guy for trying though."

"How will you compare the DNA without a living thylacine?" Connie asked.

Smith pushed the scarf up off one eye as he spoke.

"You're right, Connie, we won't have a living thylacine to compare, but there are a number of stuffed specimens across the world, I know the Natural History museum in London has at least two, Hugh, one in the main building in South Kensington and one in, where is it now, oh yes, Tring museum in Hertfordshire."

"Is there?" Hugh replied, in surprise, wondering how often he had walked past the exhibit in his frequent visits over the years. "I didn't know that."

"Specimens like that will provide hair for comparison and, I hope, our control DNA samples."

Chapter Thirty-Three

Sleeping in after another late night, it was mid-morning before Hugh found himself outside Connie's cabin. He waited while she finished getting ready, watching as she pulled her damp hair into a pony tail, it was so warm outside it would be dry by the time they got to the ranger's station.

Riding up to the white building, Hugh pointed to a large four by four parked alongside the veranda.

"Wonder who that belongs to?"

"Dunno, looks expensive – a better model than the one owned by that woman, Mrs Kameron, remember?"

"Ha, yes, but she has a station wagon, a dirty station wagon if I remember."

"Who else do we know who can afford a car like that?" Connie asked.

Hugh leant his bike against hers as he thought.

"Laura Goodman," they said in unison.

"That's not good. I swear she's dangerous," Hugh observed, "listen, that's raised voices!"

Sensing trouble, they raced up the stairs.

Laura Goodman stood in the middle of the small room, flanked by William Appleby. The kids stopped dead. Memories of their capture came flooding back at the sight of the lawyer.

Goodman waved a newspaper in the air like a sabre, slamming it on the desk, she tapped the headline with her manicured finger, her usual red varnish a splash of colour against the printed black and white page.

"This is libel," she snarled.

Hugh tried to read the headline emblazoned across the front page.

'Tasmanian Mining Corporation under Investigation for Financial Irregularities.'

Whitaker laughed, "Libel," he scoffed, "as I recall saying when you accused me of slandering you, it's libel or slander if it is untrue. That wasn't us, however, we are considering reporting you and your heavies to the police for kidnapping and assault. This, in addition to the investigation into Joe Sampi's attack," he glanced at his friend and colleague. "Or shall we call it attempted murder by Lennie Watts, who, I believe, was in your employment, will not make good reading for your investors. That situation will be re-visited if you renege on our agreement, Ms. Goodman."

"Do you think I considered your threats for more than a second?" Goodman snapped, tossing her head with such vigour that her hair swayed around her shoulders. "Go to the police and I am sure they will find your accusations farcical. What proof do you have?"

"The medical evidence as a starter for ten, and I believe Lennie Watts has been spotted near Devonport, it's a question of time before he's arrested and you can bet your bottom dollar he will squeal like a stuck pig if it means he can make a deal to save his own skin."

Goodman shook her head.

"I'm thinking you didn't say the injuries were caused as a result of kidnapping as I am sure the hospital would have reported it to the police."

Whitaker was silent for a moment.

She's called his bluff, Hugh thought.

"Someone has leaked fabricated documents to the press. That is libel. My legal team will be all over the perpetrator like a rash!" She retorted.

Appleby placed a hand on her arm, "Come on, Laura, you have more pressing engagements."

For a moment she ignored him, her eyes locked with Whitaker's, each refusing to look away.

"Laura."

"Yes, William, you're right."

She followed her lawyer out of the office in silence, walking straight to the car without a backward glance.

"What's got her so riled up?" Hugh asked, reaching for the newspaper as Sampi indicated to Connie to close the door. He scanned the article. "What's placement?"

"Something to do with money laundering," his father explained. "It would appear someone has leaked the fact Goodman's father, Craig Thomson, financed her company from proceeds accrued prior to his bankruptcy.

"Who did that?"

Sampi looked at Hugh, his expression sheepish.

"Someone made a call to our hacker friend whose name I seem to have forgotten."

"Dick Norseman?"

"Shush!" Sampi waved at him to lower his voice. "Someone," Sampi sighed, "I mean, I made a call to the man we aren't naming and explained the situation, telling him Goodman looked as though she was going back on her word to pull out of Warrugul. Our nameless friend took it upon himself to leak certain documents, although the paperwork isn't conclusive proof, so to speak, but it is a smoking gun."

"What about the libel thing?"

Sampi shook his head.

"Don't worry about that, Hugh. It's as your dad said, an accusation is libel if it isn't true. We have evidence to substantiate the claims made."

Hugh whistled.

"Thank goodness for that, she's treacherous."

"Agreed. She's as dangerous as a jack jumper."

"What's that?" Hugh asked.

"It's an ant."

Hugh laughed, "An ant!"

Annoyed he found it amusing, Connie nodded, "Yeah, their bites kill more people than sharks or snakes in a year, they are nasty little critters!"

"Anyway," Joe Sampi said, raising his voice in an attempt to prevent a squabble breaking out. "On a lighter note, we've had some good news."

Hugh's eyes lit up, "Are the DNA results in?"

Sampi shook his head, "Sorry, they'll be a few days yet."

Hugh tutted.

"Don't forget Kennedy said they take longer than they seem to on the telly," Connie reminded him.

"I know, but he said he'd put a rush on it."

"If I can finish," Sampi interrupted. "The DNA isn't ready, but the structure of the hair is a match for the samples taken from various specimens in the museums."

"That's brilliant. But we knew that anyway."

"I agree, Hugh. But Langdon is going to wait for the DNA results before taking this upstairs so to speak."

"And I've some good news too!" Andrew Whitaker announced.

"We've won the lottery..."

"Funny, son, funny, it helps to buy a ticket. No, my news concerns the development of a possible treatment for DFTD."

"Wow, go on, Dad."

"There is still a long way to go, but it's promising. A number of the universities working on the project across the world are looking into a way of replacing the missing molecule which should recognise the tumour cells."

"Does that mean your assignment will finish early, Dad?"

"I doubt it, son. There's a very long way to go."

"Good, I don't want to go home now."

His father grinned, "Ah so you don't think this is a god-forsaken-place now?"

"Oh thanks!" Connie retorted, continuing the joke, "so you thought you were coming to some primitive backwater, eh?" She grinned at Hugh's father. "Bet you thought you'd be living with country bumpkins eh?"

"Nooo!" Hugh exclaimed, turning scarlet. "I admit I was a little worried, who wouldn't be if they were moving half way around the world."

"Calm down, we're pulling your leg, son."

"The Parks and Wildlife Service seem pleased with my work. I think I stand a fair chance of having the secondment made permanent, if that's what we both want."

"See, and you thought getting away from me would be easy," Connie said, with a shy smile.

"Who said that's what I wanted?"

Whitaker and Sampi exchanged glances, "Young love," the vet teased.

The fallout from the newspaper expose was catastrophic. Within hours, news hacks from around the country were making their way to Hobart and the offices of the Tasmanian Mining Corporation. Here the news was met with a variety of responses, all of which were evasive. No one could locate Laura Goodman to make a statement about the allegations.

Investors and creditors started to gather, demanding their money. By six o'clock that evening the furore was the main story on the news stations across the State and mainland Australia. Investigative journalists with a nose for a good story were on the trail now that the connection between Laura Goodman and her father, Craig Thomson had been disclosed.

Thomson had been successful in fleeing the country before the Federal Court could declare him bankrupt. The search was on to locate his daughter.

Back in Sullivan's Creek, many of the local inhabitants were angry. They had been promised much but what had been delivered was minimal, if not amounting to nothing. Others, such as the owner of the saloon, 'Thirsty Work' had mixed feelings. It was great to get a rolling booking for bed and breakfast for two rooms but the corporation insisted on receipts and paying by corporate cheque. The backpackers and passing tourist trade usually paid in cash which could be lost in the bookwork and not declared for tax purposes.

Chapter Thirty-Four

Even from their vantage point at the top of Sullivan's Ridge, the smell of diesel permeated their nostrils, it was enough to turn Hugh's stomach.

George was supervising the clearing of the site left devastated by the removal of equipment from the Tasmanian Mining Corporation. Sampi had banned the kids from the immediate vicinity, with their track record for accidents, he explained George didn't want the responsibility of keeping an eye on them while his hands were full with this problem.

Hugh was still smarting from Mikey's parting quip saying they didn't have a play pen big enough to keep them out of trouble.

He pointed, noticing that George, along with a couple of lads he didn't recognise were beginning to dismantle the prefabricated storage facility in which they, along with the thylacine and her pups had been held captive.

Connie followed his gaze, "Yeah that was one of the most uncomfortable nights of my life."

"Agreed. My wrists are still sore."

Connie threw him a look of genuine thanks.

"I'd have never survived without you."

"Don't be daft," he replied, turning his head so she couldn't see his reddening cheeks. "So much for the environment being returned to its original state," he muttered in an attempt to change the subject. "Another one of the Corporation's blatant lies."

With the fracas thrown up by the press, the Tasmanian Government had put an immediate stop on further exploration while a full investigation was carried out into the Tasmanian Mining Corporation. As a result, all the equipment at the Warrugul site, as well as that at other locations owned and managed by the Corporation had been seized in a forfeiture of assets raid and the Parks and Wildlife Service had been given the go ahead to return the area to as near natural state as possible. The dismantling of the storage facility and portacabin were the last remnants of the exploration site to be removed.

The police had been called in to oversee the investigation into the Corporation. The fraud squad, in liaison with the Australian Securities and Investments Commission, were looking into the apparent disappearance of Laura Goodman. Their investigations revealed the pilot of her private plane had lodged a flight plan to fly to Sydney, Australia but had changed direction en-route. The plane landed in the Bahamas where she had chartered a boat to Puerto Plata, where it is believed, she joined her father, Craig Thomson, safe in the knowledge there was no extradition treaty in place between the Dominican Republic and Australia.

The newspapers were full of photographs of a dishevelled William Appleby in handcuffs following his arrest and arrival at his subsequent arraignment. It was here, he learnt Goodman had fled the country, leaving the evidence trail leading to him.

Hugh rolled onto his back and watched the clouds scurrying across the sky which was a deep azure blue. It was a beautiful day, made all the better with the knowledge that the thylacine would soon be safe. He was under no illusion the road ahead would not be easy. The population was still far from stable. Although Joe Sampi had confirmed this had been a good season for pups across the State, the species was still critically endangered, teetering on the brink of extinction.

The Aboriginal Tasmanian was confident Langdon and his colleague, Kennedy Smith had the investigation into the verification evidence supporting their sighting of the thylacine in hand. The DNA results were due any day now. For the first time since glimpsing the thylacine, he was comfortable someone else was taking control, at least for the moment.

He sat up as a sense of guilt overwhelmed him.

"Wassup?"

Noticing his expression, Connie pushed herself up so she was resting on her elbow.

"Something's up. What's wrong?"

He shook his head in a dismissive manner, "Just thinking."

Connie sat up and threw her arms around her head, "Eek, that's dangerous, run for cover!" She teased. "Or have you had an idea for an adventure?"

"I wish. No, I was thinking it feels good to know that Langdon and Smith are helping to protect the thylacine." He held his hand up, "I know this goes against everything we, or more to the point I have said up to now, but I'm glad, but then I remembered, Joe and everyone have been protecting her for decades, how do you think they feel?"

Connie slumped down onto the grass and turned over onto her back.

"Don't beat yourself up over it. I heard grandfather talking to George and Napoleon last night."

"Where was Mikey?"

"What? Oh I dunno," she said, waving the question away. "Now you've made me forget what I was going to say." She was silent for a moment. "Ah yes, I remember. I heard grandfather say he was kinda pleased the secret was out. His whole life revolved around keeping the thylacine safe but what with the likes of Spencer Tate and now the Tasmanian Mining Corporation the time was right to call in help. He said that we," she pointed at Hugh and then at herself as if emphasising the point, she was making. "We've put ourselves in danger too often and he, for one, would never be able to live with himself if anything serious happened to either of us."

Hugh was thoughtful for a moment.

"As long as the elders haven't decided to break their silence because of us, Connie."

Hearing the sound of engines revving, she scrambled to her feet and hurried to the rim, leaning over for a better look.

"Look, the lorries are leaving."

"Hey, be careful!"

"I'm fine, I'm holding on," she claimed, lurching forward as she pretended to fall.

Hugh scrambled to his feet, his heart pounding, "C... Connie!" He stopped dead in his tracks, she was messing about.

"Don't do try such a stupid stunt again," he growled.

"It was a joke, Hugh, a dumb joke."

"Yeah, I know, but I still have nightmares where I re-live the moment Tate falls over the edge. That's what I saw in my mind a moment ago, but it wasn't him falling, it was you."

A glimpse of his expression was enough to tell her he wasn't messing about; his anger was real.

"I'm sorry," she whispered. She bent over, pretending to brush the dry grass from her clothes as she hid the smile that crept over her face, pleased he was so worried about her.

"The lorries are leaving," she said, "honest, look for yourself if you don't believe me."

Taking a step forward, he peered over the edge, she was right, the lorries were leaving the area.

"Great, there's no reason why we can't go down, now. We won't get into trouble."

Connie led the way down the slope. George was standing in the middle of the devastated area, which a couple of weeks ago had been thick with vegetation, uncultured and untouched. Now it was a mess of tree stumps and churned up bushes and grass.

Hugh was aghast, close up it was worse than he imagined, much, much worse,

"This is awful," Connie said, voicing his thoughts. "Now the area's been cleared it's easy to see how much damage the Corporation has done."

George, finishing the note he was writing, looked up. Noticing their arrival, he waved and started to walk towards them.

"It's a mess, eh?"

Hugh nodded.

"I'm gutted, George. There's no way the thylacine will return here."

George checked his watch as he spoke, "Give it six months and you won't notice the Corporation were here. I appreciate the trees will take longer, but dad's trying to source some mature trees that can be brought in as well as saplings. Nature's resilient. She'll bounce back. You've seen how the vegetation is already sprouting on the site of the forest fire, and that was just before Christmas."

Hugh chewed the inside of his cheek as he acknowledged what George was saying.

"I guess you're right."

The last of the casual labour employed to help with the clear up waved as they got into their vehicle.

Connie tapped Hugh on the arm.

"Look."

He twisted his torso to see what she wanted, "Wassup?"

She was pointing towards a pocket of trees on the periphery of the mine area.

"You're not gonna believe it..."

Tutting, Hugh turned to see what the fuss was about.

"No way," he said, spotting the thylacine standing in the shadows. She sniffed the air and yapped. The pups gambolled out of the undergrowth. Connie laughed as the smallest cannoned into its siblings as it fell over itself.

"Don't tell me they've walked across the park?" Hugh asked.

"I think you've answered your own question, Hugh," George beamed as he spoke. "Unless they've hitched a lift, they've walked 'home'," he said his tone tinged with sarcasm.

Connie giggled, "Dill," she said.

Hugh held his hands up, even he had to admit it was a daft thing to say, the evidence was standing in front of him. His thylacine had returned home.

"Dad and Joe aren't going to believe this."

"Oh I wouldn't be so sure. Nothing seems to surprise Grandfather nowadays."

"Why would they return, George?"

The young man wrinkled his nose, "Dunno. It's possible another thylacine had moved into the territory even though we'd checked it out. Or it's as simple as she prefers it here. After all there's a plentiful supply of water, good food source and taking this area temporarily out of the equation, a lot of cover."

Hugh ran his hand over his face, it was unbelievable, "Whatever the reason, it's pretty damn awesome!"

"You can say that again," Connie concurred.

The trio watched in silence as the female skirted the clearing, leading the pups as she made straight for the cliff face.

"Why don't they seem bothered by us?" Connie asked.

"Good question, Connie, I've wondered that."

They looked at George expecting him to know the answer.

"Dunno, it may be that she is used to seeing us. You know, they weren't intimidated by man, that's one of the reasons for the population collapse, they were too damn easy to hunt," George explained. "We've seen her so often now and of course I fed and water her, I think she knows our scent."

They watched as the female nosed her way through the curtain of vegetation with the pups following, disappearing into the relative safety of the cave beyond.

Hugh exhaled, his thylacine was safe and she'd made her way back home.

"Dad'll be picking me up in a while. Do you want a lift back to the station?"

Connie glanced at Hugh and shrugged.

"I don't mind either way."

Hugh nodded, "Might as well," he said.

"Don't do us any favours," George quipped with good humour.

Hugh poked out his tongue.

"Charming!"

Hugh bowed, "We'd love a lift home."

George reached over and tousled Hugh's hair. Everyone knew he hated that.

There was an air of excitement buzzing around the ranger's station. Whitaker was seeing his last patient out of the door, a young spaniel which had to have a grass seed removed from between the claws of its front paw. It was still a little groggy from the anaesthetic but managed to put its front feet on the rear seat of its owner's car as he bent to lift it into the vehicle.

The vet nodded as Napoleon parked up.

"Have you had a good day?" He asked his son.

Hugh looked as though he was doing an impersonation of a Cheshire cat, his grin was so broad.

"It's been brilliant. The area at the base of the Ridge is a mess but George says we won't know the Corporation was there in about six months." A grin erupted across his face as he continued, "but you won't guess what we saw."

His father looked at their excited faces, "Go on."

Hugh scanned the area to make sure there were no strangers about. "The thylacine and her pups are back."

"No way!"

Hugh nodded, "Yes way!"

"That's fantastic news, Joe's inside, no doubt you're itching to tell him."

Hugh chased Connie up the stairs and into the office. He'd grown very fond of the old man but it was right and proper that Connie tell him what they'd seen, after all he was her grandfather.

Joe Sampi, as Connie had predicted didn't seem surprised at their discovery.

"I know they can cover huge areas when establishing a territory, so the distance back here wasn't so great for them," he said. "It seems our choice of new home wasn't quite to her liking. She is a thylacine with very discerning tastes," he laughed. "Ah, I know what I meant to say, Langdon and Smith called over today."

"What did they say?" Hugh demanded, giving Sampi his full attention.

"Hang on, I'm getting to that, young un."

"My son has never had the patience of a saint, I'm afraid."

Hugh threw his father a look of disgust.

"Ooo did you see that?" His father teased.

"Dad!"

Connie clung to her grandfather's arm.

"Go on, Grandpappy, what did they say?"

Sampi started to speak, an amused sparkle in his eyes as he told them what had happened earlier that day.

"I'm pleased to say the Parks and Wildlife Service are taking the sightings as genuine."

"But they are genuine!" Hugh interrupted.

"Indeed. Anyway, they are very pleased with the photographs, and the hair samples substantiate the evidence. The DNA results aren't through yet but Langdon insists they have been given the highest priority."

"Yes!" Hugh exclaimed. Things were turning out better than he could have imagined.

Sampi raised his eyebrows as he smiled. No one could doubt the boy's enthusiasm.

"The Parks and Wildlife service have contacted the Minister for Environment, Parks and Heritage. The thylacine is still a protected species, in spite of the World thinking it's extinct, that status was never rescinded. So that's in our favour."

Hugh pretended to wipe sweat from his forehead, "Phew, that's a relief."

"It's a shame the danger to the thylacine wasn't realised until it was too late all those years ago," Connie observed.

"Ah, but we saw what was happening and we stepped in," Sampi interjected. "As soon as the DNA results are in, Langdon says the Government will make a public statement. They have invited us to be part of the audience when they announce it to the press. That's if we want to attend."

"No way," Connie enthused.

"As far as the official statement is concerned, you discovered the thylacine. The elders don't want our involvement made public, it will inhibit our activities in the future."

Hugh was silent for a moment.

"That's not fair, Joe. You deserve the credit for what the community has done over the decades. As you've said, you have given up so much to protect the thylacine."

Sampi smiled.

"No, this is as it should be. We will remain in the background protecting them."

Chapter Thirty-Five

As predicted, with the DNA results substantiating the existence of the thylacine things moved with great speed. Warrugul National Park, along with three other sites chosen after consultation with the Aboriginal Tasmanian community were designated as thylacine sanctuaries. The legislative powers of the Tasmanian government ensured the existing protection around the thylacine was strengthened. Capture or trapping a thylacine became a federal offence carrying a lengthy prison sentence as well as a substantial fine.

A project was commissioned with Joe Sampi and Jacob Rookh acting as consultants to determine the approximate population level before any decision was taken to implement a captive breeding programme or initiatives similar to those in place to protect the Tasmanian devil.

As usual, Andrew Whitaker dropped his laptop bag onto the first empty chair as he entered the room, followed by Joe Sampi. Hugh and Connie looked up from the school project they were working on together.

"Good day?" Hugh asked.

Whitaker glimpsed over his son's shoulder to see what they were doing.

"Tiring, son."

"Can I make you a cuppa?"

Whitaker shook his head, "No thanks, son, what about you, Joe?"

Sampi smiled as he shook his head.

"No thanks, but we do have some news."

Connie put her pen down, "What's that, grandfather?"

The elderly man glanced at the vet who gave him the go-ahead to tell them.

"Do you remember saying the aboriginal community should get the credit for discovering the thylacine?"

Hugh nodded, "Yes," he said, wondering what was unfolding here.

"Good. Because your father and I have taken a decision on your behalf and we hope we have your support."

Puzzled, Hugh looked at Connie, "Go on, Joe. This sounds ominous."

"The bounty for proof of life..."

"The million or so dollars?" Connie interrupted.

Her grandfather smiled, "Yes that one. Anyway, the bounty is to be honoured."

"Wow, brilliant. I hope it's going to be given to the community," said Hugh with genuine sincerity.

"Yes and no."

Hugh raised his eyebrows.

"This is getting more cryptic by the second."

"Come on Grandfather, what do you mean?"

Sampi placed his hands on the table as he spoke.

"Your father and I think the bounty should be divided. We've spoken to the elders who are in full agreement."

"Divided, how so, Grandfather?"

Sampi moistened his lips before continuing.

"The money will be divided between the Save the Tasmanian Devil project, the thylacine sanctuaries, and the aboriginal community to help families in financial difficulty, they will be able to apply for a grant or something."

"Sounds fantastic," Hugh said. "Once the bounty has been paid out there will be no incentive to capture the thylacine."

Connie agreed, it sounded like the perfect arrangement.

"Good, we're glad you approve, but..."

Hugh stared at his father, "I hate it when there's a but!"

"But, his father repeated, "in recognition for the part you have played in protecting the thylacine a small trust fund will be set up to finance your education. There will also be some money for both Mikey and George to help them during their training programme."

"Fantastic, perhaps the boys can get the trainers they've been after," Hugh smiled.

"Funny, that's what Mikey said when we told them," Joe Sampi said with good humour.

Connie was gob smacked, tears pricked the back of her eyes.

"I, I don't know what to say," she muttered, choked with emotion. "This will mean so much to Mum, I know she's trying to save for uni. even though its years off. Hey, perhaps she can come home to work now?"

"Hang on, darl, we don't want to jump the gun. We'll talk to Mum next time she's home, okay?"

His granddaughter beamed, this was wonderful news.

Holding his hand up as if he were in the classroom, Hugh said he had a suggestion. Everyone was looking at him, his father, a little worried in case it was something that would place them in danger.

"Let's head out to Sullivan's Rise, see if the thylacine is about."

"Sounds good to me. Are you up for it, Andrew?"

"Always. Give me five minutes to change."

With the sun setting, the thylacine scratched her ear in a lazy fashion. The smallest of the three pups was sitting bolt upright beside her mother while its siblings were curled up close by.

"Dad."

"Yes son."

"I don't think I ever want to leave Tasmania. I could never leave the thylacine, or Connie, come to think of it."

Whitaker looked at his son and smiled.

"I'm glad, Hugh. Not only has this become a place of safety for the thylacine, thanks to the two of you, it's become a sanctuary for us as well. I think it's a fair bet, but if I get the offer to make my secondment permanent, I'll take it and we can make applications for permanent residency. What do you think?"

Hugh looked at his father.

"Brilliant," he said, "that's brilliant."

Printed in Great Britain
by Amazon